Shadows 10

Shadows 10

Edited by
CHARLES L. GRANT

Doubleday

NEW YORK

1987

All of the characters in this book
are fictitious, and any resemblance
to actual persons, living or dead,
is purely coincidental.

"Jamie's Grave," copyright © 1987 by Lisa Tuttle. By permission of the author.
"Apples," copyright © 1987 by Nina Downey Higgins. By permission of the author.
"A World Without Toys," copyright © 1987 by T. M. Wright. By permission of the author and the author's agent, Jeffrey Zaleski.
"Law of Averages," copyright © 1987 by Wendy Webb. By permission of the author.
"The Fence," copyright © 1987 by Thomas Sullivan. By permission of the author.
"Moonflower," copyright © 1987 by Melissa Mia Hall. By permission of the author.
"Come Where My Love Lies Dreaming," copyright © 1987 by Bob Leman. By permission of the author.
"The Finder-Keeper," copyright © 1987 by Ken Wisman. By permission of the author.
"Just a Little Souvenir," copyright © 1987 by Cheryl Fuller Nelson. By permission of the author.
"Like Shadows in the Dark," copyright © 1987 by Stephen Gallagher. By permission of the author.
"Office Hours," copyright © 1987 by Douglas E. Winter. By permission of the author.
"We Have Always Lived in the Forest," copyright © 1987 by Nancy Holder. By permission of the author.
"Just Like Their Masters," copyright © 1987 by Mona A. Clee. By permission of the author.
"Pigs," copyright © 1987 by Al Sarrantonio. By permission of the author.

The Library of Congress has cataloged this work as follows:

Shadows (Garden City, N.Y.)
Shadows. — [1] (1978)- — Garden City, N.Y.: Doubleday, 1978-
v.; 22 cm. — (Doubleday science fiction)
Annual.
Editors: 1978-   C.L. Grant.
ISSN 0884-6987 = Shadows (Garden City, N.Y.)

1. Horror tales, American.   I. Grant, Charles L.   II. Series.
PS648.H6S52   85-643084
813'.0876'08—dc19
AACR 2   MARC-S
Library of Congress   [8510]

ISBN: 0-385-23893-2
Copyright © 1987 by Charles L. Grant
All Rights Reserved
Printed in the United States of America
First Edition

Contents

Introduction

Ten years ago, I had rather ambitious plans for myself as far as my career and the rest of my life were concerned. Some of them included getting famous and obscenely rich and buying my own mountain so I wouldn't have to paint the house or have any neighbors who would keep asking me what I did for a living; some of them included facing up to my commercial (not to mention literary) failure as a sf novelist and getting on with what I really wanted to write; and some of them included becoming the editor of my own magazine, so I could publish the kind of stories *I* liked to see, not the stories I saw on the stands.

Well, I don't have the mountain (but I don't paint the house anyway), I do indeed write what I want to these days (touch wood the trend continues), and I don't have a magazine.

But there is *Shadows.*

In 1977, I submitted to several publishers a proposal for five anthologies that I hoped would showcase new and reprint material in the horror genre. I don't remember what all of them were called, but one of them was *New Gothic.* The response to the proposal was generally unfavorable; after all, I had no solid credentials as either a writer *or* an editor, and the horror market wasn't exactly exploding all over New York, much less the nation. But I did have lunch one afternoon with Karen Solem (then editor at Popular Library) and Sharon Jarvis (then at Doubleday).

Karen had been trying mightily to get my first Oxrun Station novel into the Popular Library line, but it wasn't working, and we had both been rather disheartened. At that lunch, however, Sharon had just accepted the third one *(The Last Call of Mourning,* for the Romance line, since there was no other place for it), and Karen gave me the good news that she'd be able to do the paperback edition.

We celebrated.

Then Sharon told me she loved the idea for *New Gothic;* everything, that is, except the title. I wasn't surprised. Editors hate titles. I think they'd all be happiest if we all called our work *A Book.*

Anyway, after a number of alternatives, I finally suggested *Shadows.*

We congratulated ourselves again (doing a lot of awfully mature giggling, as I recall), parted, and it wasn't until I was on my way home that it hit me that I was now stuck with doing something I'd never done before except in dreams—I was actually going to have to go out there and find stories, edit them, write contracts, pay people, and shepherd the book through the minefields of the publication process.

The idea scared me to death.

It was, now that I look back on it, probably the fact that I'd never done it before that gave me the courage to do it in the first place—the courage, as it were, of the blissfully stupid. And before long, and thanks to the hand-holding and advice of Virginia Kidd and Kirby McCauley, there were Robert Bloch and Michael Bishop and Stephen King and Avram Davidson and Ramsey Campbell and seven others . . . and there was *Shadows.*

Incredible.

But after I had turned it in, and Sharon had pronounced it not bad, it never occurred to me to do more than one volume. I'd done what I'd set out to do, and I was pleased. Perhaps even a little smug. Certainly feeling a hell of a lot better than I had in months. Then Sharon called and wanted to know who was lined up for the second volume. I think I blanched, just like they do in books; but I wasn't quite stupid enough to turn the idea down.

So I didn't.

And now there's the stalwart and ever patient Pat LoBrutto, who nags and prods and guides me just as Sharon had done, and never fails to ride vigorously to my defense against the ghouls and ogres who would just as soon see us vanish so they could stuff the list with yet another best-selling Asimov collection.

And now, God help me, there is this tenth volume, with number eleven already being shaped on my desk. It doesn't seem possible. I don't mean the passage of years, but the number of people who are still willing to write for not much money the kind of stories you and I like to read—quiet, literary, autumn night horror; dark fantasy;

fireplace and hearth stories—that, despite the onslaught of slasher/glitzy/gore-inspired fiction intended for those with an attention span of zip, continue to survive.

If it had been work, and since I'm a damned lazy person, I would have quit a long time ago. But it isn't work, not really. All I do is read the stories that come in, pick the ones I like, and stick them in an envelope to send to Pat, who gets the ball rolling on the publication end.

This isn't work; this is fun.

So now I'm going to take the opportunity to correct something that has bothered me since 1978. In the autumn of that year, *Shadows 1* was chosen as the Best Anthology by the World Fantasy Awards. I don't remember what I said when I picked up the award on behalf of those first dozen writers, but I damned well know what I didn't say—

To every writer who has ever submitted a story, to every writer whose story was selected—thank you a thousand times over, and know that I realize how truly inadequate that is. Because there would be, quite literally, no book without you; there would be, quite literally, no place for the new folk in dark fantasy without you; and I would, quite literally, still be dreaming about somehow, in some way, gathering shadows from corners and attics and closets and deserted October streets and putting them into print.

Number ten, then.

Each a shadow, each a silhouette, each a promise that nightmares aren't restricted to dreams.

Charles L. Grant
Newton, New Jersey
1987

Shadows 10

I've said it before: Lisa Tuttle doesn't write nearly enough to satisfy her fans. But she is a writer more careful than most, determined there be no mistaking her design or intent. In dark fantasy that's vital. We're dealing with people here, people who come up against shadows cast by no light. And to set one against the other carelessly only makes both story and writer seem extraordinarily silly. "Jamie's Grave" is not silly; it's a perfect Shadows *story.*

JAMIE'S GRAVE
by Lisa Tuttle

Mary sat at the kitchen table, a cup of tea gone cold by her left hand, and listened to the purring of the electric clock on the wall.

The house was clean and the larder well stocked. She had done the laundry and read her library books and it was too wet for gardening. She had baked a cake yesterday and this wasn't her day for making bread. She had already phoned Clive twice this week and could think of no excuse to phone again. Once she might have popped across the road to visit Jen, but she had been getting the feeling that her visits were no longer so welcome. There had been a time when Jen was grateful for Mary's company, a time when she had been lonely, too, but now Jen had her own baby to care for, and whenever Mary went over there—no matter what Jen said—Mary couldn't help feeling that she was intruding.

She looked at the clock again. In twenty minutes she could start her walk to the school.

Clive said she should get a job. He was right, and not just for the money. Mary knew she would be happier doing something useful. But what sort of job could she get? She had no experience, and in this Wiltshire village there was not much scope for employment. Other mothers already held the school jobs of crossing-guard and dinner-lady, and what other employer would allow her to fit her working hours to those when Jamie was in school? She wouldn't let someone else look after Jamie—no job was worth that. Her son was all she had in the world, all she cared about. If she could have kept him home with her and taught him herself, instead of having to send him to school, Mary knew she would have been perfectly content. She had been so happy when she had her baby, she hadn't even minded losing Clive. But babies grew up, and grew away. Jen was going to find that out in a few years.

Mary rose and walked to the sink, poured away the tea, rinsed and set the cup on the draining-board. She took her jacket from the hook beside the door and put it on, straightening her collar and fluffing her hair without a mirror. The clock gave a dim, clicking buzz, and it was time to leave.

The house where Mary lived with her son was one of six bungalows on the edge of a Wiltshire village, close enough to London, as well as to Reading, to be attractive to commuters. After the grimy, cramped house in Islington, the modern bungalow with its large garden and fresh country air had seemed the perfect place to settle down and raise a family. But while Mary had dreamed of being pregnant again, Clive had been dreaming of escape. The house for him was not a cosy nest, but a gift to Mary and a sop to his conscience as he left.

Five minutes' leisurely walk brought the village school in sight. Mary saw the children tumbling out the door like so many brightly colored toys, and she reached the gate at the same moment as Jamie from the other side.

Jamie was involved with his friends, laughing and leaping around. His eyes flickered over her, taking in her presence but not acknowledging it, and when she hugged him she could feel his reluctance to return to her and leave the exciting, still new world of school.

He pulled away quickly, and wouldn't let her hold his hand as they walked. But he talked to her, needing to share his day's experiences, giving them to her in excited, disconnected bursts of speech. She tried to make sense of what he said, but she couldn't always. He used strange words—sometimes in a different accent—picked up from the other children, and the events he described might have been imaginary, or related to schoolyard games rather than to reality. Once they had spent all their time together, in the same world. She had understood him better then, had understood him perfectly before he could even talk.

She looked at the little stranger walking beside her, and caught a sudden resemblance to Clive in one of his gestures. It struck her, unpleasantly, that he was well on his way to becoming a man.

"Would you like to help me make some biscuits this afternoon?" she asked.

He shook his head emphatically. "I got to dig," he said.

"Dig? In the garden? Oh, darling, it's so wet!"

He frowned and tilted back his head. "Isn't."

"I know it's stopped raining, but the ground . . ." Mary sighed, imagining the mess. "Why not wait until tomorrow? It might be nicer then, the sun might come out, it might be much nicer to dig in the garden tomorrow."

"I dig tomorrow, too," Jamie said. He began to chant, swinging his arms stiffly as he marched, "Dig! Dig! Dig!"

During the summer they had taken a trip to the seashore and Mary had bought him a plastic shovel. He had enjoyed digging in the soft sand, then, but had not mentioned it since. Mary wondered what had brought it back to mind—was it a chance word from his teacher, or an enthusiasm caught from one of the other children?—and realized she would probably never know.

He found his shovel in the toy chest, flinging other toys impatiently across the room. Not even the offer of a piece of cake could distract him. He suffered himself to be changed into other clothes, twitching impatiently all the while. When he had rushed out into the garden, Mary stood by the window and watched.

The plastic shovel, so useful for digging at the beach, was less efficient in the dense soil of the garden. As Jamie busily applied himself, the handle suddenly broke off in his hands. He looked for a moment almost comically shocked; then he began to howl.

Mary rushed out to comfort him, but he would not be distracted by her promises of other pleasures. All he wanted was to dig, and he would only be happy if she gave him a new shovel. Finally, she gave him one of her gardening spades, and left him to it.

She felt rejected, going into the house and closing the door, staying away from the windows. He didn't want her to hover, and she had no reason to fear for his safety in their own garden. Had she waited all day just for this?

The next day, Saturday, was worse. Mary looked forward to Saturdays now more fervently than she ever had as a child. On Saturdays she had Jamie to herself all day. They played games, she read him stories, they went for walks and had adventures. But that Saturday all Jamie wanted to do was dig.

She stood in the garden with him, staring at the vulnerable white bumps of his knees, and then at his stubborn, impatient face. "Why, darling? Why do you want to dig?"

He shrugged and looked at the ground, clutching the spade as if she might take it away from him.

"Jamie, please answer me. I asked you a question. Why are you digging?"

"I might find something," he said, after a reluctant pause. Then he looked at her, a slightly shifty, sideways look. "If I find something . . . can I keep it?"

"May I," she corrected automatically. Her spirits lifted as she imagined a treasure hunt, a game she might play with him. Already, her thoughts were going to her old costume jewelry, and coins . . . "Probably," she said. "Almost certainly, anything you find in our garden would be yours to keep. But there are exceptions. If it is something *very* valuable, like gold, it belongs to the Queen by right, so you would have to get her permission."

"Not gold," he said scornfully.

"No?"

"No. Not treasure." He shook his head and then he smiled and looked with obvious pride at his small excavation. "I'm digging a grave," he said. "You know what they do with graves? They put dead people inside. I might find one. I might find a skellington!"

"Skeleton," she said without thinking.

"Skeleton, yeah! Wicked, man! Skellyton!" He flopped down and resumed his digging.

Feeling stunned, Mary went inside.

"And that's what you phoned me about?" said Clive.

"He's your son, too, you know."

"I know he's my son. And I like to hear what he's doing. But you know I like to sleep in . . . you could have picked a better time than early on a Saturday morning to fill me in on his latest game."

"It's not a game."

"Well, what is it, then? A real grave? A real skeleton?"

"It's morbid!"

"It's natural. Look, he probably saw something on television, or heard something at school . . ."

"When I was little, I was afraid of dead things," Mary said.

"You think that's healthier? What do you want me to say, Mary? It'll pass, this craze. He'll forget about it and go on to something else. If you make a big deal about it, he'll keep on, to get a reaction. Don't make him think it's wrong. Want me to come over tomorrow and take him out somewhere? That's the quickest way to get his mind on to other things."

Mary thought of how empty the house was when her son was gone. At least now, although he was preoccupied, she was aware of his presence nearby. And, as usual, she reacted against her ex-husband. She was shaking her head before he had even finished speaking.

"No, not tomorrow. I had plans for tomorrow. I—"

"Next weekend. He could come here, spend the night—"

"Oh, Clive, he's so young!"

"Mary, you can't have it both ways. He's my son, too. You can't complain that I take no interest and leave it all to you, and then refuse to let me see him. I do miss him, you know."

"All right, next weekend. But just one day, not overnight. Please. He's all I have. When he's not here I miss him dreadfully."

Mary stood by the window watching Jamie dig his grave, and she missed him. She could see him, and she knew that if she rapped on the glass he would look up and see her, but that wasn't enough; it would never be enough. Once, she had been the whole world to him. Now, every day took him farther from her.

She thought of Heather, Jen's little baby. She thought of the solid weight of her in her arms, and that delicious, warm, milky smell of new babies. She remembered how it had felt to hold her, and how she had felt when she had to give her back. She remembered watching Jen nurse her child. The envy which had pierced her. The longing. It wasn't Jen's feelings which made Mary reluctant now to visit her but her own jealousy. She wanted a baby.

She went on standing by the window for nearly an hour, holding herself and grieving for the child she didn't have, while Jamie dug a grave.

For lunch Mary made cauliflower soup and toasted cheese sandwiches. Ignoring his protests that he could wash his own hands, she marched Jamie to the bathroom and scrubbed and scrubbed until all the soil beneath his fingernails was gone.

Twenty minutes later, a soup moustache above his upper lip, Jamie said, "I got to go back to my digging."

Inside, she cried a protest, but she remembered Clive's words. Maybe he did want a reaction from her. Maybe he would be less inclined to dig a grave if his mother seemed to favour it. So, with a false, bright smile she cheered him on, helped him back into his filthy pullover and wellies, and waved vigorously from the back door, as if seeing him off on an expedition.

"Come back in when you get cold," she said. "Or if you get hungry . . ."

She turned on Radio Four, got out her knitting and worked on the sweater which was to be a Christmas present for her sister in Scotland. She worked steadily for about an hour. Then the panic took her.

A falling-elevator sensation in her stomach, and then the cold. It was a purely visceral, wordless, objectless fear. Her shaking fingers dropped stitches and then dropped the knitting, and she lurched clumsily to her feet.

If anything happened to Jamie she would never forgive herself. If she was too late, if anything had happened to him—

She knew he was safe in the back garden, where there was nothing to hurt him. She knew she'd had this experience before, and there had never been anything threatening her son. Logic made no impact on the fear.

He was so fragile, he was so young, and the world was so dangerous. How could she have let him out of her sight for even a moment?

She ran to the back door and out, cursing herself.

She saw his bright yellow boots first. He was lying flat on the ground, on his stomach, and she couldn't see his head. It must have been hanging over the edge, into the hole he had dug.

"Jamie!" She didn't want to alarm him, but his name came out as a shriek of terror.

He didn't move.

Mary fell on the ground beside him and caught his body up in her arms. She was so frightened she couldn't breathe. But he was breathing; he was warm.

Jamie gave a little grunt and his eyelids fluttered. Then he was gazing up at her, dazed and sleepy-looking.

"Are you all right?" she demanded, although it was clear to her, now the panic had subsided, that he was fine.

"What?" he said groggily.

"Oh, you silly child! What do you mean by lying down out here, when the ground's so cold and wet . . . you'll catch your death . . . if you were tired, you should have come in. What a silly, to work so hard you had to lie down and take a nap!" She hugged him to her, and for once he seemed content to be held so, rubbing his dirty face against her sweater and clinging.

They rocked together in the moist grey air and country silence for a time, until Jamie gave a deep, shuddering sigh.

"What is it?"

"Hungry," he said. His voice was puzzled.

"Of course you are, poor darling, after so much hard work. It's not time for tea yet, but come inside and I'll give you a glass of milk and a biscuit. Would you like that?"

He seemed utterly exhausted, and she carried him inside. Although he had claimed to be hungry, he drank only a little milk and seemed without the energy even to nibble a biscuit. Mary settled him on the couch in front of the television, and when she came back a few minutes later she found him asleep.

After she had put Jamie to bed, Mary went back to the garden to look at his excavation.

It was a hole more round than square, no more than a foot across and probably not more than two foot deep. As Mary crouched down to look into it she saw another, smaller hole, within. She didn't think Jamie had made it; it seemed something quite different. She thought it looked like a tunnel, or the entrance to some small animal's burrow. She thought of blind, limbless creatures tunnelling through the soft earth, driven by needs and guided by senses she couldn't know, and she shuddered. She thought of worms, but this tunnel was much too large. She had not been aware of moles in the garden, but possibly Jamie had accidentally uncovered evidence of one.

She picked up the spade which Jamie had abandoned, and used it to scoop earth back into the hole. Although she began casually, she soon began to work with a purpose, and her heart pounded as she pushed and shovelled furiously, under a pressure she could not explain to fill it in, cover up the evidence, make her garden whole again.

Finally she stood and tamped the earth down beneath her feet. With the grass gone, the marks of digging were obvious. She had done the best she could, but it wasn't good enough. It wasn't the same; it couldn't be.

As she walked back into the house, Mary heard a brief, faint scream, and immediately ran through to Jamie's room.

He was sitting up in bed, staring at her with wide-open yet unseeing eyes.

"Darling, what's wrong?"

She went to him, meaning to hug him, but her hands were covered with dirt from the hole; she couldn't touch him.

"What's that?" he asked, voice blurred with sleep, turning towards the window.

Mary looked and saw with a shock that the window was open, if only by a few inches. She didn't remember opening it, and she was sure it was too heavy for Jamie to lift by himself.

"I'll close it," she said, and went to do so. Her hands looked black against the white-painted sash, and she saw bits of earth crumble and fall away. She felt as disturbed by that as if it really had been grave-dirt, and felt she had to sweep it up immediately.

When she returned to the bed Jamie was lying down, apparently asleep. Careful not to touch him with her dirty hands, she bent down and kissed him, hovering close for a time to feel the warmth of his peaceful breathing against her face. She loved him so much she could not move or speak.

In the morning Jamie was subdued, so quiet that Mary worried he might be getting ill, and kept feeling his face for some evidence of a fever. His skin was cool, though, and he showed no other signs of disease. He said nothing more about wanting to dig, nothing about graves or skeletons—that craze appeared to have vanished as suddenly and inexplicably as it had arrived.

It was a wet and windy day, and Mary was glad Jamie didn't want to play in the garden. He seemed worried about something, though, following her around the house and demanding her attention. Mary didn't mind. In fact, she cherished this evidence that she was still needed.

When she asked what he wanted for his tea, the answer came promptly. "Two beefburgers. Please."

"Two!"

"Yes. Two, please."

"I think one will be enough, really, Jamie. You never have two. If you are very hungry, I could make extra chips."

He had that stubborn look on his face, the look that reminded her of his father. "Extra chips, too. But please may I have two beefburgers."

She was certain he wouldn't be able to eat them both. "Very well," she said. "After you've eaten your first beefburger, if you still want another one, I'll make it then."

"I want two—I know I want two! I want two now!"

"Calm down, Jamie," she said quietly. "You shall have two. But one at a time. That's the way we'll do it."

He sulked, and he played with his food when she served it, but he did manage to eat all the beefburger, and then immediately demanded a second, forgetting, this time, to say "please."

"You haven't eaten all your chips," she pointed out.

He glared. "You didn't *say* I had to eat all my chips first. You *said* if I ate one burger I could have another—you *said.*"

"I know I said it. lovey, but the chips are part of your dinner, too, and if you're really hungry—"

"You *said!*"

His lower lip trembled, and there were tears in his eyes. How could she deny him? She couldn't bear his unhappiness, even though she was quite certain that he wasn't hungry and wouldn't be able to eat any more meat.

"All right, my darling," she said, and left her own unfinished meal to grow cold while she went back to the cooker. Clive would have been firm with him, she thought, and wondered if she had been wrong to give in. Maybe Jamie had wanted her to say no. The thought wearied her. It was too complicated. He had asked for food, and she would give it to him.

Jamie fidgeted in his chair when she put the food before him, and would not meet her eyes. He asked if he could watch TV while he ate. Curious, she agreed. "Just bring your plate in to me when you've finished."

A suspiciously few minutes later, Jamie returned with his plate. The second beefburger had vanished without a trace. There were only a few smashed peas and stray chips on the plate. Jamie went back to watch television while Mary did the washing-up. Almost immediately, above the noise of the television, she heard the back door open and close quietly. When she rejoined Jamie he seemed happier than he had all day, freed of some burden. They played together happily—if a little more rowdily than Mary liked—until his bedtime.

But after she had tucked him into bed, Mary went out into the dark garden. In the gloom the whiteness of a handkerchief gave off an almost phosphorescent glow, drawing her across the lawn to the site of Jamie's excavation.

Like some sort of offering, the beefburger had been placed on a clean white handkerchief and laid on the ground, on the bare patch. Mary stared at it for a moment, and then went back inside.

Mary usually woke to the sounds of Jamie moving about, but on Monday morning for once she had to wake him. He was pale and groggy, with greenish shadows beneath his eyes. But when she suggested he could stay home and spend the day resting in bed, he rallied and became almost frantic in his determination to go to school. He did seem better, out in the fresh air and away from the house, but she continued to worry about him after she had left him at school. Her thoughts led her to the doctor's. She didn't mind waiting until all the scheduled patients had been seen; she paged through old magazines, with nothing better to do.

Dr. Abden was a brisk, no-nonsense woman who had raised two children to safe and successful adulthood; Mary was able to trust her maternal wisdom enough to tell her the whole story of Jamie's grave.

"Perhaps he found his skeleton and didn't like it so much," said Dr. Abden. "There, don't look so alarmed, my dear! I didn't mean a human skeleton, of course. You mentioned seeing something like a tunnel . . . isn't it possible that your son came across a mole—a dead one? That first encounter with death can be a disturbing one. Perhaps he thought he killed it with his little shovel and so is guiltily trying to revive it . . . Perhaps he doesn't realize it is dead, and imagines he can make a pet of it. If you can get him to confide in you, I'm sure you'll be able to set his mind at rest. Of course, he may have forgotten the whole thing after a day at school."

Mary hoped that would be the case, but it was obvious as soon as she saw him that afternoon that his secret still worried him. He rejected all her coaxing offers of help, pushing her away, hugging his fear to himself, uneasy in her presence. So Mary waited, kept the distance he seemed to want, and watched.

He was sneaking food outside. Biscuits, bits of chocolate, an apple . . . she meant to let him continue, but at the thought of the mess eggs and baked beans would make in his pockets, she caught his hand before he could transfer food from his plate to his lap.

"Darling, you don't have to do that," she said. "I'll give you a plate, and you can put the food on that and take it out to your little friend. Just eat your own meal first."

His pale face went paler. "You know?"

Mary hesitated. "I know . . . you're upset about something. And I know you've been leaving food outside. Now, why don't you tell Mummy what's going on, and I'll help you."

Emotions battled on his face; then, surrender.

"He's hungry," Jamie said plaintively. "He's so hungry, so, so hungry. I keep giving him food, but it's not right . . . he won't eat it. I don't know what he . . . I don't want . . . I can't . . . I'm giving him everything and he won't eat. What does he eat, Mummy? What *else* does he eat?"

Mary imagined a mole's tiny corpse, Jamie thrusting food beneath its motionless snout. "Maybe he doesn't eat anything," she said.

"No, he has to! If you're alive, you have to eat."

"Well, Jamie, maybe he's dead."

She half expected some outburst, an excited protest against that idea, but Jamie shook his head, an oddly mature and thoughtful expression on his face. He had obviously considered this possibility before. "No, he's not dead. I thought, I thought when I found him in my grave, I thought he was dead, but then he wasn't. He isn't dead."

"Who isn't dead? What is this you're talking about, Jamie? Is it an animal?"

He looked puzzled. "You don't know?"

She shook her head. "Will you show him to me, darling?"

Jamie looked alarmed. He shook his head and began to tremble. Mary knelt beside his chair and put her arms around him, holding him close, safe and tight.

"It's all right," she said. "Mummy's here. It's all right . . ."

When he had calmed she thought to distract him, but he returned to the subject of feeding this unknown creature.

"Well," said Mary, "if he's not eating the food you give him, maybe he doesn't need to be fed. He might find his own food—animals usually do, you know, except for pets and babies."

"He's like a baby."

"How is he like a baby? What does he look like?"

"I don't know. I don't remember now—I can't. He doesn't look like anything—not like anything except himself."

It was only then that it occurred to Mary that there might be no animal at all, not even a dead mole. This creature Jamie had found was probably completely imaginary—that was why he couldn't show it to her.

"He can probably find his own food," Mary said.

But this idea obviously bothered Jamie, who began to fidget. "He needs me."

"How do you know that? Did he tell you? Can't he tell you what sort of food he wants, then?"

Jamie shrugged, nodded, then shook his head. "I have to get something for him."

"But he must have managed on his own before you found him—"

"He was all right before," Jamie agreed. "But he needs me now. I found him, so now I have to take care of him. But . . . he won't eat. I keep trying and trying, but he won't take the food. And he's hungry. What can I give him, Mummy? What can I give him to eat?"

Mary stopped trying to be reasonable, then, and let herself enter his fantasy.

"Don't worry, darling," she said. "We'll find something for your little friend—we'll try everything in the kitchen if we have to!"

With Jamie's help, Mary prepared a whole trayful of food: a saucer of milk and one of sweetened tea; water-biscuits spread with peanut butter; celery tops and chopped carrots; lettuce leaves; raisins; plain bread, buttered bread, and bread spread with honey. As she carried the tray outside, Mary wondered what sort of pests this would attract, then dismissed it as unimportant. She pretended to catch sight of Jamie's imaginary friend.

"Oh, we've got something he likes here," she said. "Just look at him smacking his lips!"

Jamie gave her a disapproving look. "You don't see him."

"How do you know? Isn't that him over there by the hedge?"

"If you saw him, you'd probably scream. And, anyway, he hasn't *got* lips."

"What does he look like? Is he so frightening?"

"It doesn't matter," Jamie said.

"Shall I put the tray down here?"

He nodded. The playfulness and interest he had shown in the kitchen had vanished, and he was worried again. He sighed. "If he doesn't eat this . . ."

"If he doesn't, there's plenty more in the kitchen we can try," said Mary.

"He's so hungry," Jamie murmured sadly.

He was concerned, when they went back inside, about locking the house. This was not a subject which had ever interested him before, but now he followed Mary around, and she demonstrated that both front and back doors were secure, and all the windows—particularly the window in his room—were shut and locked.

"There are other ways for things to get in, though," he said.

"No, of course not, darling."

"How do my dreams get in, then?"

"Your dreams?" She crouched beside him on the bedroom floor and stroked his hair. "Dreams don't come in from the outside, darling. Dreams are inside, in your head."

"They're already inside?"

"They aren't real, darling. They're imaginary. They aren't real and solid like I am, or like you are . . . they're just . . . like thoughts. Like make-believe. And they go away when you're awake."

"Oh," he said. She couldn't tell what he thought, or if her words had comforted him. She hugged him close until he wriggled to be free, and then she put him to bed.

She checked on him twice during the night, and both times he appeared to be sleeping soundly. Yet in the morning, again, he had the darkened eyes and grogginess of one who'd had a disturbed night.

She thought about taking him to the doctor instead of to school, but the memory of her conversation with Dr. Abden stopped her. This was something she had to cope with herself. There was nothing physically wrong with Jamie. His sleeplessness was obviously the result of worry, and the doctor had already reminded her that it was her duty, as his mother, to set his mind at rest. If only he would tell her what was wrong!

That afternoon Jamie was again subdued, quiet and good. Mary actually preferred him like this, but because such behavior wasn't normal for him, she worried even while she appreciated his nearness. They sat together playing games and looking through his books, taking turns reading to each other. Later, she left the dishes to soak in the sink and watched her son as he sat with his crayons and his coloring book, wondering what went on in his mind.

"Has your little friend gone away, to find food somewhere else?" she asked.

Jamie shook his head.

"We could put some more food out for him, you know. I don't mind. Anything you like."

Jamie was silent for a while, and then he said, "He doesn't need food."

"Doesn't he? That's very unusual. What does he live on?"

Jamie stopped coloring, the crayon frozen in his hand. Then he drew a deep, shuddering breath. "Love," he said, and began coloring again.

He was no longer worried about the doors and windows, and it was Mary, not Jamie, who prolonged the bedside chat and goodnight kisses, reluctant to leave him alone. He didn't seem afraid, but she was afraid for him, without knowing why.

"Goodnight, my darling," she said for the fifth or sixth last time, and made herself rise and move away from the bed. "Sleep well . . . call me if you need anything . . . I'll be awake . . ." Her voice trailed off. Already, it appeared, he was sleeping. She went out quietly and left his bedroom door ajar. If he made a sound, she would hear it.

She turned the television on low and slumped in a chair before it. She was too tired to think, too distracted to be entertained. She might as well go to bed herself, she thought.

So she turned off the television, tidied up, turned out the lights and checked the doors one last time. On her way to her own bedroom she decided to look in on Jamie, just to reassure herself that all was well.

Pushing the door open let in a swathe of light from the corridor. It fell across the bed, revealing Jamie lying uncovered, half curled on one side, and not alone.

There was something nestled close to him, in the crook of his arm; something grey and wet-looking, a featureless lump about the size of a loaf of bread; something like a gigantic slug pressed against his pyjama-covered chest and bare neck.

Horror might have frozen her—she couldn't have imagined coping with something like that in the garden or on the kitchen floor—but fear for her son propelled her forward. As she moved, the soft grey body rippled, turning, and it looked at Mary. For a face there was only a slightly flattened area with two round, black eyes and no mouth.

In her haste and terror Mary almost fell onto the bed. She caught hold of the thing and pulled it off her son, sobbing with revulsion.

She had expected it to be as cold and slimy as it looked, perhaps even insubstantial enough that the harsh touch of her hands could destroy it. In fact, it was warm and solid and surprisingly heavy. And it smelled like Jamie. Not like Jamie now, but like Jamie as a baby—that sweet, milky scent which made her melt inside. Like Jen's baby. Like every helpless, harmless newborn. She closed her eyes, remembering.

Mary pressed her face against the soft flesh and inhaled. No skin had ever been so deliciously, silkenly smooth. Her lips moved against it. She could never have enough of touching and kissing it; she wished she was a cat and could lick her baby clean a hundred times a day.

Responding, it nuzzled back, head butting at her blindly, and she unbuttoned her blouse. Her breasts felt sore and heavy with milk, and she longed for the relief of nursing.

Somewhere nearby a child was crying, a sound that rasped at her nerves and distracted her. Someone was tugging at her clothes, at her arm, and crying, "Mummy," until she had, finally, to open her eyes.

A little boy with a pale, tear-stained face gazed up at her. "Don't," he said. "Don't, Mummy."

She knew who he was—he was her son. But he seemed somehow threatening, and she wrapped her arms more tightly around the creature that she held.

"Go to bed," she said firmly.

He began to weep, loudly and helplessly.

But that irritated her more, because he wasn't helpless; she knew he wasn't helpless.

"Stop crying," she said. "Go to bed. You're all right." She pushed him away from her with her hip, not daring to let go. But as she

looked down she glimpsed something grey and formless lying pressed
between her breasts. For just a moment she had a brief, distracting
vision of a face without a mouth, always hungry, never satisfied. She
thought of an open grave, and she closed her eyes.

"He needs me," she said.

At last she felt complete. She would never be alone again.

Within the protective circle of her arms, the creature had begun to
feed.

Not long ago, I visited a writers' conference in Oklahoma, fully expecting to meet (as has happened before) blue-haired retired women and bald retired men who wrote diaries, doggerel, and cute stories about cute pets. Well, they weren't there, thank god. But Nina Higgins was, a delightful woman who vowed to send me a story as soon as she could get back to her typewriter in Tulsa, assuring me that she knew what I meant when I said "shadows." She was right. This is it, her first published story, and I'm pleased to be able to present it, and her, to you now.

APPLES

by Nina Downey Higgins

"It's mother," Mitchell said, trying to read Heather's reaction as she poured coffee. "She follows me everywhere." He glanced at the apartment window for a convincing amount of time.

Heather never veered her gaze from him. "That can't be, Mitch."

He glared at Heather, who was now sitting across from him at the table. She was thinner than he remembered. He didn't recall when he'd seen her last, but he supposed it was about the time of her father's death. Remembering was troublesome. As she had been. "Mother hates me."

"Mother's dead." Heather's expression bordered on boredom. "I'm quite sure she has forgiven you all your shortcomings. Anyway, what can she possibly do to you now?"

After all these years, he was still uncertain of his feelings toward his stepsister. They were actually the same age, only the harsh lines had not yet eroded the skin around her eyes. Her dark hair, rolled up in a French twist, made him feel unkempt, made him feel much older than his twenty-eight years. His own straggly hair touched his shoulders. Hitchhiking several hundred miles hadn't helped.

"It's easy for you to be flip. No one's after you. You don't know what it's like." He jammed the fork into the sausage link. The tines stuck in the thin casing of meat. "She wants revenge, I tell you. Because I left you when you were . . ." He didn't have to pretend to swallow a lump. It was the sausage. "You were just a little kid." He managed to throttle out the words.

She shrugged. "We were both kids. I've done all right for myself."

"Yeah." He tossed a crust of biscuit onto his plate and stared at her lounging dress. Chiffon, or crepe, or something. It looked very expensive. He looked down at his faded jeans, which seemed to get baggier every day. "And your stepbrother is so far down on his luck it'll take an oil rig to dredge him up."

She tossed him that look—the one that said *What else is new?* "You'll find a job, Mitch," she said as she cleared the table.

He grunted. "You call cleaning out latrines and washing dishes *jobs?* Mother always said I'd never amount to anything. 'Can't even hold a decent job,' she said. 'Someday when your poor mother is dead, you'll be sorry,' she said."

Heather paused in her trek to the sink. He'd have sworn, even though looking at the back of her head, that she'd smiled.

The high-pitched shriek of the teakettle punctuated secrets about him that both his mother and Heather harbored. The little hammers tapped at his temples. Coffee slipped through his teeth, wetting the tip of his tongue. "Turn that thing off, will you?"

Heather raised an arm, and for a moment, he thought she'd been about to strike him. "What do you want from me, Mitch? Why did you come here?" There was something brazen about the way she went to the stove to turn off the flame.

Sweat beaded across his upper lip. The soft curves of Heather's body disturbed him. The room was suddenly very warm. "I thought we might get reacquainted. Look, I won't stay long. I'll get a job, get my own place."

He watched the deep-set stains spread across the porcelain edges of the sink. He rubbed a hand over his chin, discovered his beard was matted and grimy. He needed a shower.

"You can't stay here," she said as though she could see right into his mind.

He choked on a swallow of coffee. "What do you mean?"

She sighed noisily. "I have my own problems. Besides, we wouldn't get along."

He tried on the surprised and hurt look. "We got along okay when we were back in California. I kept your old man from slapping you around, didn't I?"

Heather folded her arms. "Leave him out of this. And just because he married your whining, self-centered mother doesn't make me responsible for you."

"You really hate me, don't you?"

"For Chrissake, Mitch. It isn't that. You'd be . . ." She glanced toward the bedroom. "You'd be uncomfortable here."

Mitch kicked the table leg, stood and flung the chair away from him. "Just where would I be comfortable? Answer me that, will you?"

She shook her head. "I guess it is partly my fault, isn't it? My father and your mother. What a pair, huh?"

Mitch scowled. "Remembering is like bobbing for apples. The things just keep popping back to the surface. Sometimes they smack you right in the face."

She laughed. "I know exactly what you mean. All right, *brother.*" She said it as though he were another apple to reckon with—the bad one of the bunch. "But only this once. And only if you'll promise to look for a job right away. And I'll even spring for lunch." She dug out a loaf of bread and began to make sandwiches. "We'll bury the hatchet for one night."

He winced at her choice of words. As she went to work preparing him a sack lunch, the room became a merry-go-round of churning colors. If only he could get off the ride. Heather was his last chance.

After she'd gone into the bathroom and closed the door, Mitch caroused around the kitchen. Then he moseyed quietly over to the teapot, reached in, and fished out three dollars and a handful of change. Good old Heather, he thought, glad that human creatures never changed their habits.

"See you later?" he said to her as she left.

She waved at him, then stole a glance over her shoulder, went back to close the bedroom door. "See you later. And good luck."

Clutching the brown paper bag in his left hand, he opened the door to a wave of sultry heat. He caught a bus to town, where thousands of staggered windowpanes caught the blaring rays of the sun. In spite of the summer morning, a chill crept up his backbone and sifted through the hair at the nape of his neck. This was not going to be pleasant. The day was already an eternity that sapped his strength.

Maybe his mother had been right. Maybe he really was a good-for-nothing. Maybe she really was here, looking over his shoulder, waiting for him to fall flat on his keister. The story of his life.

Business establishments which always shook their collective heads and professed their redundant apologies. *Had to lay off . . . not hiring now . . . the economy, you know.*

After his third random attempt at seeking employment, and following the consumption of his peanut butter sandwiches while sitting on a wooden bench, a Chinaman with a broom chased him from a vegetable stand while emitting a string of foreign obscenities.

Mitch ran, dodging the shadows under the eaves. Once he caught a glimpse of himself in a shop window—an emaciated, bearded ghost who paralleled his lanky movements. He crossed a rubbish-filled alley, and when the sun crossed over the top of the sky, the shadows shifted. And it was the first time he'd known for sure.

Someone was watching him. Could it be Heather? She'd be at work at her secretarial job, not giving him a second thought. He looked around him, at the people going about their business, and thought that the heat was getting to him.

Checking his shirt pocket to be sure the three dollars were still there, he slipped, unnoticed by the apathetic shoppers, into a bar and ordered a beer. The hillbilly tune bleating from the jukebox echoed his mood. It was too early to go back to Heather's apartment. She would know if he'd lolled around, even for a few hours. He'd simply have to make the beer last a long time. Maybe scrape up enough change to buy another. Drinking was good for him. It dulled his senses; gave him courage; diminished the cudgeling effect of life's rejections.

He hadn't meant to let it get so late. But when he wandered outside, he was greeted by a velvety grey cloak of dusk. As he walked, night fell swiftly, like the blade of a guillotine. A shadow, shapeless but definite, followed him like an invisible panther. He turned. "Who's there?"

No one. Nothing. All the same, he picked up his pace. Houses slipped nonchalantly by. And still it came, catching up to him. He could feel it breathing on him.

"What the hell . . . ?" He jogged, his breath coming in ragged spurts. Beating the sidewalk with the soles of his shoes, his sobs caught in his burning chest, until at last he was on Heather's street.

Emitting a little cry, he ran inside the apartment and turned the lock. He stood against the inside of the door, his legs spread as though he were about to take flight. His eyes closed. His heart pounded. Minutes passed. He was dimly aware of soft music playing.

He opened his eyes. Safe inside, he thought. But safe from what? Had the beer turned him into a whimpering bundle of paranoia? He felt a twinge of anger when he realized that Heather wasn't home. Then in the next moment, he found himself wondering why the lights were burning if she wasn't home.

The bathroom door was closed. Perhaps she was in there. He listened at the door but heard nothing.

"Heather?" he called out with caution. Now he heard water dripping in the shower. The soft music continued to serenade him. He called to her again, this time placing his hand on the doorknob and gently pushing open the door.

Blood jetted into his veins. The shower curtain was closed. The smell of soap and talcum powder was fresh. But no sound came to him, except for the slow, tantalizing drip of the water.

Whether from concern for Heather or from his own morbid curiosity, he yanked back the curtain. There was no one there. He felt like screaming. Instead he laughed aloud. She must have come in, showered, and gone out again. On the floor stood tiny puddles of water. They seemed to give off a greenish hue.

When the music stopped, he realized it had been coming from the adjoining apartment. It dawned on him that the place was not so welcoming in the evening hours. The rooms were overheated. A film of haze filled the pores of the air. But at least he was safe. Inside, he could relax.

In the refrigerator, he found some red wine and a steak—which he broiled for himself. He attacked the juicy meat until his belly was full. Then he wandered through the apartment.

Peeking into Heather's bedroom, Mitch was at once aroused by the sweet mingling aromas of perfumes and colognes. He picked up a bottle from her dresser top. He barely had time to register the thought that the bottle's contents were a man's cologne when the front door opened.

He hurried into the living room. She didn't speak, but rather behaved as if he weren't there. "Where've you been?" he demanded.

She glared at him. "I'm going to bed. You can sleep there. On the sofa." She pointed the way.

The ballpeen hammer that drove at his temples wouldn't stop. "Where did you get those fancy clothes?"

She didn't look at him. "Tomorrow, Mitch. You must go tomorrow." She started toward her room, then hesitated at the door. "And stay away from my teapot."

He had but a minute's warning, but he had no doubt that the beer and wine and steak were coming up. He clapped a hand over his mouth, ran to the bathroom. He threw up, the remnants of his mother's voice ringing in his ear. *You'll be sorry when I'm dead and gone* . . . The flushing of the toilet lopped off her words.

He staggered to the sofa. Get a good night's sleep, he told himself. Tomorrow, he would go out and get a real job. Be like Heather. Tomorrow. He sank into the fabric of the sofa.

The haze in the room had thickened. When he tried to close his eyes, he heard the first of the sounds. He raised his head; looked toward the window; heard . . .

A stretching sound, like wood expanding, then a dripping, like partially frozen liquid. He inhaled. Listened.

A warm gust of wind filtered through the window screen, followed by a buzzing quietness. Night sounds. Nothing else. The shade, halfway down, displayed reels of street movie shadows. He breathed.

And he slept. And in his sleep, he saw green glowing images winding through back alleys, curling tentacles of mist. And the men of the town chased him with brooms and rakes and hatchets while Heather's voice crooned *if in fact there is anything to forgive* and the Chinaman brought down the long, slender blade of a sword toward a red apple which was sitting atop Mitch's head.

Mitch sat up. He was sweating profusely. Who had screamed? Himself? A cat, perhaps. He lay awake for a long time.

When he awakened the next morning, Heather's bedroom door was ajar. He peered inside. Her bed was tidily made, but she was gone. He stretched, sniffing the air, pleased to discover she'd left him fresh coffee. In the light of day, the apartment looked cozy, the air looked clear. He breathed deeply, then he remembered.

She'd only given him one night. The old hackles rose up into his craw. He'd have to go out job hunting today or get out of the apartment.

Yesterday, no one had offered to hire him, nor even to interview him. He hadn't even left his name with anyone. Most had openly shunned him. And if last night's dream had been any indication, he'd have the same rotten luck today.

Over coffee, he shuffled his thoughts. Maybe he would just make a day of it here. Get a six-pack. Watch the soaps. Stretch the one allotted night into two. He was the expert at it, after all.

But Heather was no dummy. She would know if he just sat around all day. Heather knew everything about him. With the old double-headed monster of guilt and resentment gnawing away at his insides, he showered and brushed his teeth, then dressed in his last clean change of clothes.

In the teapot, he found a twenty. Despising and yet relishing her carelessness, he snatched the money and went out to be swallowed up by the world. But of course it had been his mother who had chewed him up and spit him out because he'd been the replica of his father.

He wondered why he wasn't dead. He had, of course, thought of suicide. But how would he do it? He had never been able to think of a painless way. He could just step into the street and allow a semi to run over him. But what if he just bounced off the windshield—like the apples that bobbed up and down in the water—why, with his luck, he'd land squarely on his feet again.

So he had no choice but to alter his ways. Find a job, even if it was the degrading manual labor sort. He couldn't blame Heather for not wanting him around. But they'd stuck together during their growing-up days under the most adverse of conditions. They could, unlike his mother and her father, pull together now.

Near the first busy district, he saw Heather about a block away. She was getting into a cab with a man. Mitch hailed a cab for himself and had the driver follow them.

The lead taxi stopped in front of a shabby-looking hotel and the couple got out and ducked quickly inside. For a moment Mitch sat there, his mind listing, then crossing off, plausible excuses. The revelation jolted him. "I'll be damned," he muttered. "She's a hooker."

The cab driver glared at him in the rear-view mirror. "You gettin' out here or what?"

Mitch felt a mixture of relief and anger. "Take me to the nearest bar."

The establishment was a place called Cleary's. It was a place where he could sit and revel in all life's screw-ups.

Heather was rich. Well, maybe not rich, but a far site better off than he was. So who'd messed up his life? Surely not himself. He'd used the hauntings of his mother as an excuse for failure. Now it was time for him to wake up and face the real world. And tomorrow, without fail, he was going to do just that. But for now, he still had enough money left to put some bread and butter on the table of Mr. Cleary.

When the twenty bucks was gone he sauntered out of Cleary's, confident that he had enough information to blackmail her into letting him stay for as long as he liked. He rode a bus to Heather's end of town, keeping well ahead of the shadow, which was after all an abomination of his past and not his future. He jogged the remaining blocks to the apartment in the gathering darkness, laughing aloud as he entered.

Inside, his laughter subsided. From the square of living-room window, the moonlight disappeared as a corrugated shadow crossed the pane of glass. The blood coursed, grosgrain rivulets of liquid, through his limbs. Something was behind him. Something had *come in* with him. Had slipped past the doorjamb like a rat.

He looked toward Heather's bedroom and saw nothing but the haze of light that filtered from beneath her door.

She was already in bed. He'd have to wake her up, to tell her what he'd done. When he tried to walk, the room seemed to swell, to press his chest muscles together. He could barely breathe. Slowly he inched forward, pausing at her door.

In the bedroom he heard Heather sigh, then turn over in her sleep. A green mist seeped and curled from beneath her door. The same green mist that had awakened him last night.

He heard a mewling sound, then Heather began to moan. The thing he'd let into the apartment was in there with her.

Mitch turned the doorknob and pushed the door slowly open.

The room was filled with the thick green mist. A nauseating stench overpowered him, reeled him backward. Green tentacles tugged at his clothing, caressed his skin as he pushed his way into the facsimile of his dream.

"Heather, wake up! You have to get out!"

She rose slowly, coming upright on the bed, covers pulled snugly up to her nose. Her hair stood up as though she'd been electrocuted. A green hand gripped Mitch's throat. He made a choking sound.

Heather impaled him with icy eyes. "I tried to warn you, Mitch." Her voice was muffled. "I tried to tell you, but you wouldn't listen."

Mitch lay on the floor, gasping for breath. "What . . . tell me . . . what?"

Inch by inch she slid the covers down. Her mouth curved into a smile. "It's father."

I have been an unabashed fan of T. M. Wright ever since I read his first novel, Strange Seed, *a superior work of dark fantasy. Since its appearance in 1978, Mr. Wright's energies have been directed primarily toward producing such fine books as* The Woman Next Door *and* Nursery Tale. *His latest is* The Waiting Room. *Now, he has taken his distinctive style into the short story, and the following piece is his first appearance in* Shadows.

A WORLD WITHOUT TOYS
by T. M. Wright

When the County Water Authority tore up part of St. Paul Street so new pipe could be laid—the old pipe had been there nearly seventy-five years, and, according to records, had never been patched—they found a small green clapboard house in the storm sewer twenty feet below street level. Only the front of the house and its rusted tin roof were visible from above; there was a chimney, half of it gone, and small sections of the roof's cap were missing, exposing portions of the framing beneath.

Subsequently, two people from the local historical society were summoned. They peered down at the house and exclaimed that it was, indeed, of great and consuming interest, if only a way could be found to get down to it. A way was found. Workers widened the big hole, a ladder was carefully lowered in, and the two people from the historical society climbed down with hard hats firmly in place and encountered the front door of the house.

One of these people, a man in his late forties who was wiry and bright and always wore colorful bow ties, said, "Should we knock?" and chuckled.

The woman with him, also in her late forties, her name was Blanche, said through tight, thin lips, "This is hardly a joking matter, Alex. This house could be of extreme historical importance. And you know, of course, that there may be people in it."

Alex gave her a feigned look of alarm. "People? You mean *dead* people?"

"Yes," she told him grimly, "dead people," and she stepped forward in the few feet between the ladder and the oak front door and tried the brass knob. She stepped back.

"What's the matter?" Alex asked.

"It's locked," she said. "The door is locked. It was something I hadn't expected."

From above, a workman called, "You people okay down there?"

Alex said, "What do you mean it's locked?"

"I mean it won't open. I need a key."

"Maybe the people who live here stepped out for a few minutes." He smiled. "Maybe we can leave them a note and tell them when we'll be back."

She gave him a hard look. "Alex," she proclaimed, "if there *are* people here, in this house, then I would say that in all likelihood it is their *mausoleum.* So my guess is that they'd be even less responsive to your so-called humor than I am. If that's possible."

Alex continued smiling. "Well put," he said.

Again the workman twenty feet up, at street level, called down, "Are you people okay?"

Blanche called back, "We have a problem. The house is locked."

"Locked," the workman said, parroting her.

"Maybe," Alex suggested, "we can get in through a window."

There were three windows in the front of the house—two, with lace curtains drawn, to either side of the door, and one very tall and narrow window six or seven feet above it, in what apparently was the attic. Blanche and Alex could not get to either lower window easily because there was water pooled around the house; since the house rested on what appeared to be a natural limestone hump, they had no idea how deep the water could be ("You got some troughs down there," a workman had told them, "that you could step in and never come out of. It ain't no place for no one to go walking around alone").

Alex got back on the ladder and climbed it so he could peer into the attic window.

Blanche called to him, "Do you see anything?"

He called back, "Yes. I do."

Blanche waited a few moments for him to continue. When he didn't, she called, *"What* do you see, Alex?"

He answered, "I see . . . toys."

"Toys?"

"Yes. A rocking horse. Some blocks. Wooden blocks with the alphabet on them. A train set. And a doll . . . no, two dolls. Raggedy

Ann, I think—Blanche, I think it's a Raggedy Ann and a Raggedy Andy." He smiled. "*I* had a Raggedy Andy."

And I had a Raggedy Ann, Blanche thought, but she said nothing and within a few seconds had chased the thought away.

"That's about it," Alex called. "Toys," he murmured, and when Blanche looked up at him through the gloom below the street, she saw a tiny, quivering smile on his face.

"Come down from there," she told him.

Reluctantly, he came down.

She said, "It's remarkably well preserved," paused, continued, "And it has no business being here, but it *is* here, of course, so it's something we'll have to deal with." She studied the house a moment. "I think that it is possibly pre-Victorian, and, well preserved though it is, it lacks character, of course, so it is clearly the house of a laborer of the day—"

A workman called down, "You two gotta come up outa there now."

Blanche called back, "I'm sorry, we can't do that. We have hardly begun our investigation—"

"You don't come up outa there you're gonna get awful wet."

"I'm sorry?"

"It's gonna rain, sister. It's gonna rain hard."

Blanche noticed then that the light had changed, that it had grown even more deeply sullen than when they had come down the ladder. "We *must* get into this house. You can understand that, of course."

"You got about a minute and a half, then you're probably gonna go swimmin'."

"Dammit!" Blanche whispered.

On the way back up the ladder, she looked briefly into the attic. Alex, ahead of her on the ladder, said, "You coming, Blanche?"

She said, "This is a strange place. This is a very strange place. I'm not at all certain that it makes me comfortable." She paused. She realized that she wasn't sure what she was talking about. "There's light in that room," she said, meaning the attic. She said "room" because that's the way it looked—like a child's room that no child had ever used because it was too much in order, too much as if in waiting.

"Not possible," Alex said.

"I'm aware of that," she said. "I was speaking . . . metaphorically." She closed her eyes in brief embarrassment. She added, "You understand that, of course."

"Of course, Blanche," he lied.

She finished, "I would say, in fact, that this house makes me extremely uncomfortable."

"I think it's great," Alex said.

And she told him, her tone very serious and very instructive, "Alex, I believe that you are forty-seven years old going on twelve." It was very similar to what she'd told him many times before—"Alex, I believe that you are forty-three years old going on thirteen," . . . "Alex, I believe that you are forty-five years old going on ten," . . . "Alex, I believe that you are forty-two years old going on fourteen." She kept him in adolescence because that was very reassuring to her.

It rained that night. It was not a gentle rain, not comforting or restful, not the kind of rain that soothes and heals. It was a torrent, as if an ocean were draining, and the things that got caught in it—hoboes, night workers, trees, cats, flowers—were marked by it and their lives made shorter because of it.

Blanche was sent stumbling to her window by it and she watched in awe and fear as it wailed at her in a fury that there were things beyond her control, after all. It was not something she would have admitted aloud, although she understood it. There were many things that she understood. Things about the world she'd grown into and become a part of—a world made up of meetings, and lunches, and decision-making, and exhaustion. A world she'd moved about in for centuries. A world that pinched. A world without toys.

She stood for a long time at her window. She watched the storm reach a peak, then watched it groan back to practically nothing, then, as if it were relieved or sated, almost instantly to nothing at all. Then it was morning and there were shiny black streets and a peach-colored sky. And there were people, too. They moved tentatively, like small animals, out of their houses. And they nodded at each other and began to piece their worlds together from the debris left behind by what the earth had hurled at them the night before.

When, late that morning, Blanche arrived at the hole in the street and looked down she saw that sunlight was bouncing gaily off the sides of the hole all the way to the bottom. She saw as well that the house was not there.

She looked at a workman standing beside her. She gave him a small, incredulous, quivering smile. "The house isn't there," she said.

"I know it isn't," he said.

Alex came up alongside her then. "The storm washed it away, Blanche," he told her.

She shook her head slowly. She said, "How could the storm do that?"

The workman said, "Hell, lady, there was a lot of rain last night. It had to go somewhere." He nodded at the hole. "That's where it went."

Alex repeated, "And it washed the house away, Blanche. I'm sorry."

"Sorry?"

"It was probably of great historical importance," he explained, and adjusted his bright bow tie.

She said nothing. She looked stunned, Alex thought. He said, in order to comfort her, "Chances are, Blanche, that it broke up." He had no real idea why such a statement would comfort her. He might have decided, had he examined it, that it would have comforted her because there was much work to do elsewhere. And besides, working below the street was a dirty business, and smelly, too, and was without a doubt extremely dangerous.

"Broke up?" she said.

He nodded. "Yes. Broke up. Into pieces."

"And?"

"And so . . . and so . . ." He smiled. "It got swept away and is beyond us and we can get on to other things."

She shook her head. "Alex, we have to go and find it."

He shook his head. "We can't do that. We're not equipped to do that."

She looked from his face to the hole in the street, then back to his face. She said, "Alex, that house was of great . . . *historical* importance. And besides . . ." She stopped. She looked confused.

"Besides?" Alex coaxed.

"Besides," she said, "there were toys in it."

The workman said, "Toys?"

"Yes," she said, "in the house."

"Toys?" the workman said again, as if it were a word he just then had encountered.

Alex explained, "There was a rocking horse. Yes. And a train set. And some blocks."

"With the alphabet on them," Blanche cut in, smiling a broad, childlike smile that Alex had never seen on her before. "And a Raggedy Ann and Raggedy Andy."

The workman shrugged. "Well, they ain't there no more, and that's about as true as yesterday."

It was a week of storms, all of them as angry and as destructive as the first, all of them interrupted, during the day, by sunlight and still, clear air. It was a week that sat on Blanche like a bullfrog, a week that she moved about in leadenly from place to place, from responsibility to responsibility, as if her world were some grim amusement park where the carousel horses didn't move and the funhouse consisted only of darkness and the prize for knocking over milk bottles on the midway was a trip back in time to do it all over again.

To grow up all over again.

To be here. And be precisely who she was.

"Did you ever wonder," Alex asked her at the end of that week, "how it got there?"

"It?"

"The house below the street."

"No," she told him. "I never wondered. It was there, that was all we needed to know. It was all anybody needed to know."

Alex smiled. They were in a big gray brick Victorian on Mount Hope Avenue and they were trying to decide if it qualified for landmark status. "Or *why* it was there, Blanche? Did you ever wonder *why* it was there?"

"No," she answered at once, as if the question frightened her.

"You don't need to know very much, do you, Blanche?"

"Sorry?" she said, though she knew what he meant.

He explained, "You don't need to look around the edges of things. You don't need to see around corners. You've got your eyes glued only on the road ahead."

"No," she told him. "No," she repeated thoughtfully, as if to herself. "I *do* want to see around corners. I want that very much. But I don't know how."

Alex adjusted his bright bow tie. Adjusting it was a nervous habit and he often adjusted it when it didn't need adjusting. He was nervous because he wanted to tell her something that had pounced on him just then but that he didn't have the nerve to tell her. He wanted to tell her that he cared for her.

"It's possible," he said, "that the house under the street wasn't there at all."

He didn't know *why* he cared for her; perhaps it was a fault within himself that had caused it, some growth had taken over a lobe of his brain and had made him stupid. He'd worked with Blanche for five years, and in that time she had said only one kind thing to him— "I'm sorry about your hamster, Alex; *I* had a hamster once."

"Yes," she said now, in the gray brick Victorian on Mount Hope Avenue, "I know. It's possible that the house under the street wasn't there at all."

This surprised him. "But it *was* there," he said. "I was only . . . joking. It was only a joke."

"The room we looked at could have been anything," she said. "It could have been a concoction. It could have been a dream, Alex."

He looked at her and saw that she was smiling oddly, as if at the memory of something that warmed her slowly from the inside, like pudding. "But it *was* there, Blanche," he insisted.

"And now it's gone," she said. "And that's what matters. It matters that it was there, under the street, and now it's gone, and we can . . . get on to other things." It sounded to Alex like a plea. She looked away, as if embarrassed.

"I care for you," he said, but it was to himself, in his head, in preparation for saying it aloud, and he didn't say it aloud because it didn't make any sense to him.

That night, Blanche threw her cool sheets off her cold legs, put on her terry-cloth robe and her blue slippers, and padded to the window that overlooked her street. *The rain has stopped,* she told herself.

She smiled. Light from a streetlamp below bounced off her face, then off the window, and she saw her reflection. It was, she realized, the first time in forty years that she'd seen her own smile.

Suddenly she wished she had a cat. Something to talk to. She didn't know for sure what she'd say to it, but she knew that she would make sounds at it and that it would respond in its way. Maybe she'd tell it what she'd been afraid to tell herself all these years—that there really was a world made up of Raggedy Anns and Raggedy Andys, toy trains, and wooden blocks. A world that didn't pinch. A world that was buried as deep within her as the house and its wonderful attic room were buried beneath the street.

She talked to her smiling reflection. She said, "And all I have to do is find it." She turned from the window. She hesitated. Her smile broadened. She slipped out of her blue terry-cloth robe and her slippers. She dressed. And she walked out of her apartment and into the night.

Later that morning, toward noon, a workman at the hole in the street, where the house had been, handed Alex a hard hat and told him, "The hole wasn't closed up, mister, 'cuz we wasn't finished workin' in it." He paused very briefly, then continued, "You know that it's gonna rain?"

"Yes," said Alex.

"An' you know," the workman pressed on, "that if you get caught down there and it's rainin' real hard then you'll drown for sure. There are troughs you could walk into and never come out of—"

"I know that."

The workman shrugged. "You got your lamp?"

Alex held up the battery-powered lantern that the foreman of the work crew had given him.

"Good," said the workman. "There ain't no lights."

"I know," said Alex, and a moment later he was climbing down into the hole in the street on the same ladder that Blanche had used eight hours before.

He could hear the other rescue workers. He could hear bits of conversations, grumbled curses, and he thought as he listened that those men could be anywhere in the maze of tunnels under the street, that he could head in their direction and get to where he thought they were and find that they were somewhere else entirely.

But he knew this, also, as he listened to them: he knew that they were not going to find Blanche. He knew that *he* was going to find her.

He could see their lights, then, and he realized that they were moving in his direction. He stayed still. He said nothing. He did not call out to them, as he'd been told. For a few moments he watched their lights—softened by reflection from half a dozen wet stone walls —then he turned and walked in the other direction, through ankle-deep water; as he walked, the dull orange light of his lantern showed him only the angles of dark walls intersecting other dark walls.

He walked this way—slowly, through the ankle-deep water—for ten minutes. Then he saw the house.

And at that same moment, he heard from far behind him, "I found her. God, I found her!"

He smiled. *No,* he thought, *no, you haven't found her.*

"Bring a light," shouted the same voice. "Mine ain't much good no more. Bring a light."

The house was listing in the tunnel, like a ship beginning to sink, the left side in one of the troughs he'd been warned about, so his lamp could not show him much of it—only the lower right-hand window, some of the right-hand wall, green clapboards trailing off into darkness, and the softly glistening front edge of the rusted tin roof. And all of the attic window, too, which he could see very well because it was illuminated from within.

He heard then, from far behind him, "It's her. God, it's her!"

And another voice answered, "How are we going to get to her?"

No, Alex called to them in his head, smiling, *no, you're mistaken, that's not her at all. No. She's here!*

He set his light down on a ledge near where the tunnel wall intersected the floor.

He moved forward through the ankle-deep water toward the little house under the street. He longed to peer into the attic window but he couldn't; even though the house was listing, the window was still too far above him. He stepped up to the door, saw the soft reflection of his lamplight on the brass knob, reached out, grasped the knob hard.

He heard from far behind him, "She's rolled over. I can see her face!"

"Can you get to her?" shouted another voice.

"I don't know," answered the first voice. "I don't know. Get me a line."

Alex turned the knob. "Blanche?" he whispered. The door was locked.

He heard from behind him, and above—at street level, he guessed —"Come on outa there!"

He shook his head. *No,* he thought. He stepped back from the door and peered up through the gloom below the street and into the attic. He saw the attic ceiling; he saw a shadow on it, he saw the shadow move.

And he watched as a small face—the face of a child—appeared at the attic window.

He heard from behind him, and above, "It's gonna rain! Get outa there!"

He smiled at the face of the child in the window. The face smiled back. "Blanche," he whispered.

The child's lips mouthed his name: "Alex."

From behind him, he heard again, "It's gonna rain, dammit! Get outa there!"

"We can't! We ain't got her. We ain't got her yet!"

"She'll have to wait. Get outa there. Now!"

Alex stepped up to the front door of the house under the street. He grasped the knob. Turned it. The door opened.

Above, at street level, the rain started. It was not a gentle rain, not comforting or restful, not the kind of rain that soothes and heals. It was a torrent, as if an ocean were draining.

And Alex stepped into the house.

It's strange country below the Mason-Dixon line. There's something about the South that brings out a type of nightmare found nowhere else in the country. It's called Southern Gothic. Wendy Webb, whose first story this is, is a nurse, a sometime magician's assistant, and she knows Gothic indeed. It's less a style than a state of a mind that knows that all we see is not all there is.

LAW OF AVERAGES
by Wendy Webb

The young man rubbed a well-manicured hand over his day-old beard. It didn't matter anyway, he thought. No one would see his face. He reached into the crumpled grocery bag at his side and pulled out the black cloak. Slipping it over his head, he adjusted the neck string and pulled the hood down over his head. They would know who to look for. The instructions were explicit: the school bus stop—near the abandoned lot. Five A.M. The man in the black cloak.

He peeled back the plastic top on the Styrofoam coffee cup and took a sip of the steaming liquid. The Breakfast Hut to-go bag already showed signs of a spreading grease stain from his hash browns-slathered-and-lathered, and the grilled egg sandwich would be cold by now anyway. Besides, he thought, the whole thing would be over within two hours. He tossed the bag and looked at his watch. They'd be here any minute. He took another sip of coffee.

The state car approached quietly down the one-way street, and stopped, idling softly in the morning air. The hooded man rose, folded the grocery bag into halves, then quarters, then slipped it into the back pocket of his trousers. He approached the car slowly and heard the automatic locks pop open. He slid easily into the passenger side of the front seat, noticing that the driver, in his crisp blue uniform, was new at the prison. They always sent the rookies to pick him up. He wondered if it was a kind of initiation.

"Hi," he said. "I'm Barnes. I'm here to take you to State." Then a moment of awkward silence. "But I guess you already knew that."

The hooded man stretched and leaned back in the seat.

"Beautiful day, isn't it?" Barnes said.

The hooded man looked out at the passing neighborhoods. Soon it would be tired, colorless buildings, then the slums and, finally, the prison—back entrance.

"I mean," Barnes said, "a beautiful day for some of us. At least for one it won't be so great."

At least for one, the hooded man thought.

Silence again. The young recruit seemed nervous with the quiet. He tapped out some private tune on the steering wheel, then reached for the radio as if for accompaniment. "How do you like that?" he announced. "No radio. Must be some guy's idea of budget cuts."

Shut up. Why can't the kid just shut up? the hooded man thought. He liked it quiet. Solitude was his sanctuary. He patted his breast pocket for a cigarette, then changed his mind. Identifying even a smoking preference was more information then he cared to reveal. He looked out at the gray dawn, creeping up on the day. Silent. Calm. Quiet. It gave him room to think. To plan.

"Say, have you read the latest on that serial killer? You know, the one they call the Penknife Murderer? Boy, that guy needs to be locked up. The electric chair is too good for him. Carvin' people up into little pieces and stuff." Barnes shuddered suddenly. "God . . ."

The kid was scared all right, the hooded man thought. He could smell it—smell the fear before the kid even knew he had it. He liked to make people scared. It gave him the upper hand. And it was a sign that he was above average. Well above. Even his father had admitted it. Finally. But then he had to, didn't he? He had breathed deeply the scent of his father and his father's fear. And he remembered.

Barnes's hand moved slowly to the automatic lock button and pushed. For safety, the hooded man thought. He smiled under the hood.

The entrance doors rumbled open, then closed behind the hooded man and his entourage. His black cape muffled the squeak of tennis shoes and ragged corduroy. He knew this route like the back of his hand, but formality and the solemnity of the occasion warranted the ritual once again.

He knew that even now twenty-four witnesses were taking their seats in the viewing room. A lottery hand-picked most of them from around the state; bribes chose the rest. All of them would be twisting in their seats to find the maximum viewpoint. It was a once-in-a-lifetime experience—for all concerned. Except for the hooded man.

The rubber of his tennis shoes marched in rhythm with the patent leathers of his escorts. He wondered if bits of drying mud fell with each step, leaving a clue to his whereabouts prior to the 5 A.M. rendezvous: and his identity. It wouldn't do to reveal who he was. Not even the warden could put a name or face to him. He was simply a man who pulled the switch at the designated time, and got one hundred and fifty dollars for his effort. Cash.

The entourage passed death row, and the holding room where the condemned man was sequestered. The hooded man paused briefly and sniffed the air. Not yet, he thought. But soon enough. He looked at the wall separating himself from the prisoner on the other side, and thought he could almost see what was happening.

The condemned man would finish his last meal of steak (medium rare), and strawberry shortcake (with whipped cream and chocolate sprinkles), then reach for the phone. His last phone call would be to his mother. He would apologize for the pain he had caused her.

It was all so predictable, the hooded man thought. But then getting information on the prisoner had been easy, thanks to his predecessor's quirks. Besides, it was a matter of personal pride to know all the details of a subject. It was proof that he was methodical, controlled—above average.

The entourage turned as one and stepped briskly towards the death chamber: a drill team practiced in its precision. They were met by a stocky, gray-haired man in worn work clothes. His belt was weighted down on one side with a collection of tools neatly packaged in holsters. Black letters on a khaki patch over his left shirt pocket introduced the prison electrician as "Bob."

"I charge the generators every Tuesday to make sure they work right."

The hooded man nodded. He pulled the black material a little further down over his face.

"A week before an execution," Bob said, "I run the generators every other day. It'd be a whole lot easier if the local power company would supply us with the juice. But you know how that is, public relations and all." Bob glanced sideways for any reaction to this, but the hooded man remained still. "I'll let you know when the power is up. Then it's your turn."

The hooded man knew what would happen next in the prisoner's cell:

"It's time now," the guard would say. His voice would be almost sympathetic.

"I love you, Mom." The condemned man would try to say more but his voice would crack, then falter. The telephone headset would fall into its cradle and echo a barely audible ring. He'd then rub a leather-rough, dry hand over damp eyes.

The hooded man took his place next to Bob, the electrician, and in front of the voltage switch. It was a simple matter of flipping the L-shaped lever from left to right. Bob would be responsible for moving it back again—when the time was right.

Twenty-four witnesses craned their necks for a better view of the black-clad executioner. His predecessor could take credit for that too. One man's demise was another man's gain, he thought. The hooded man grinned, knowing that he would be the sole topic of speculation and rumor long after talk of the mass murderer's electric death had subsided. All had heard of him, in one form or another. A few had even seen him. Fewer still lived to tell the tale. And no one knew him as the hooded executioner.

He noticed the carefully groomed gentleman in row two, witness twenty-four, trying for a better seat. But no one would budge, not even with the offer of cash.

The heavy chamber door closed behind the condemned man. He shuddered with the "click" of the lock and wiped away the beads of sweat that gathered on his shaved head. Two guards pushed him gently into the old oak chair and stood on his feet. A kick to the prison administrator would only delay the process.

"The state versus William Danforth," the administrator said. "In accordance with the law of the state, you are hereby condemned to death by means of the electric chair. Do you have a final statement?"

Danforth raised his eyes to meet those of the administrator. An icy-cold hardness displaced any fear. He stared at the administrator as if trying to remember his every feature, then looked to the witnesses. "No, nothing." The cloaked man nodded in agreement. What could he say? Anyone who could have slaughtered a family so deftly, yet leave an eyewitness, could only be considered an amateur.

Danforth winced as his arms were jammed back and leather-strapped into the chair. His shaved calves were electrode-dotted, and equally secured. Thick bands of leather crossed his chest, with one thinner strand holding his forehead so that his jaw thrust out in an effect of almost belligerence.

Yes, there would be a kind of belligerence, the hooded man thought. Danforth's guilt was in being caught. Being caught was average—below average. It took planning, deliberation and knowing your subject to be better than others. It was a question of personal standards, a law of sorts. He had the strength of the law, his law, and with it the ability to take lives. But sometimes throwing a switch wasn't enough. He could feel his jaw tighten at the thought. Electricity was merely a stepping-stone to the mastery of certain skills. There was victory in what he did, had to do yet. It was logically correct. Reasonable.

An opaque black hood fell over the condemned man's head and face. The cloaked man could see the shape of Danforth's lips with every inhalation of his quick, short breaths. His clenched fists strained against the heavy leather straps.

On a nod from the administrator, Bob pushed the preliminary button that cranked up the generator. A low hum traversed the floors of the prison and crept within the walls of the death chamber. Small reverberations of energy rippled under their feet.

The hooded man looked toward the viewing room from the corner of his eye. Watching the effect of impending death was the best part. He knew a greedy anticipation would settle on their faces as the switch was thrown, only to be followed by shock and stunned surprise. Then confusion oozed in, as if each person were frantically reviewing the reasons for being there in the first place. As they shuffled out, lost in their own emotional turbulence, he would feel only disappointment, then anger at their weakness. Anger turned into strength. Strength to power. Then slowly, a calculating, deliberate plan took form. A plan that would cause an intimacy of himself and one other. An intimacy that could happen only once. And that one would feel his power, he thought, and see his strength.

The witness caught his eye again. The large, tanned gentleman had dressed well for the occasion. His expensive, tailored suit hung in neat, crisp folds, and that alone made him different. But there was something more. He leaned forward in his chair, chin resting on clasped hands, intent on every movement within the chamber. Unlike the other witnesses, who seemed predictably nervous, this man was watchful, almost . . . calculating.

He was a man of means by the look of him, the hooded man thought, an out-of-towner for sure. And probably one who wouldn't be above bribing a prison official if it suited his purposes. The hooded man could almost smell the rich, earthy cologne the gentleman would assuredly be wearing. Perhaps seeing a man electrocuted was some kind of a thrill—a vicarious sacrifice of sorts. He felt his mouth begin to water. A man like that could have anything he wanted, except, possibly, a hand in his own death. Yes, he thought, this man's reaction to death would be worth watching.

It was time.

The executioner grasped the lever in a strong hand. His nostrils flared as he breathed deep the smell of fear. The scent of Danforth mingled freely with others in the room. Adrenaline raced through his body, followed by exhilaration. He flipped the lever easily to the right.

Leather groaned and creaked as the voltage raced through Danforth's body. The toes of his shoes flipped up from the floor, pulling the restraints as far as they would allow. His fists became trembling knots. A small stream of spittle inched out from under the hood.

The generator hum faded. Then as suddenly as it started, it stopped.

The doctor who would pronounce Danforth irrevocably dead was being ushered into the chamber.

And yet, the hooded man thought, it was all so—unsatisfying. He would have to content himself with something else, something better. He wiped his mouth with the back of his hand, and glanced at the witness. The man's fleshy, well-manicured hands, punctuated by heavy gold rings, were pressed solidly against the glass. The grim emptiness etched on his face implied that he too had hoped for something better. And so it would be.

The witness turned suddenly to leave.

Slow, the hooded man thought, he'd take his time with this one. Slow and careful. There were plans to be made. Careful plans. The labyrinth of prison halls would lead him past a window view of visitors parking, then outside. Just enough time to get a quick look at the gentleman's car and license plates. It was all the information he needed. Then they would both be satisfied. One above-average man to another. It was the law, their law.

He hoped the man would be wearing the rich cologne at his death. It would be a way to remember him apart from the others.

The guillotine, the gas chambers, the levers to electric chairs—all fading memories now. It was time to look to the future.

Yes, he thought, fingering the penknife through ragged corduroy, the cologne would be a nice touch.

This is not Mr. Sullivan's first appearance in Shadows, *but it's certainly his most intriguing. When he sent it to me, he said, "The story says it's ready." A story does that sometimes. Whether you like it or not, it refuses to submit to your well-intentioned tampering, resisting all attempts to "make it better" because it knows damned well it's ready for the mail. A good writer quickly learns to trust this instinct. So, now, "The Fence," disturbing and chilling.*

THE FENCE
by *Thomas Sullivan*

Spring quarter at Nebraska U. wasn't an hour dead before they were on the road. The four of them. Homebound.

Roger had the last exam—Advanced Nuclear Physics—and he sprawled in the back seat seemingly exhausted, his olive eyes closed like bivalves behind their Coke-bottle lenses. Janine tried to give his long legs room. She had the same puffy lips, the same slender hands, even the same ponderous glasses—except where his had tortoise frames her metal wires were encased in clear lucite and looked like transparent birds' legs with the bones running down the middle. If you saw the two of them walking together on campus, you thought, *brother and sister* . . . Certainly not lovers. Which they were.

The differences between the couple in the front seat, on the other hand, were profound. Sheryl rode shotgun. She had straight, raven hair and amber eyes that never gave up thinking, and just now they were thinking Jay-Jay was driving too fast. She was as smart as Roger, but somehow she had entered into a love-hate relationship with wise-ass, not-too-bright, helmet-head Jay-Jay. Hyphens seemed always to define him. Clichés and qualifiers. Cup-and-saucer eyes. Close-cropped hair. Mr. Toad with a wire-brush buzz. No one was sure whether he had gone to any exams at all. It hardly mattered though, Sheryl believed, so long as he caught footballs in the fall for the people who paid his scholarship. The problem now was slowing him down without challenging him.

"Jay-Jay, my boy, sonic booms cause rockslides," she said.

He gave her his John Belushi stare and added a mile or two to their velocity.

"It is not true that speeding is a mark of sexual potency," she observed.

"You've taken a survey?"

"Oh, Jay-Jay, you're so macho. I can't wait for you to get through puberty."

He palmed his fuzz, thought about it, slowly fashioned a reply. "The altitude's making you horny, you know that, babe?"

"Ah, your death wish." She smiled her Gioconda smile and stared out the window.

The smug silence seemed to suit everybody, a quartet of college students on the way home to Utah. Youth and ease. Only there wasn't much ease in the back seat. Because Roger had come awake just as they sideswiped a semi outside North Platte, and now he was chattering nervously about fuel economy in a voice he hadn't used since adolescence.

Sheryl had known this was going to happen, had known Jay-Jay would get bored and start to drive like the asshole he fundamentally was, and she knew that if she put her objections to him directly it would get worse. If anyone had control of Jay-Jay, she did; but not now, not in his brand-new yellow Sentra, courtesy—some said—of appreciative alumni. She had sat next to him as much to be near the brake as to snipe. A year of verbal sparring was coming to an end and she wanted to hang something terminal on him before his leaded foot hung something terminal on all of them.

But it was Janine who devised a way, even though by that time they were already through Denver and ascending the Rockies.

"I think I've got to go to the bathroom," she announced, leveling her eyes at Jay-Jay in the rear-view mirror. Which is to say he could see her glasses with their vague blue lakes. "Jay-Jay, I really do."

"Bladder ought to have less pressure on it up here in the mountains. Right, Roger?"

"Negligible factor," said Roger.

The car continued at lethal speed. Guardrails and vistas and a creek bed blurred alongside. Then they passed a chocolate-brown sign: REST STOP NEXT RIGHT.

"Jay-Jay," said Janine. "Slosh, slosh."

Sheryl glanced into the back seat. "Jay-Jay doesn't understand that, he's all crap."

They went by the rest stop.

"You creep," Janine said.

Everybody was quiet for a while then. They ate up highway with the same eager roar and suffered the same silent indigestion of anger. The traffic began to thin and seemed to travel in clusters, as if the ups and downs of the foothills exerted a rubber-band effect. Overhead the Colorado sky likewise thinned to a vaporous blue, implying that God was tiring of humans and running out of statements to make. The land, too, grew devoid, taking on a bigger-than-life simplicity. Nature's palette had gone all to rusty browns and distant, mountaintop spasms of white.

"Tell you what, Janine," Jay-Jay said presently, as if the conversation had never lapsed, "there's a tunnel up ahead, I'll stop in there."

"I don't really have to go, Jay-Jay. But you're driving too fast."

There actually was a tunnel through the mountain, a dark hole in the red stone like a gaping mouth in an inflamed face. The road descended in a long, sweeping curl posted: HEADLIGHTS ON.

But Jay-Jay made no move toward the dash.

Sheryl glanced across, her brows rising exotically. She could tell by the way he was chewing gum like it was the last play of the Cotton Bowl that he was about to go for the marbles. *Don't do this,* she commanded him silently, *don't do this . . .*

"We could crash head on!" shrilled Janine. "Turn the damn lights on!"

"There's always a light at the end of the tunnel," Jay-Jay said matter-of-factly.

And then they were into it, and the sound of the tires came off the walls like a shriek. There actually was a bright pinpoint far out in front of them. But for all they knew it might have been the onrushing headlight of a motorcycle or a utility-panel bulb on the tunnel's flank. And in between was what? Animals? Potholes? Rocks fallen from the invisible walls carved out of the mountain? The beacon ahead remained small, the car screamed, darkness occluded, and suddenly the small bright oval at the far end of the tunnel vanished.

They all started shouting after that, all but Jay-Jay, who was fumbling at the dash. And when the car lights came on, the venting voices knifed off as if sound and light could not co-exist. The walls were curving. Curving and curving and curving. And descending. Fear curving and descending. But then the oval burst upon them again, and they shot free of the belly of the mountain.

No one spoke while the countryside flew past, the same country-side as before—a creek and a vista and a guardrail—only beyond the guardrail was a fence.

Sometimes she could really hate Jay-Jay, Sheryl thought. For a junior he could be incredibly sophomoric. If she looked at him now he would be chewing his gum a little more slowly, and he would throw her that big empty grin of his, like they had just done something wonderfully clever. Someday fate would nod the wrong way and then it would be all over. For Jay-Jay. For those who were with him. *But not today,* the grin would say. So she didn't look at him. She looked in the vanity mirror. Roger and Janine were huddled directly behind her, their Coke-bottle lenses making them look like contrite kamikaze pilots. How the hell did they ever grope into each other behind all that glass? she wondered. How had they ever discovered each other in the first place, for that matter?

Jay-Jay made a noise which might have been a grunt or a laugh. "Hey, Roger, how do you figure it? First you see it, then you don't. How do you figure the light went away, Herr Physicist?"

"Maybe you drove up the walls."

"Captain Loop-the-loop, that's me."

Roger pushed his glasses up with a long slender finger. "I suppose we could've been looking from one end to the other at first, and because the headlights were out we didn't see that the roadbed dipped below the horizontal while the ceiling remained—"

"Golly, wow, Roger." Jay-Jay lived in two-dimensional space.

They were cruising at the legal speed limit now. Whatever needed to be proved was proven. At least they thought it was the legal speed limit. There were no contradicting signs to mitigate the double nickle.

There were no signs of any kind.

And that was when Sheryl made the first observation about the single feature which had been introduced after the tunnel. The one that had taken awhile to accumulate in her mind. The one that went on and on and on . . .

"Look at that fence," she said.

They all looked. It was just a fence.

"Yeah, that's a fence all right," Jay-Jay agreed finally.

"What on earth is it for?"

"Cattle."

"I don't see any cows."

"Sheep then."

"Where?"

Jay-Jay shrugged, blinked his round, round eyes. "They hide in the bushes. Leap out at sunset."

"It's fenced on both sides," Sheryl said.

"That's because they put the road through the middle of the range, ninny." He was chewing gum at speed again, some new novelty churning in his mind.

Sheryl saw it coming but kept on arguing. "That's no range fence. Look how high it is."

"I told you, the sheep leap at sunset."

"Deer leap," Roger said, shifting around in the back seat. "It's probably to keep deer from crossing the highway and colliding with cars."

"How thoughtful, but it's still a weird fence," Sheryl reiterated. "They must have a post every four feet. And what are those other sections?" She flicked a finger at the horizontal crossbeams that overlaid the fence every several hundred yards.

"Gates," Jay-Jay said.

"For what?"

There were no roads, no rutted paths or trampled grass leading to any of them, but they did look like gates.

"Revised theory." Roger brightened. "We are looking at a missile base."

They gave that a half minute's speculation. Janine punctuated it with a sneeze.

"Missile bases are posted," Sheryl said, plucking a Kleenex from the box on the dash and handing it back. "They have warnings all over. You can see buildings or a Jeep or something."

Roger began to elaborate. "It hasn't been developed yet or maybe it's underground. It might be a large tract for something like the MX. I wonder how far we are from the Rocky Mountain Command Center."

Jay-Jay hit the brakes. The Sentra came to a full stop and began to back up. They all saw it then. Sheryl said, "Oh, my God."

One of the gates was open.

It was open less than a foot, but Jay-Jay had been looking for an opening. He parked on the narrow shoulder, got out.

" 'Don't fence me in,' " he quoted.

"I think Mr. Toad has found a new adventure," Sheryl imparted to the back seat, and turning her amber eyes on Jay-Jay again, "Leave the car keys," which produced the only uncertainty on his otherwise eager face.

With a cavalier shrug he tossed them over and waded off through the grass. At the gate he shouted back, "It's electronic!" and eased through sideways.

And that was when the funny thing happened.

Because the gate simply swung shut. Jay-Jay spun around, faced it square, reached out one big ham-hock hand, pushed, then jerked his fingers back. They all saw it, heard it. A blue-white flash, a popping sound.

"That's just ducky," Sheryl said. "Now we know what it's for. It's a speed trap that lures you out of your car and incarcerates you without a trial. Damn clever."

She got out and stretched her ample but well-proportioned figure. Then she picked her way through the grassy ditch to the fence, Roger and Janine following.

"I didn't close the damn thing," Jay-Jay said.

Roger waved his long fingers over and around the rails, like a magician playing with the space around a levitation to disprove hidden wires. "You must have brushed against it. Or you formed a static electricity connection that started it moving. Or maybe it was so delicately balanced—"

"What happens if I grab this sucker with my shirt wrapped around my hands?" Jay-Jay demanded.

"It probably isn't lethal. But you'd never hang on."

The rocky plateau at the base of the fence looked inviolable. Sheryl scuffed it with her shoe. "There's always the sheep leap. How's your pole-vaulting, Jay-Jay m'boy?"

"Sweat not the temporary dilemma." He gave a careless look over his shoulder. "Maybe the Secretary of Defense will show me out."

"This is going to be cute," Janine said.

But it wasn't.

It was boring.

Jay-Jay simply disappeared over the ridge, his bullet head making him look like a marine recruit marching off to boot camp. They waited. After a while Roger called his name. Then they went to the car and waited some more. Janine was sneezing more or less steadily now. Allergies, she said. An hour passed. Two. They argued, but in the end Sheryl got out of the car carrying her blue windbreaker and returned to the fence.

"Jay-Jay!" she shouted. "We're going for help!"

The air seemed too thin to support sounds, and the words fell flat on the earth a few feet away. Then she spread the windbreaker, which had a note pinned to it, over a bush facing the fence.

Sheryl drove slowly at first, clutching the wheel as if to hang on to something. Roger sat beside her, somehow taller-looking in the front seat. Or had the posture of everything changed? The stark red landscape seemed insidiously empty. A pale butterfly lurched up and was dashed on the windshield.

"You know, I haven't seen anything but insects since we came out of the tunnel," Janine said slowly, leaning up behind Roger.

"Meaning what?"

"I don't know. How come there aren't any cattle or sheep? How come there aren't any dogs? How come there aren't any signs?"

"Because we've only come about ten miles, that's why." Roger sounded annoyed. He didn't like irrational things or innuendos that trailed off like receding radio stations. Add rhetorical questions.

"I haven't even seen any of those little squirrelly things along the road," Janine murmured.

"The smokies fly helicopters out here."

"Cute, Roger." She searched the sky outside the window. "Haven't seen any of those either. Maybe we should speed like hell and pick up an escort."

A pensive silence set in. The road, the fence and the endless red plateau hemmed in by blue mountains swept past mile on mile. Everything was beginning to look more and more like a painted backdrop, like a stage set. *Hello? Is this Kansas?* How could four people going home on well-traveled I-70 in bright sunlight suddenly become three disoriented souls lost and isolated with a fourth wandering around in a pasture like Little Boy Blue?

Then Sheryl said in a voice low with uneasiness: "You're right, Janine. There aren't any animals."

"We just haven't seen any," Roger corrected.

"There aren't any animals." Janine said it forcefully, angrily. "There aren't any animals just like there aren't any signs."

"How do you know there aren't any animals?"

"Because there aren't any carcasses."

She was right. They hadn't seen anything dead or alive since the tunnel. Before that the shoulder had been dotted with the usual carnage.

"I see a hawk," Roger said, grasping the frames of his glasses as though he were focusing binoculars.

"Where?"

"There." He pointed skyward at a slowly wheeling silhouette. "Hawks eat animals."

"It's a very lean hawk," Sheryl conceded sulkily. "When it comes to hawks, Roger, you've got eyes like an eagle."

"He *must* be lean," Janine said with initial calm. "Lean or lost or maybe he eats college students on the way home because I'm telling you *there aren't any animals out there!*"

She took consolation in another Kleenex, and it sounded like more than just allergies now.

Roger let her scintillation wane a moment. He didn't like emotional outbursts any more than he liked irrationality and innuendo. They all came out of the same subjective morass, as far as he was concerned. When the nose blowing and sniffling came to an end, he said: "Maybe it's the radiation."

"What radiation?" from Sheryl.

"The missile base. Whatever the military has over there would explain the lack of signs, too. They don't want anyone knowing where they are. This is a nowhere place. You move on, you avoid it—"

"Except for that." Janine's finger arched into the front seat, pointing through the windshield at what neither of them had noticed.

It was a house behind the fence, a very modest house. Adobe walls, pipe stack, stick roof. And there was an old couple in front of it, a man and a woman, their faces as baked and worn as red mud bricks. They had on faded clothes, mismatched clothes. The man's trousers were too long, his sleeves too short. The woman wore a dingy dress and a man's hat. *American Gothic.*

Sheryl braked hard. "So where's the road in?"

"Who cares?" Janine was laughing. "Thank God we've found someone."

They pulled off, got out, scrambled toward the fence.

Sheryl waved. "Helloo-o!"

But there was something oddly lapsed in the old couple's expressions—the expressions of their bodies—like the frozen tension in startled cats. It wasn't just apathy. It was *poised* apathy.

"Hello! Can you tell me where the road in is?"

She began to doubt that they heard. Or if they did, that they were processing what she was saying. But she saw by the keen glimmers in their eyes that they were not senile, that they grasped the urgency of the moment. Maybe they just didn't speak English. She offered a pantomime of gestures to go with the explanation: "There were four of us, but one of us got through a gate and now he's trapped on your side of the fence. We're trying to get him out, only we can't find the road."

They looked in the direction she indicated.

"Do you speak English?"

"They're afraid of us," Roger whispered behind her.

"Offer them money," Janine said.

Roger fished out a five-dollar bill. "We'll pay you to help us," he said. "Is there something that way? Where's the nearest town?"

Sheryl sighed. "Put your filthy lucre away, Roger. The Junior Chamber of Commerce is DOA."

Wearily they returned to the car. Sooner or later the fence had to end. As she pulled away, Sheryl glimpsed the old couple in the rearview mirror. They were walking now, walking in the direction of the tunnel.

A sense of abandonment beset them in the little car. They had left Jay-Jay, but wherever he was in the red vastness, he had escaped the constraints of a predestined road between two narrow barriers. *Don't fence mo in,* he had said. And then he had gone out for a pass, secondary unknown.

They began to see more houses now. Nothing you could call a village, just widely scattered dwellings, impoverished-looking, like that first one. There were no cars, no antennas. A handful of distant figures seemed to acquire an extra degree of immobility at their passing, as if taking wary note of strangers.

"I think we're looking at a reservation," said Roger, "Navajo or Anasazi or something."

Sheryl smiled sweetly. "The atomic hawks and their nuclear IBMs . . . Indian Brave Missiles."

"You mean that's a *fenced* reservation?" Janine scoffed.

"Why not?"

"Roger, this is a free country. I can't believe you said that."

"There was a resurgence at Wounded Knee or someplace a few years back, wasn't there?"

"That was a couple of radicals, we're talking about a fence that's going around miles and miles of . . . of—" Janine's voice was climbing in frustration.

"A fence with gates," Sheryl put in to defuse her.

"A fence with gates . . . yeah. To herd buffalo through or something. Boy, you've come up with some crazies today, Roger. The great Treaty of the Fence."

And that was when they saw the old gas station, and maybe it was coincidence, but the sign on the pump said: RED CHIEF.

For the past several hours they had been struggling to articulate reality against a tide of surrealism, and now they had arrived in Oz where the answers must be, where clean asphalt if not yellow brick had led. But their arrival occasioned no evident response. They idled onto the apron, shut off the engine, and still uncertain of their surroundings, they rose slowly out of the car like an air mattress inflating.

There was a figure behind the window of the office, a figure sitting in a chair with its feet up against the glass, watching them, as if they had no choice but to come in and make their inquiry. Sheryl led them through the doorway into a room devoid of commerce except for a cash register.

"Where are we?" she demanded, thoroughly out of touch with social graces.

The grizzled mask of a man who had spent decades staring out of the cool, cavernous shade of a gas station at the wavering heat of a plateau assayed her. "You're in a gas station," he said.

"A gas station where? Show me on a map. Don't you have a map?"

"We're all out." He said it with an edge to his voice.

"You're all out of *maps?*" She didn't know why, but she began to feel a gnawing generalized suspicion. "Well, maybe I'm not. Maybe I've got one in the car. Will you show me where we are if I bring it in?"

His eyes, as blue and pupilless as Janine's through her glasses, remained steadfast. "If it's a good one," he said evenly.

Janine intervened then. "Look," she said and her voice was trembling, "we've just had a bad experience. There were four of us, we were on our way home to Utah from college, and one of us got behind that fence out there and now he's trapped."

The grizzled mouth got harder but the blue eyes seemed to soften at Janine's plea or perhaps just at Janine. "How did he get behind the fence?"

"A gate was open, and when he went in it snapped shut."

"Foolish thing to do."

"We tried to tell him that."

"Will you help us, mister?" This from Roger.

The quilted face went to his now and seemed to decide two to one that they deserved pity. "Nothing I can do for your friend," he said, "but Utah's that way."

"Where the hell's the nearest town?" Sheryl flared.

"Please," Janine said, "you can understand, we can't leave our friend."

"I can understand, but there's nothing you or I can do about it."

"Why not?" Roger said flatly.

"Ain't my fence."

"Whose is it?"

"Don't know. But it runs a long way. You'd best get on to the next town before nightfall."

"Which is?"

"Don't know. Never been there."

They felt the gap between the man and themselves widening now. Sheryl was smiling —a soft, sick little smile, as if she had determined that this was all futile and inevitable.

"How do you know there is a town?" she put to him.

"Always a town. Ain't there?"

"Where's the nearest police post?" asked Roger.

"Next town, I imagine."

"Don't you ever see them?"

The blue eyes fled to the window. "It's quarter to five," he said. "You'd better get started. Nightfall comes about nine—"

"Where's your phone?"

". . . better gas up, too."

"We've got half a tank," said Sheryl.

"Better gas up. No more stations before the next town."

The town he didn't know about, they were thinking.

"Gas up and go," he repeated. "Get clear of the fence by night-fall."

"Why?"

". . . it'll be raining down the road. Just—"

"It's not raining," Roger said. "There isn't a cloud on the horizon."

"It'll be raining. Raining hard. Just keep driving. If you can't see the road just keep driving. When you get through it, you'll see where you are. Then you can go to the next town and"—he smiled wanly—"get the police."

"Don't you have a phone?" Sheryl demanded.

He got up stiffly from his chair, went out to pump the gas.

"What about a radio or a TV?" Sheryl persisted, following. "What about a newspaper?"

"Six dollars and fifty cents," he said when he was done pumping.

Roger counted out the money carefully. "We're going back for our friend," he said softly.

The washed-out eyes attempted to engage his. "Listen, son, you've got four hours of daylight. Take my advice—I don't often give it—and get the hell on down the road."

Roger met his gaze. "We don't know what you're hiding here, or why you're going to so much trouble to scare us, but if you won't help us get our friend out, then we'll have to do it ourselves."

They stood staring into each other's face for a few more seconds, and the chasm between them went soaring open. Then Roger lowered himself into the car, took the wheel and turned the yellow Sentra back in the direction they had come.

"Radio!" Sheryl said as if it was a revelation, and she turned the car radio on. It was mostly static, but with a half turn of the dial she brought in Denver. In disgust, she flicked it off.

"What did you expect?" asked Janine.

"I don't know," Sheryl snapped, and it was the last time anyone spoke for half an hour.

And even when they saw the blue windbreaker with the note hanging from the bush, it was observed in an emotional silence. For one thing, Jay-Jay wasn't there. And for another, the old couple were.

They were standing just inside the fence, their baked, red mud faces studying every move the young people made.

It shook them.

The old couple. Finding this spot. Finding it so quickly. They had seemed so passionless.

"Have you seen our friend?" Roger shouted at them. "Are you going to help us look? He went that way."

He pointed behind them, but they never batted an eye. They simply stood behind the gate and looked back.

"What are you waiting for?" Janine screamed at them, and she answered herself with a failing, ". . . waiting for."

They got back in the car then. Sat and thought and stared at the couple staring back. The old Indians, or whoever they were, were not afraid of them after all.

"It's five-thirty," Roger said. "The tunnel is closer. We'll keep going back until we find help."

They drove faster now, faster than Jay-Jay had driven. The tunnel was a handful of miles away. They would reach it in ten minutes.

Or fifteen.

Twenty at most.

After that Janine began crying. Soft sobs, growing.

"Shut up, Janine," Sheryl said when it began to feel contagious.

"There's no tunnel, it's not there anymore," Janine babbled.

"Shut up."

Whimpering.

Roger stopped the car in the middle of the road. It was nearly six-thirty. He gripped the top of the wheel in both hands and suddenly turned it hard around.

Back. Back. They were going back. Back to the bush and the blue windbreaker. The old couple were still standing there.

Back past the distant dwellings, whose owners were waiting at the gates now.

Back past the gas station. The quilted face was nowhere to be seen, but they noticed an open cargo hauler behind the building, and it was piled high with dismantled auto parts. A row of car doors in particular was visible, each with window smashed.

Roger sped up to seventy-five, and the little Sentra began to shudder. It was nearly eight-thirty when Janine began babbling again. They were going by whole villages now and the people were gathering at the gates and Janine was saying, ". . . there aren't any animals, there aren't any carcasses . . . there aren't any cemeteries . . . and there aren't any farms!"

Roger understood, and he wondered—if they were Indians—what kind of treaty they had signed and when. Because they were all waiting for nightfall and he had the accelerator to the floor and there weren't any farms or cemeteries or dead animals along the road because the gates would be open soon and he had the wipers on now for the rain even though they had so far to go, so far to go, and the people had rocks in their hands already all along the fence, the fence, the fence that was there to protect tourists during the day until the gates opened and the reservation came out to harvest the animals on the highway.

There's something about Texans. I don't know what it is, but they're not like normal people. I'm not talking about the stereotypical braggart here; I'm talking about the writers. They're just slightly around the corner from the rest of us, and in some cases, they somehow manage to make the turn around that corner the most unsettling few steps we'll ever take. Melissa Mia Hall is rapidly becoming an expert at altering such landscapes; she has the soul of the poet, but I'm not sure about her heart.

MOONFLOWER
by Melissa Mia Hall

This is the first summer Jacob Roy has noticed since his childhood. The others have slid by in a mesh of days spent working in air-conditioned offices and nights washed away in vodka. He's stopped drinking this past winter when threatened with the loss of his latest job, a comfortable teaching position in his hometown university.

Jacob wants to notice this summer. He dangles, halfway off his unmade bed, unmade because he hasn't got up yet; he dangles, smiling lazily at the light slipping in from the window. Jacob's come home. He's just turned forty and he's come home, after years of teaching at a variety of colleges, never winning tenure, barely scraping along, thanks to his heavenly addiction to Mother Courage. The light stretches closer to his island. Jacob turns over and gives the ceiling his benediction. He's a holy man now that he's a recovered alcoholic. And, by God, he loves it. That's why this summer he's not teaching. He's not going to do anything but find out what he wants.

He's been sleepwalking through his life, unable to settle down, unable to want to settle down, his personal life a series of missed connections, his professional life a list of unkept promises. But now he's wide awake, his body and mind clear and alive. Opportunities beckon. This summer he's not going to rush things. He's going to get up, dress, go out into the world and see what he's been missing.

Today's the first day of the rest of his life. He always laughed at that poster board saying, that trite beatitude of the late sixties, but now he appreciates it. Now the light streams into his bedroom with its bare walls and untidy piles of books. He's lived in this rented house long enough to have gotten a semblance of order established, but it needs more doing. More—something—more—identity. He screams out a wild laugh and yells out to the stillness, "I must find myself!" It seems as if all the triteness he has abhorred (and ridiculed in his English Literature and Popular Culture from a Twentieth Century Perspective classes) for the past twenty years at last makes a wonderful, if bizarre, sense. With an exuberant push, he jumps out of bed and looks in the mirror over his cluttered dresser. His receding hairline has receded yet more. His mustache looks grayer, more distinctive, perhaps, than it did last year. Yes, he most definitely looks more attractive, the better to dazzle the young ladies. He has always had a fondness for young ladies but a reluctance to get involved. He rubs his unshaven cheeks and decides to grow a beard again. He's just too lazy to shave. It's his special summer, a summer in which he plans to do nothing but see.

"I'm going out for a walk," he announces brightly, "—a leisurely promenade." He turns on the radio and heads for the kitchen. The coffee is ready, thanks to the timer on the coffee machine. But first he drinks his orange juice (not spiked with anything, so the flavor is a bit dull). Then he gets his toast ready, to be eaten without butter, with his newly acquired spartan finesse. After wiping the crumbs from his mustache, he eats a banana and pours his coffee. He drinks it black, of course, two cups, one after another. He does not read the newspaper. This summer he will not read. He has grown tired of reading.

The radio announcer blurts out a quick dose of weather information. Jacob listens to this with another smile on his lips. No rain, today, another hot summer day. Summer doesn't dillydally in the South; it hits early and stays long. A long hot summer. He sits on the edge of the kitchen table and finishes his last cup of hot coffee. An old Supremes song sputters out over the airwaves and he jumps. Marion loved that song. He feels young and in love. Aborted love. He shouldn't dare to call it that. He just let a friend get too close, expect too much. Jacob makes himself block out her face and searches for a substitute but there aren't any. He knows better than to, say, fall in love with a student. He's had colleagues who have done so, to their eventual misfortune. It's not a wise thing to do. He stomps out of the kitchen and goes to the front door where he can look out at the neighborhood. The houses are shaking off the night. The sun rises and sends out a protective warmth. He needs to go outside. He needs to know this neighborhood again. He wants to stop and smell the roses. He giggles at his new tendency to think in overworked clichés. Bending down, he tightens the shoelaces on his Reeboks and grabs the house keys off the coffee table. He stashes them in the pocket of his old jean cutoffs. Nobody wears cutoffs anymore but it doesn't matter. He has resolved to not go to the shopping mall for anything, except maybe a movie. This is where he plans on staying this summer—this neighborhood, the one where he was born. He wants to remember home. His eyes mist over. This is a weak moment he did not want to face.

Down the street is the place where his house was. Some purchaser bought the house and decided to tear it down after a small fire destroyed a large portion of it. Then he evidently changed his mind and did not build a new house. The lot has remained unsold for the last couple of years—that's what he was told by a fellow professor who lives a few blocks over on Ridgemount.

The house he's renting is one the Farleys used to live in, a family of three children, all of them boys and bullies. One of them, Conrad, wasn't too bad, kind of mean (his idea of fun was setting lizards on fire), but fun. He sort of liked Conrad. He sleeps in the bedroom that belonged to Conrad's parents. It's strange, to live in a house half known. He never went into that room when he played with Conrad. He uses Conrad's room for his study. He seldom enters it except during school. This summer he's locked the door.

Jacob warms up on the porch. He makes a big show of stretching and slapping his arms about, does a few jumping jacks and lifts his head and breathes noisily. He feels great. The birds chirp and cluster in the pecan tree out on the lawn. Out of the corner of his eye he watches a squirrel scamper up into the arching branches. Doesn't want to look directly at it. Not yet. He might see Conrad dangling from a branch, daring him to climb up. He did not realize when he returned to this town how much he loved his childhood. Course, his teenage years was another matter entirely. Didn't make the football team or the basketball team and, although he made the baseball team, he'd been lousy. Couldn't get dates. James Hawkins called him Snot-Face in front of the cheerleaders and then creamed him in a fight over something forgotten. Jacob shivers and shuts off that memory. Some things are best forgotten.

Full morning, now, full and bright; he forces himself to experience

it. He checks to see if he locked the front door. When he was a kid
nobody locked their front door, but the neighborhood is not as safe
as it used to be. Before the spring semester came to a close, a house a
few blocks over was robbed. Jacob doesn't use his VCR much but
he'd hate to lose his camera equipment or his tape deck.

"Here I go, out into the bright blue yonder—" he says, glancing
around to see if anyone else is outside yet. There's one old guy put-
tering about a neat vegetable patch. Jacob decides to walk the other
way. He's not ready to be enormously friendly. He could manage a
cheery wave. The old man glares at him and fumbles with the water
hose. Jacob jerks his hand down and starts to run. He hadn't intended on running (do these shoes have the right kind of soles?). He
slows down to a walk so he can see better. Once past the grumpy old
man, Jacob glances around eagerly. Most of it he remembers, the
houses and the yards, some are in need of repair, a couple look
vaguely alien because of additions. One house appears extremely odd
because its thirties look has been submerged in a compilation of
contemporary renovations. He squints at the satellite dish on the side
and wonders who lives there. Surely not Mrs. Beaker. He remembers
Mrs. Beaker's peach pies and her daughter Caroline who gave him
his first kiss (Mrs. Handley's third-grade class, recess) and his first
rejection (she turned down the valentine he gave her in fifth grade).

He swallows a sudden lump in his throat and belches. He's got to
stop drinking coffee. And the minute he thinks that, he realizes he
never will. He enjoys belching. Some dogs are barking at him. Luck-
ily they are fenced in. He likes dogs, but these are chows and one of
them has some nasty-looking buck teeth. Maybe he'll get him a dog.
Last winter he read a book called *Shakespeare's Dog*. He might just
look into it. A collie might be nice, like Lassie.

Suddenly he sees a jogger up ahead. She's wearing an earphone,
plugged into something. Her body is magnificent. He gawks in open
awe for a few minutes. He's shy but not that shy. He smiles at her as
she goes by but she doesn't seem to appreciate it, too involved in
whatever speaks in her ear. Probably a motivational tape. Beetho-
ven? No, she has a sneer on her face. Has to be the Rolling Stones.
Still, she runs like a gazelle, her muscles in attractive array, propel-
ling her forward with lucid grace. Jacob pats his stomach bulge in
self-defense. Somehow seeing her does not send him into a morass of
guilt. Some people run. Others walk. Still others sit.

"I'm walking this summer," he says to the air. Now the sun is climbing steadily. He chooses to walk down by the cemetery. It's behind his house and not a macabre place, but rather nice. The water sprinklers are on and he walks down the winding paths inside the gates with a sense of peace and satisfaction. He used to play here when he was a boy. At night he'd slip in with Conrad once in a while. Then it was a little scary. In the daytime, though, it's just a pleasant shady place, well taken care of and useful. The markers are endless, however, today and too mute. He leaves the cemetery struck by an intruding thought about the jogger. Her shorts were cut entirely too high up. He doesn't know why it should bother him. Buttocks are sexy when they look as good as the jogger's did, bouncing up and down. But still, he regrets the tendency of women to show so godawful much.

As he leaves the cemetery, he notes the scudding mounds of clouds. For a moment, he prays that it won't rain and then resolves that, if it does, he'll continue on his walk.

He heads for the neighborhood closer to where his house used to stand. He's sad about it no longer being there, but vestiges of his mother's garden yet linger and the creek behind the house still attracts children. He sees two kids heading there right in front of him with fishing poles. He never caught anything in that creek except a head cold. Maybe he should warn them, but that would probably spoil their fun. There are at least tadpoles, maybe some crawdads, who knows. It's incredible watching the boys. They look so much—well—like the past. Do kids still fish? Evidently. If he had a boy, he'd take him fishing. It's been ages since he did anything like that. What's the matter with him? What's happened to him?

Veering off to the left, Jacob watches someone leave for work, a man driving a Volkswagen. A businessman. His wife stands on the porch holding a baby on her hip. Jacob tries to appear nonchalant. She waves at her husband's taillights and the baby stares right at Jacob. Babies always look so smart. Looks right into his soul and starts crying. He hurries past their house. The sun's getting terribly bright and hot. The sweat rolls down his back and streams from his forehead. He's not ready for so much exertion. He's walked and walked and his bladder is full and he's hungry.

The houses are alive with people now. In and out they go—people watching him suspiciously, not used to his appearance on their street. His right ankle begins to hurt. He stepped on a stone back a few blocks. Small, though, why should it hurt so bad? Then he remembers breaking his ankle when he was ten years old. Down by the creek. Or was he twelve? Thirteen? He's gone past the creek and the vacant lot where his house used to be. He can't go there when there are others around. He ought to go back home, well, to his house. Jacob turns around and starts for that direction, which takes him before the vacant lot again. He can't help staring at the twisting mass of dark leaves in the old flower bed bordering the creek. He wonders if they are the old moonflowers. Why, he's never seen them before when he's driven past in the evening. Surely not. He's driven past so many times, certainly he would've seen them—glowing white flowers in the dark. But they are pretty far back from the street. A pain shoots through his chest. Gas, he thinks, from the pizza he ate the night before. The sun beats down on his head. A sunburn on the pink place where his hair has receded the most would not exactly thrill him. Suddenly the entire walk seemed like a stupid thing to do. He can't see a whole summer doing this. The days reach forth, days of walking and seeing nothing of any use. He ought to be working, saving money for his old age or even traveling. It's been awhile since he went to Europe.

His house slides into view. It almost looks as if no one lives there. Next door an old woman turns off her lawn sprinkler, straightens up with a groan and stares at Jacob.

He stares back at her defiantly. She hits her head with a gasp— "Little Jake Roy! My God, how you've grown! You look just like your father!"

Before he realizes it, Jacob finds himself looking over his shoulder, expecting to see somebody else. His height shrinks a good two inches. Jake. He shields his eyes from the glare of the sunlight and tries to see her better. Stooped, white hair threaded in spots with gold, this old woman apparently knows him but he doesn't know her. She hobbles towards him, oblivious to the wet grass. Can someone be that glad to see him? How can she remember him? His hands touch his own face wonderingly. The little boy is in there somewhere, certainly the teenager. That's what she must remember. He doesn't move. He anticipates dread. He has an apprehensive thought that she might kiss him. Old women do that. Pinch his cheek, maybe. She comes closer and closer until she's there in front of him in a faded rose print housecoat, her pale white skin fragile as very old paper. Touch her and she will crumble. He takes in a gulping breath. Looking down, he meets her eyes, eyes of a youthful blue-violet that sparkle and snap with memories he does not share.

"Don't you remember me?" The sparkle dies down unwillingly. "Jake, I'm surprised at you. All this time I kept thinking the reason you hadn't said anything was because you were too busy, settling in at the university and all. But now, I see it's because you really don't remember me. I can't imagine—" Her words descend into a whistling sigh. "Jake."

The voice stirs something way back. A breath of wind. A smell. He feels uneasy standing there, looking down at her. He's much taller now, back to his mature height.

"Jake, look at me."

He obediently looks at the shriveled old lady with the hump on her back. Or is there a hump? She sees him staring at her rounded, stoop shoulders.

"Not enough calcium," she says. "I never could abide milk—except with cookies."

Chocolate chip cookies. They melt in his mouth.

"Mrs. Christopher!" she says.

Vaguely, a memory of something forbidden oscillates, flashes of color. It disturbs him that it's not something concrete. Mrs. Christopher. "It's nice to see you again, Mrs. Christopher. I didn't mean to be rude, honestly. Life can get rather hectic on a college campus."

She creeps across the grass and goes to his front porch. Jacob follows her reluctantly, resentful of her automatic presumption that he would. Follow her. She throws herself into the rickety wooden lawn chair that was there when he moved in. It wobbles alarmingly. He doesn't recall it being there when Conrad lived here. Probably left over from the last tenants. Without a word, Jacob sits in the matching chair across from her. "Would you like to go inside? Would you like me to fix some iced tea?"

"Oh no, don't go to any bother over me. I just want to sit a spell with you, look at you, you know, and talk. You look pretty good. Your parents would've been so proud of you."

His mouth goes dry as kindling.

"My man's been dead for a good ten years now. Reckon I'll be along presently. But not too soon, I hope. Lord, how time flies."

His head crackles with a headache. Her voice is irritatingly corn-pone. No wonder he can't remember her. He touches the side of her chair absently, aware of the lavender talcum smell of her. Her hand, blue-veined and trembling, reaches out to touch his.

"I can't tell you how good it is to see you. How you been? No family? No wife? No kids? I should've had kids. God said I wasn't fit for any. I guess. I don't mind but sometimes I think it was a judg-ment. What about you?"

Jacob pulls his hand away, acts as if he has to scratch an itch on his neck. Her familiarity begins to chafe. "Oh, came close a couple of times but—I suppose it's still a possibility."

"But you been happy?"

Jacob visualizes his last good drunk, what he can, that is. Mostly he remembers waking up in a New Orleans flophouse without his billfold. Then he catches her cataract stare behind the thick glasses. She can't really see him that well. How could she remember him? Maybe the cataracts have been removed? He avoids the intent spider-like gaze, stands and pops his knuckles. "You bet."

"That doesn't sound too convincing, Jake."

Where does she get off calling him that awful name? He slaps at a persistent mosquito. "If you'll excuse me, ma'am, that's an awfully dumb question. How have you been?"

"Lonely."

"I'm sorry. I can imagine losing your husband must've been terri-ble. It's good to see you again. I'm sorry to seem as if I'm rushing you, but I have some work to do on an article I promised an editor friend of mine."

He refuses to dwell on the hurt springing into her expression, the fumbling of her body rising from the chair, the joints audibly creak-ing. "Probably almost noon already. Don't want to miss my pro-grams. I always watch 'All My Children.' Little Jake, it sure is fine to see how you turned out and all. I knew you'd make a handsome man." Her watery gaze dilutes him. Jacob makes a chapel out of his hands and touches his lips with his fingers.

"I'll be seeing you."

She nods sadly and moves across his porch into the relentless sunshine. Jacob rushes into the house and blinks at the darkness. He sits shakily in the davenport and wonders what to do next.

He's had too much sun, too much exercise. He has to go to the bathroom. Pee and a shower, in that order.

The water arouses him, the water like a thousand warm fingers reminding him of the forgotten past. He turns on the cold water and cries some. Exhaustion can do that. He doesn't make a habit of crying. But maybe he shouldn't have tried to come back home.

After the shower he eats a huge ham and cheese sandwich and drinks a large glass of V-8 juice. He watches the soap operas and falls asleep after "General Hospital." When he wakes up it's late afternoon and he knows he's got to go down to the creek. He wants to see the moonflowers again. Barefoot, he goes to the front door and looks out through the glass screen door. He remembers real screen doors, the feel of mesh against skin, how it smelled, the metallic sweetness commingled with the scent of fresh air. Now glass keeps out the air. A fly hits against the glass where his forehead rests. He can't go out now; there are too many people on the streets, couples strolling, children playing, people driving by, coming home or going out for dinner. Too many people. He might have to talk. Someone else from the past that he doesn't remember might see him and come up, marveling at his paunch or his baldness. He'll wait, wait till it gets thoroughly dark.

The phone jangles; he rushes to pick it up, his lips breaking into an incredulous smile of relief. He grips the phone like it's a football. He's about to make a pass. "Hello? Hello?" The phone hisses and fusses, then goes dead. For a few minutes, after he's put the phone down, he waits to see if it will ring again. It doesn't.

Night falls. Jacob shuffles around the house, turning on lights, adjusting the air conditioner. Standing in front of a vent, Jacob exalts in the cool air ruffling the hairs on his face. He walks through the rooms, looking at pictures and riffling through books and papers at random, searching for clues to the life he's lived before he returned to this little town. Turner reproductions, Lautrec prints, a preponderance of outgrown Hemingway and Fitzgerald, anointed by a cluster of poets and British science fiction. Packets of newspaper book reviews he's written that are yellowing and disintegrating. Files of unpublished short stories written in his twenties, scholarly magazines that he's supposed to read and doesn't. Piles of *Omni,* the *New Republic, Esquire* and *Playboy.* A token *New Yorker.* He snatches a photo album and names each face frantically. There's Marion—or is that Marsha? Diane? Gina? That's old Joe Bridges and Harry Winston. Old what's-his-name and what's-her-face. The names start to disintegrate. He puts the album away with a small shudder. Too many party hats and too many questions.

He glances at the clock. It's almost 9 P.M. The time has gone by amazingly quick. He can go find the moonflowers now. He peeks out the curtains at his street. Lights shine from many windows but he doesn't see much outdoor activity. His nerves rattle. Maybe he'll read the Follett he picked up the other day. Or Dick Francis. No, he has to go out. He puts on his shoes. No one will notice him. He pulls on a sweatshirt with the sleeves cut out. He checks the pockets of his shorts for his keys and leaves the house abruptly, forgetting to turn off the T.V.

Night air is not like day air. The moon is softer, fair, like a woman's face smiling down upon him. He runs, then walks down to the block where the vacant lot is. And the creek. A white cat crosses his path and he smiles, seeing it as a benevolent omen of good luck. The confusion of the day sloughs off him like dead skin removed by a loofah.

The closer he gets to the creek, the happier he becomes. This is what he meant to do, this is what he meant by seeing. This is important. He arrives at the vacant lot. He stands on the curb and tries to picture the house. It wasn't all that important, but the white flowers beckoning him towards the creek are. He hurries through the weeds and grass. It's his old backyard. The moonflowers are huge, trumpet-shaped, related to morning glories. Lush, crawling all over creation, tumbling down towards him, sending out waves of a heady fragrance he has not smelled since he was—fourteen—fifteen—? He kneels in the midst of them, burying his face in their fragrance. His mother loved them. His father tolerated them for her sake, called them a nuisance, the way they take over everything. And he was right, a spasm of uneasiness passes through Jacob as he regards one vine curling around his leg. Quelling this anxiousness, he looks down to the creek. There's been enough rain so there's water enough to reflect pieces of sky peering down through branches of trees much larger than he remembered.

He climbs down the embankment, sits down on a large, flat rock that seems very familiar but he's uncertain if it was there when he was little. He snaps off a stick from a straggly bush and ripples the water with it. Crickets sing and locusts hum. Peace settles around him like a cloak of soft velvet. The smile keeps returning. He ignores the mosquitoes for a while but then knows he can't stay much longer. Tomorrow night, before he comes, he'll spray himself with insect repellent.

"Jake—" the voice whispers behind him. Startled, Jacob leans back and looks up the embankment where a white head looms. For a moment he thinks it's a moonflower come alive. But then the head grows a body, a female body, arms reaching down for a hold, unbound breasts swaying, hands spread out, searching. She clambers down to squat beside him, an exotic animal exuding a familiar smell he can't quite place, but when he does, a wrenching fear tightens his mouth and sends a chill down his spine.

"Surprised? I seen you looking, boy." The pretty hand touches his wrist, a hand smooth and strong. Her nude body pushes against him. "It's warm, isn't it, though? No one saw me come. We're safe. Not even St. C. knows where I am tonight. Just you."

The nudity scares him, the disturbing whiteness, a luminous lack of color. He'd say she was a ghost but he knows Mrs. Christopher is not dead. Her fingers pluck at his clothes. He pulls away from her, frightened and intensely aware of the neighborhood surrounding them. He hears the train. His parents will find out. His parents will come home and discover he's not in bed. His mother knows where he likes to go on summer nights. Down to the creek. Jacob pinches his naked thigh. He's awake.

She comes down on him with a determination that appalls him. She won't let him alone. She's tearing his clothes off. He's crying, telling her to stop it, it's not funny. She laughs. He whimpers. Momma might see them. She'd kill her. She would. Let go. She sticks a breast in his mouth. She rakes his chest with her nails. Her breath is hot like a wolf's or a bear's. He's small and she's so big. Let go. He kicks at her. "Don't, Mrs. Christopher, let me go, please—"

"You know you want it—you all want it."

"Stop it, please, Mrs. Christopher." She grabs it and it's lite it's not a part of him anymore and she takes hold and won't let go. He burns up inside and the world splits apart and the creek swallows them whole. The moonflowers are laughing. The moonflowers know.

Jake pushes her away and she laughs again, not at all an old woman's laugh. He scrambles to his feet and looks up at the moon

far advanced in the sky. It's so late. He needs to be in bed. She points
at his pitiful naked body but it's not pitiful; he's a man, a grown man.
He can't go home naked. He looks around for the remnants of his
clothes. Mrs. Christopher is holding his shorts. "So come and get
them," she says.

"Hush, Mrs. Christopher, please hush—" he cries. He has on his
shirt and he starts to make a run for it but he has to have his shorts.
"Oh, God, I'm bleeding, Mrs. Christopher—" And it's true, there's
blood running down his thigh. "Oh God, I'm hurt, I'm hurt bad," he
blubbers. But she's gone, splashing down the creek. "My shorts!" he
cries once more in a guttural whisper.

She doesn't stop, the bell-like sound of her laughter recedes. She
waves his shorts. Can a boy be raped? Shame runs down his cheeks.
He moves through the moonflowers and prays that no one sees him.
The back door is still open and the house is silent. No one's back yet.
His parents haven't come back from the party. He stretches out on
the bed and cries.

"Jake?" Jacob claws the dirt of the creek bank. His memory has
done enough damage, reality must not deepen the pain. He whirls
around and braces for another apparition. But it's the wind, surely.
Clouds kicking up in the west—the scent of rain floats down.

He climbs to his feet and says the old name again, "Jake." How
he's hated that name all these years. He walks through the twisting
moonflowers. He keeps touching his shorts reassuringly and, as he
reaches the block where his house waits, he sees the ambulance
parked out in front of Mrs. Christopher's.

A great leaden weight prevents his feet from reaching his house.
He just stands and stares at the activity going on in her house. Emergency medical help. A group of neighbors, none of whom he knows,
talk and gesticulate in her halo of porch light. Another group clusters in the circle of street light at the corner.

A woman nudges him. "Did you know her? Mrs. Christopher?
She died a couple of hours ago. Everyone's trying to figure out who's
the next of kin. You're not related, are you?"

"No," he says with a flare of triumph and profound pleasure he
knows he should be ashamed of. He's relieved that she's dead.

"You live here, don't you? Aren't you that professor who used to
live down the street a long time ago? Then you knew her, didn't you?
Jake? She was always talking about you."

He sees that this woman is the jogger. In this light, her buttocks are frightfully huge. He steps back as she steps forward. "No, she must have confused me with someone else," he lies.

"Oh," the jogger says. "Well, I got to get back to my kids. They'll be scared if they wake up and don't find me. My husband works at night."

Jacob looks at the woman blindly. "Moonflowers bloom at night."

"Yeah, sure, mister." The woman sidles away from him with increasing velocity. She thinks he's crazy. She gives him a sour glance and an uncertain goodnight.

They take the dead woman out of the house on a stretcher. The summer night enfolds the object within its impartial embrace. Jacob hums a wordless tune as he watches the activity. He doesn't want to go into the house alone. He feels like being with someone but not with her. His teeth start chattering. Silently groaning, he finally unlocks the front door. The living room is sunny with lamplight. The T.V. chatters happily and Jacob walks to his bedroom very slowly. The light's on in there, too. It illuminates the wilted object on his bed with cruel insistence. He will always remember Mrs. Christopher.

Another writer who doesn't publish enough for all those who enjoy him is Bob Leman. From his first appearance in F&SF *some years ago, he made his mark as a writer whose stories, whether sf or fantasy, were not to be taken lightly. Now that he's retired, he's promised to be more prolific. And if ever there's someone who ought to be seen and read more, it's him; and I couldn't be more pleased to have him in* Shadows, *this for the first time.*

COME WHERE MY LOVE
LIES DREAMING
by Bob Leman

Listen.

The House is speaking.

It speaks softly, just below the level of intelligibility, a whisper that might almost be nothing more than a draft of wind blowing through the tall rooms. It speaks invitingly, seductively, lovingly; it says, Come to me, let me protect you. Oh, come, it says. I love you.

But there is no one to hear it. It has been uninhabited for more than forty years, and it stands alone on a hilltop, miles from any other house. A wall surrounds the property. It is true that the gate is a rusted ruin and stands open, so that anyone passing on the county road might turn in and follow the lane through the trees to the house, but no one ever does. The house stands empty. It stands empty and calls softly for someone to love, and no one comes. Sometimes the drafts of wind make a noise almost like weeping.

There are houses that hate and houses that love. They are old houses, mostly, built in the days of dedicated craftsmen for men who hoped to found dynasties and therefore decreed houses that would give appropriate shelter to the princelings who would follow. Sometimes, as these houses were rising, when the circumstances were right, when the workmen were all superior craftsmen and the materials were all of the very best, and when someone—the architect, perhaps, or the owner—had conveyed something of his vision to the workmen, then, very occasionally, these men would find themselves working together with such smooth precision that they seemed more a single creature than a crew, and the recalcitrant stone and wood and metal with which they worked somehow became docile and amenable to the tools that shaped them, and the house would grow to completion like an organic thing, leaving all these people well satisfied and pleased with themselves. Such a house sometimes has a soul.

This soul is a *tabula rasa,* or perhaps an empty vessel; the people who live in the house will write upon the tablet or fill the vessel, and so will determine what the soul of the house will become. If anger and hate and malignity are the emotions that fill the house, if the thoughts of the inhabitants are malicious and turned to crafty plotting, if the sounds to be heard are blows and shrieks and the sobbing of despair, then this evil will drench the house and soak into its very fabric and substance; its soul will harden and shrivel and become malign. Such a house is a house that hates.

But this house is otherwise; this house was once filled with the glee of little children and the heat of young love and the warmth of affectionate domesticity. The sound it had heard most often was laughter, and the dominant emotion in its shaping was love. Its soul had bloomed in that warmth. This is a house that loves.

Loves, but has no person to love; for more than forty years has had no person to love. In 1942 Ensign Peter Colby went off to war, and his wife Priscilla closed the house for the duration and found an apartment in Norfolk to make a home for him to come to when his ship was in port. When the little ship went down in the North Atlantic she did not return to her house, but neither could she bring herself to sell it. It was to her an enchanted place where she had known three years of unalloyed happiness with her young husband; the memories were too fresh. The house's contents were sold at auction under her instructions but in her absence, and the house was locked up. She never returned.

When she died, the nephew who was her residuary legatee lost no time in offering the house for sale. It did not move quickly. It was a costly property, twenty miles from town, and the house itself was in need of extensive internal refurbishing after the long neglect. The purchaser would have to be someone with plenty of money and a taste for isolation, and such people were few and far between in that end of the state. The nephew listed it with a real estate firm that handled high-priced property on a national scale, and when their advertisements in glossy magazines drew nibbles, they retained Fred Watkins, a local realtor, to show the property.

"There she is," Watkins said. He and the customer were standing at the bottom of a shaggy slope that had once been a lawn, looking up at the house.

"Seems to be in pretty good shape," the customer said. He was a lean man in his early thirties, wearing a tweed jacket and cavalry twills.

"Oh, it's been kept up, Mr. Knapp," Watkins said. "Mrs. Colby saw to that. She didn't want to live here, but she loved the house. I think maybe she always thought she might come back here to live sometime."

"Is that a stable?" Knapp said.

"It was when it was built. Old Joe Potter converted it to a garage sometime in the twenties. Room for eight cars in there."

"I'd want to reconvert. I have horses."

"How about family, Mr. Knapp?"

"A daughter. Katy. She's eight. My—I'm a widower. My mother-in-law lives with us. We have a cook and a stable man, husband and wife. That's it."

"You can't see it from here," Watkins said, "but there's a small house back there for the help. You want to go into the house, now?"

"Yes, I think so. Then check the little house and the stable. The grounds could use some work."

"My goodness, yes. But it's a very handsome house, wouldn't you say?"

It was a large house of the school of Wren, solidly built of gray sandstone. The structure was balanced and symmetrical and indeed elegant, but it had also an air of gravity and decorum, something *Bürgerlich* and almost smug. To Webster Knapp it seemed to make a statement: I am a fine house; I was a credit to that decent and successful man, my builder, and I will be a credit to whoever owns me, if he is worthy of me.

"How old is it?" Knapp said. "Who built it?"

"Man named Stubbs," Watkins said. "Cyril Stubbs. Built it in 1845. His father was the canalboat and riverboat man. One of the biggest fortunes in the country at the time. Young Stubbs set himself up here to be landed gentry, but the people around here never quite caught on to what he was up to, and in due course he came to be very well liked. Served a number of terms in the legislature, as a matter of fact. Had nine children, and lived until 1895, died a very old man.

"The house went to his eldest son, Godfrey. Godfrey was a widower with no children. He died in 1903, and left it to a bunch of nieces and nephews. They sold it to Joe Potter, the glass man. Joe died in 1931, and his widow sold it to Wallace Colby. When Colby's son Peter got married, Colby gave him the house. Peter was killed in the war, and of course you already know that his widow kept the place standing vacant until she died a few months ago. The seller here is her heir."

They had been walking toward the house as they talked, and had reached the front door. Watkins unlocked it, and stood aside for Knapp to enter. The moment he stepped across the threshold, Webster Knapp knew he had come home, come home to stay.

It was not a sensation he had encountered before, this feeling for a house. He had never in all his life really felt that he had a home at all, until his marriage, and then home was wherever Sally was; the house did not matter. His boyhood had been spent in boarding schools and big houses in Virginia and Switzerland and the South of France, where, much of the time, he was the only resident apart from the servants. His parents had divorced when he was small, and both had married and divorced a number of times since. They were careless persons, rich enough to be irresponsible without incurring disaster, not fond of anything remotely intellectual, devoted to unceasing recreational activity: yachting, skiing, polo, gambling; and always drink and love affairs, and sometimes drugs.

The small Webster Knapp was an unhappy boy, his money notwithstanding. The only person he loved, his nanny, moved on to another household when he went away to school at seven, and he never saw her again. He formed few friendships at school; he was bad at games and tended to cry easily, so that he was fair game for the mob cruelties of schoolchildren. His closest associates were misfits like himself, and it generally happened that such boys moved from school to school, just as Webster did; most often budding friendships were aborted early.

He was a loner at the university, joining no clubs, taking part in no extracurricular activities, having no love affairs, forming no friendships. He did the required work, but no more than that, and always without enthusiasm. He kept two horses, and rode daily; it was the one activity at which he excelled. He had long since decided that he liked horses better than people.

After graduation he went to live at his mother's house in Virginia, because the only thing he really wanted to do was to ride and train his horses, and there were stables and grooms at that house. It was hunting country, and the hunt gave him an occasional opportunity to shine; he was really very good on horseback. And the only time that he felt good, felt really alive, was when he was in the saddle.

Then, one day, in a manner that seemed in retrospect to be a ridiculously prosaic preliminary to an event of enormous importance, Sally Pogue came into his life. He went to dinner at the house of a neighbor, and among the guests he had not met before was Sally. He was smitten, instantly and permanently; even before she said, "How do you do?" he knew that his life, bad as it had been, would hereafter be infinitely worse unless he could capture and keep this merry little person.

His courtship was clumsy and gauche, but it was furiously single-minded, and as abjectly sincere as that of a dog seeking affection; in two weeks she succumbed. She told him later that she probably would have done so on the evening they had met, if he had pressed matters; she had, she admitted, been struck by the same bolt that had felled him.

Knapp was almost unable to grasp the fact of his good fortune. His gray and featureless life was suddenly painted in brilliant colors, the drone of his daily routine converted to delightful music. The young man who had been unable to love because he had not been loved had found love, and he loved totally and without reserve. He loved the open, freckled face and the compact little body and the alert and well-trained mind. She had, no doubt, certain imperfections —she was, after all, human—but the imperfections were to be treasured as part of her. He was wholly astonished by the great good fortune that had fallen to him, and enormously grateful.

For the first time he was pleased that he had money; she was to have whatever she desired, if money could buy it. In the event, she desired very little. She had money of her own, and she was not given to conspicuous consumption or display. They found a satisfactory farm in Maryland, and her horses joined his in the stable. Her mother "gave" them the Mackinsons, George and Leah, stable man and cook. They furnished their house with gleanings from her mother's attic, their aim being to replace the shabby and heterogeneous collection with new pieces as over time they found precisely what pleased them most. But somehow they never got around to replacing most of it, and they lived quite happily among the shabby furnishings, which in fact neither of them had ever examined with a critical eye. The house was comfortable and shabby and strewn with a horsey disorder that suited both of them very well. They were too much involved with each other to give much thought to their surroundings.

When Sally became pregnant, Knapp was not quite sure whether he was pleased or not. He had taken for granted that they would in due course have children, but he was by no means certain that he wanted them so soon. He found that he was made uneasy by the idea of sharing Sally's love with someone else, even their baby, and after the little girl's birth he sometimes felt actual pangs of jealousy. He loved the small Katy, but the mother came first. Sally always came first.

And then she died, was killed, and went away from him and left him forever. He did not handle his bereavement well. His grief was extravagant, excessive, crippling. His mind reeled erratically from grim depths of black depression to spasms of red rage, from hopeless despair to wild resentment. He locked himself in his room because he did not believe in public displays of emotion and could not control his emotions; there in solitude he howled and beat at the walls with his fists and cursed the God he did not believe in.

For a time he thought about avenging her death, about slowly and painfully taking the lives of the four young thugs—two male and two female—who killed her, the creatures who were all able to walk away from the twisted interlocked wreckage of the two cars where Sally lay dead, the four inhuman freaks who, the state trooper said, continued to bob their heads and snap their fingers to the rock music that blared from the unaccountably intact radio of their destroyed old car. "High as kites," the trooper said. "There was half a dozen joints and a couple six-packs in the car. Must of been going eighty, anyhow."

But he saw after a while that revenge would be barren and that life somehow had to go on; he remembered that there was a motherless little girl whose life had to be put back together and set on the right track. He forced his mind to leave the mad seesaw it had ridden for so long, and to think about what must be done. His own future, he thought, lay plain and bleak and arid before him, an endless vista of an empty dry land where old bones parched. He saw no relief of his grinding sense of loss, of his terrible longing for his lost Sally. But he had a duty, and only his sense of that duty kept him alive and sane. Katy came first, now; she must be taken care of.

Sally's mother had come to live with them after the accident, as soon as it became apparent that Knapp was failing to cope with his grief and that someone had to see to the child. She was, fortunately, fond of Knapp, and altogether devoted to Katy, her only grandchild. When Knapp, struggling to regain his equilibrium, proposed moving to a wholly new place, somewhere without reminders of Sally, she agreed to go with them, so that Katy should have some bulwark of normality in her life until Knapp should have recovered.

Thus it was that Webster Knapp found himself with Fred Watkins, entering the old house in Goster County, entering it and feeling instantly that he had come home at last. He turned to Watkins and said, "I like it. I'll take it."

Watkins was tongue-tied for a moment. This was not how houses were sold, certainly not houses as costly as this one. He said, "But— Well. Good. You've made a wise choice. Uh—do you want to go through it?"

"Oh, yes," Knapp said. "By all means. I'm anxious to see it all. I must say I like it very much."

The rooms were large and well proportioned, the kitchen old-fashioned and in need of modernization, and the heating system, which was based on a hand-stoked coal furnace, would have to be replaced. But, all things considered, it could be ready for occupancy in a very short time. "Let's go sign the papers," Knapp said.

When they left the house to go back to town, Knapp's spirits, which had risen while they were inside, fell at once to their usual quiet despair, but he made no connection between the two events. He telephoned his mother-in-law to alert her to the necessity of planning for the move. She said, "What's it like, Webster?"

"Oh, it's great, Liz. Just great. You'll like it. So will Katy."

"How many rooms?"

"Why—I don't know. I didn't count. Enough. Oh, plenty of room. You'll like it."

"Webster, tomorrow you must check the rooms—how many bedrooms, bathrooms, all of them. Count them. Take a tape measure and measure them. Draw a diagram. I'll need some idea where things are to go. Will you do that?"

The next day Knapp got the key from Watkins, bought a tape measure, and drove out to his new house. Once again he felt a small glow of pleasure as he entered, a sense of being sheltered and comforted. What luck, he thought, what a stroke of luck that I found this house. He went about his inventory of rooms somewhat dreamily. He was in an unaccustomed state of mind, experiencing the emptiness that comes with the abatement of great pain, a certain blanking out of thought, so as to keep at bay the apprehension of a return of the pain. When he had finished his measurements he went out to examine the garage and evaluate the possibilities it had for conversion to a stable, but he found it difficult to concentrate. It came to him that, having given the building a once-over, it might be well to step back into the house, and think about it there.

But once he was inside, he did not think about it; he did not, in fact, think about anything. He simply stood inside the door and felt —not at peace; that had been lost with Sally—but better. Better than he had felt for a long time.

Renovation of the house, as is usual with such things, took longer than had been expected; it entailed laying several miles of gas pipeline to fuel the new heating system and a general breaking into walls to install ductwork. It became Knapp's conviction that his presence was necessary for the work to proceed properly, and he succeeded in making a nuisance of himself during all phases of the work. Renovation of the small house proceeded in parallel, so that both were ready for occupancy at about the same time. The grounds and the stable were still unfinished, but work on them would not interfere with occupancy of the houses, and as soon as the school year was over for Katy, Knapp moved his family in.

He was surprised and disappointed that their enthusiasm for the house was considerably less than his own, that they were, in fact, no more than dutiful in commenting upon it; but he supposed that in due course they would come to agree with him. The Mackinsons were much pleased with the little house, and Mrs. Mackinson was delighted with the gleaming technology of the new kitchen, but apart from that she seemed to have reservations about the big house, and Mackinson apparently felt the same, although he was a taciturn man, and it was hard to be sure.

Knapp was somewhat intolerant of their attitudes. The excellence of the house in every respect was, he thought, blatantly obvious, and those who felt otherwise were displaying flaws in themselves, not in the house. He knew the house better than anyone, surely; he had been present every day while the work was going on, and had examined every inch minutely. He believed that there was no place on earth that he would rather be than in his study at the back of the house on the first floor. For no reason that he could think of, Sally seemed somehow less distant and perhaps not wholly lost while he was in that room. And that was important, very important. Although the ferocious edge of his grief and rage had been somewhat blunted by the passage of time, his longing for Sally had not abated in the least, and in his study the pain was tempered somewhat. He spent a great deal of time there.

His mother-in-law worried about him. She saw a man who appeared to have made a partial recovery from a state of mind that was, from a layman's point of view, insane or near insanity; but still, something was not right about him. He went about with an air that suggested dissociation from his surroundings, with a detachment indicative, she almost believed, of a conviction that she and Katy and horses and all were not necessarily real, that reality lay somewhere else. And her suspicion was that his reality lay in the study where he spent so much of his time. He would sit for hours in the big leather chair, doing nothing whatever, probably not even seeing the landscape outside the window through which he stared, possibly not even thinking. He made no secret of it; the door of the room stood open, and when anyone entered he was aware of it, and he responded when he was spoken to, although with the detached air of someone humoring lesser beings.

Then he took to closing the door of the study. He had begun to have conversations, and they were the most private of private affairs. The conversations were with Sally. She had come back to him.

Not in body. When she first appeared he had tried to embrace her, and his arms passed through her as through empty air. But she was there, solid enough in appearance if not to the touch, dressed in jodhpurs and boots, the dear freckled face as merry as ever. He knew he had the house to thank for this boon. He knew that the house loved him, and wanted him to be happy, and had recreated Sally from his thoughts and memories. And it was all right. If he could not have her in the flesh, this would do. Would do very well. But it had to be altogether private. No doubt she would be invisible to anyone else, and if he were to be discovered talking to empty air, there might be talk of putting him away somewhere.

But one day Katy ran howling through the house, screaming for her grandmother. Liz took her in her arms and hugged her and tried to soothe her and break the hysteria. When at last the child was able to speak, she said, "It was Mama, Gram. I saw Mama. In the hall. But she wasn't Mama. She was—She was—" She did not know how to explain what had terrified her.

As soon as Katy's panic had been allayed, and she was safely in the kitchen to have hot chocolate with Mrs. Mackinson, Liz marched into Knapp's study. "Webster," she said, "I don't know whether it's you or this house that's causing it, but Katy is a badly disturbed child, and something has to be done about it. Let me tell you what just happened. Katy was hysterical. She thought she saw— well, she thought she saw her mother, she said she saw Sally in the hall."

Knapp leaped up, highly elated. "She did, she did," he said. "She saw Sally. Sally's here. The house brought her back. I thought I was the only one who could see her, but Katy can, too. It's wonderful. She's becoming more real all the time. Liz, isn't it wonderful?"

"Webster, are you crazy? Wonderful? The child was absolutely terror-stricken. What she thought she saw was horrible, horrible. You should have seen her, heard her. You're infecting her, Webster. I'll say it right out: you're not rational anymore, and Katy is suffering for it. I tell you, something has to be done. She shouldn't be here."

"Liz, Liz," he said. "This is exactly the place for us all. Don't you understand? Sally's here. Katy can have her mother again, and you your daughter. We have our Sally back. And in a house that loves us."

She stared at him, horrified. "Webster," she whispered. "Oh, Webster."

From the kitchen came a shriek, and another and another, as repetitive and with the same strident urgency as an ambulance siren.

Knapp sprinted down the hallway and into the room. Mrs. Mackinson was backed into a corner, seemingly trying to back herself through the wall, screaming and screaming. Katy sat frozen at the table, pale as snow, her eyes wild. Knapp gave Mrs. Mackinson a brisk slap. It broke the rhythm of her screaming, and her eyes partially cleared. "Ghost," she said. "Oh, my God. Sally. Mrs. Knapp. Ghost."

Knapp was overjoyed. "She saw her, too! She's real! Thank God. Thank God. She's real."

"You *are* crazy," Liz said, cradling Katy in her arms. "I'm going to leave, Webster, and I'm going to take Katy with me. You can have her back when you've straightened yourself out. And the first thing you ought to do is to get out of the house yourself."

Mrs. Mackinson suddenly regained control of her muscles, and bolted from the room. They could see her from the window, running full tilt toward the little house. Knapp said, "Oh, I don't think you ought to take Katy away, Liz. She needs her mother."

Liz gave him a cold glare. "I'm going to take her," she said, and then, to Katy, who was clinging to her fiercely, "Come along, sweetheart. Let's go up to Gram's room."

In the hall they met the ghost. Liz had not until that moment believed that it existed. Her first thought was, Yes, it is Sally, and then she saw what had so terrified Katy and Mrs. Mackinson: it was a figure so idealized that there was in fact no real resemblance to a human being at all. It was a semblance of Sally modified into a quite inhuman perfection, a thing as disturbing as a window mannequin endowed with movement and pretending to be alive. It said, "Katy. Mummy. I love you." It was an idealization of Sally's voice, eerie in its purity and perfection.

Katy screamed, *"Go away, go away!* Please, please, go away." The figure turned and disappeared through the door of the study. Clinging tightly to each other's hands, grandmother and granddaughter ran to the safety of Liz's room. They collapsed upon the bed, holding each other.

Knapp had remained in the kitchen, and was making himself a pot of coffee. He whistled as he bustled about. The bad days were over at last, he was thinking. The family would be complete again, and they would be happy together in the house that loved them. Liz had not seen Sally yet, that was why she was being so unreasonable. Once she and Sally had talked it over, everything would be settled. It was going to be great, just great.

Mackinson came into the room. Knapp said, "Mack! Sit down. Have some coffee."

Mackinson said, "We're quittin', Mr. Knapp. Leah won't stay out here anymore at all. She says she's goin' to be gone before night, and I can come with her or stay here, whichever, but either way she's goin'. It seems shameful to quit this way after all the years with the family, but there's no movin' her. I'll be comin' back with a truck for our things. Tell Miz Liz we'll write her. It's disgraceful to leave this way—I come to work for her father when she was just a little girl, knowed her all her life, almost, and Miz Sally too, and now little Katy. But I know better'n to argue with Leah when she's as set as this. Have *you* seen this ghost, Mr. Knapp?"

"There's no ghost, Mack. Sally's back, that's all. Scared Mrs. Mack, I guess. Don't know why, nothing scary about her. You know, you oughtn't to leave us this way."

"Sally's ba—? Uh, yeah. Yeah. Well. Well, I'll be goin' now, Mr. Knapp." And he went out.

Too bad, Knapp thought. It would be hard to get along without the Mackinsons. He'd have to see to the horses by himself, now, and Liz would have to do the cooking. And she wasn't much of a cook. Still, it was no doubt for the best. He was quite sure Sally would think so, too. He'd better tell her about it.

In the hall he met his mother-in-law and his daughter. They were carrying suitcases. Liz said, "I'm taking Katy away, Webster, out of this house. You know as well as I do that she can't live around that— that *thing*. Even if it's not real, Katy and I both saw it, or thought we saw it. Can't you see how horrible it is, Webster? That's no more Sally than that doorknob is. There's something wrong with this house. I can't bear to be in it. And it's worse for Katy. Don't you try to stop us, now."

"Oh, I won't, Liz," Knapp said. "I expect you'll be back. Sally and I'll miss you both."

"Oh, Webster," she said. "Poor, poor Webster. Goodbye." Little Katy, pale and tense, was tugging at her hand, and she allowed herself to be led out of the house. After a little while Knapp heard the sound of the departing car.

"Alone at last," Sally said. Knapp turned. She was not there.

"Where are you?" he said. He could speak to her now without actually talking aloud.

She said, "I don't think we need the image anymore, do you, Webster?" She too was talking without actual speech.

"No," Knapp said, elated again. "No, of course not. I know you're here. You're all around me, aren't you?"

"Of course I am," she said. "I love you and I'll always be all around you." And he knew it was true.

After that Knapp was very happy. To be well loved is, after all, one of life's deepest and purest pleasures, and Knapp knew he was loved. Love was around him, always. There was no need anymore for the image of Sally; she and the house were part of each other, and the house's love was her love. Knapp knew contentment at last, after all the long suffering. The unbearable tensions of grief and regret were behind him now, and with these relaxations came a certain lethargy, the drowsiness that follows relief. He found that he was content to do nothing at all, to lie in bed all day long, or to slump immobile in his chair while the sun rose and set and rose again.

Leaving the house, even for a short time, was an enervating and distressing experience. In the house, time did not exist, and there was only a drowsy, blissful present; but outside, with the door closed behind him, time's grim claws caught at him, trying to haul him back into the stream, to force him to think of duties and responsibilities, to bring into his mind Katy's pale, frightened face as her grandmother took her away. It was better to stay inside, to luxuriate in easeful contentment, to be wholly separate from time as it passed in the world outside.

He discovered one day that the horses were dead. The man who delivered the groceries said, "My God, Mr. Knapp, what the *hell* is that smell out there? My God, it's awful."

"Smell?" Knapp said. "I don't smell anything. How much is the bill?" The man took his money and departed hastily, intimidated by both Knapp's manner and his gaunt, unshaven, wild appearance. After he had gone, Knapp stepped outside the back door and sniffed. There was indeed a powerful and horrible stench, coming, it seemed, from the stable; when he opened the stable door the smell almost felled him. The horses lay dead and rotting, dead of thirst and hunger, unfed and unwatered for—he had no idea how many days or weeks. He felt an unaccustomed stirring of regret and remorse, and then a wave of astonishment that he could have so neglected his beautiful horses, could have condemned them to such horrible deaths. He was engulfed by emotion, suddenly, washed by sorrow and self-condemnation. My God, my God, he thought, and bolted for the house.

The bad feelings gradually subsided, once he was inside, and he felt very sleepy. As he was settling into his chair, the house said, "You see, Webster, it's very bad out there. I think you should stay inside from now on, don't you?"

"Oh, yes," Knapp said. "Yes, I think I'd better stay inside."

Time passed in the world outside the house, and inside it Knapp lived in his daze of timeless euphoria. In the early days of his life as a hermit the telephone had rung often and long, each time shattering his precious peace, and after a while he had the service cut off. He rented a very large box at the post office, and simply allowed his mail to accumulate there. He had placed a standing order with a market in town to make weekly delivery of a list of comestibles he had prepared, and each week a load identical with that of the week before arrived, until he could no longer bear the intrusion of the delivery man into his life of peace, and he canceled the order. He had discovered that he was seldom hungry nowadays.

Autumn came, and brought frosts to the world outside, and the trees became violently beautiful; and then it was winter, and the world was white and still and beautiful again. But in the house Webster Knapp did not see these changes, nor would they have meant anything to him if he had seen them. He kept the house dark, now, every curtain drawn tight against the light of the day. He could feel the love more deeply when it was dark and perfectly silent and he sat all alone in the great dark house.

But then he had company. With the coming of the cold, a tribe of field mice moved into the house, and settled down for the winter. Knapp did not mind. They were so small and shy and timid that their presence did not disturb him, and after a time he even came to like them. He believed that the house loved them, just as it loved him, and if that was the case, they were, in a sense, his brothers and sisters. After a time they lost their fear, and indeed seemed to become fond of him; when he groped his way from one room to another he always heard around him a faint sound of scratching, of a host of tiny nails scrabbling over the polished floors. It was as if the whole tribe felt compelled to stay close to him all the time.

Knapp believed that it had been a long time since he had last eaten —weeks, perhaps—but he felt no hunger, not even when he opened cans or boxes of food for the mice. He was very weak, and he knew that the weakness was a consequence of starvation, but he merely noted the fact; it had no emotional impact upon him. He came to dislike rising from his chair, and no longer fed the mice. They seemed to find adequate nourishment elsewhere, however, and remained lively and inquisitive, often running across his feet, and sometimes up his trouser legs. Knapp thought vaguely that they were nice little fellows.

You're nice, too, the mice said.

"I'd really better get something to eat," Knapp said aloud. He tried to rise from his chair, but was too weak to do so. He gripped the arms of the chair and pulled himself erect. He stood for a moment, took a tottering step, and collapsed to the floor.

Listen.

The house is speaking. I love you, it says.

I love you, too, says Webster Knapp. He lies on the floor in front of the armchair, curled like a fetus. He has not moved for more than a week. The mice scurry around and over him, sit upon his cheek, nestle close. We love you, the mice say to Webster Knapp. I love you, too, he says to the mice.

The tiny footsteps of the mice cause a minute stir in the dust that is settling upon him. A spider has begun to spin a web anchored at his ear and stretching across his face. There is no sound, there is no light.

There is only love. Love.

Ken Wisman has a friend in Connecticut who lives in a Victorian house where things disappear and are replaced by other things. Crows are notorious for that sort of thing, as we who pay no attention to cities know full well. We also know, as Ken does, that crows aren't the only answer. Sometimes you have to go hunting for something else, especially when it's obvious that crows, either in Connecticut or Ken's Massachusetts, haven't quite yet learned the knack of using a key to open the back door.

THE FINDER-KEEPER
by Ken Wisman

Thursday was hot. Muggy. The kind of July day that was thick and electric, threatening to storm.

Maggie stood in the kitchen, iron in her right hand, left hand resting on the ironing board. The steam of the iron only added to the heat and increased her feelings of claustrophobia.

Why doesn't Brad have his damned shirts laundered? Maggie thought irritably.

The answer came easily. *The house.* The two-hundred-and-fifty-thousand-dollar Victorian house that Brad had to have, but was a hundred and twenty-five thousand dollars more than they could afford.

Maggie ran the iron over a button and accidentally popped it from the shirt. She cursed under her breath: "To hell with Brad and his expensive antique."

She upended the iron and glanced out the window. The sky was filling with black clouds.

Maggie pressed her cheek against the glass. So damned hot. A buzzer sounded from the cellar, startling her. Maggie went to the cellar door and paused. It was a truly beautiful Victorian house with a great deal of charm—except for that cellar. Dark. Damp. Filled with spiders and small, skittering things.

She took the steep, wooden steps slowly, descending toward the buzzing Maytag. The washer and dryer were across from the foot of the steps. Maggie kept a big red flashlight on the washer. Invariably, when she reached the appliances, she grabbed the light and flashed it around the room.

To the right of the appliances was a pile—or rather a wall—of junk that must have been accumulating for a hundred years. There were ancient chests and broken chairs and tables with their surfaces scarred and ruined. Brad called it a treasure trove of possibilities and often talked about salvaging and restoring—but Maggie had never actually seen him touch any of it. Personally, the pile of junk gave her the creeps.

Maggie threw the clothes into the plastic basket. Then a noise in the junk pile caught her attention. She grabbed the big red flashlight and aimed it. Something skittered into the shadows.

Maggie grabbed the basket of clothes and took the cellar steps two at a time. At the top, she bolted the door and listened to her heart beating out of control. After a moment she felt a little foolish. She put the basket on a table and sorted.

Brad's stuff in one pile. Their daughter Andi's in another. When she was done, she was left with three of Andi's socks—all unmatched.

It was really the last straw. The heat. The scare in the cellar. And now the carelessness and inconsideration of that child . . .

The door opened at the front of the house. Andi called and came into the kitchen. She took one look at her mother's red and irritated face and wished she was somewhere else.

"How many times do I have to tell you to take better care of your things?" Maggie said. "I've got three knee socks here that you begged me to buy. And not one with a match."

"But, mommy—"

"Don't 'but' me!" Maggie shouted. And she saw her self-control melting away in the July heat. "I'm sick and tired of throwing money away—"

But Andi turned and ran from the room.

Maggie sighed. She had lost it. Truly lost it. And poor Andi had taken the brunt.

Maggie found Andi face down in her pillow.

"Hey, squirt," Maggie said, rubbing Andi's back. "Your mother is truly sorry."

Andi wriggled under her mother's touch.

"Come on," Maggie said. "Talk to me."

Andi flipped over. "What does 'financial burden' mean, mommy?"

That one took Maggie off balance. "Where'd you hear that?"

"You and daddy," Andi said. "The other night. When you were yelling."

"Discussing, dear," Maggie said, and she smiled. "It's what happens when you buy something you can't afford. Your father goes out and works two jobs, and your mother does all the menial tasks because you can't have them done for you. By the way, where are those three missing knee socks, young lady?"

"The finder-keeper must have them by now."

"Fantastic. Do you think you could ask the finder-keeper to give them back?"

Andi laughed. "He never gives anything back, mommy. You know —Finders keepers, losers weepers."

"Just who is this finder-keeper and why won't he give anything back?"

"He lives in the cellar."

"A great thing to tell your mother who's half neurotic about the basement to begin with."

Brad came home in a mood as dark and foreboding as the storm that had broken loose outside. Maggie had supper ready but Brad ate listlessly. The two jobs were taking their toll.

Maggie tried her usual ploy of snapping him out of his mood. She steered the conversation to Andi, who was his pride and joy.

"Andi's got a new imaginary," Maggie said.

"Oh," Brad said, jabbing at a carrot.

"Tell daddy about him," Maggie said.

"He's a real one, daddy," Andi protested. "He lives in the cellar and collects all the things people lose."

"Maybe we could charge him rent," Maggie said. "At the very least we should get him to get rid of that pile of junk in the cellar."

"Oh, that's not his," Andi said. "He actually lives in back of all that stuff through a hole in the wall. He's got tons of junk in his caves."

Brad showed a spark of interest. "How does he get all his junk, sweetheart?"

"Anything that falls behind the sofa or bureau or under the rug is his."

"How does he get the stuff without anyone seeing him?" Maggie asked.

"He moves around in the floors and walls and pulls small things in through the cracks and little holes," Andi said.

"Must be pretty skinny," Brad teased.

"Oh, daddy. The finder-keeper has no bones."

Friday, promptly at 11 A.M., Biddy Jameson came over for her weekly visit with Maggie. Maggie loved the old lady. Seventy-six (if she was a day) with grey hair pulled back severely in a bun. No makeup. Thin-lipped and plain. She looked the archetypal, strait-laced, New England lady—and was anything but.

Eleven A.M. to 3:30 P.M. was Maggie's and Biddy's "happy hour." Around noon they uncorked a bottle of wine or Maggie rolled a joint and they sat and passed the pungent stick back and forth.

This day, Maggie took out her plastic bag of marijuana, and the old woman fetched the papers.

"I completely agree, dear," Biddy said. "It's truly the worst of days to drink wine. What with this humidity we'd both wind up with headaches by two."

"It really kills me," Maggie said. "I mean the way you—smoke and all."

"Back in the thirties I used to go with a musician," Biddy said. "In New York. He turned me on, you might say."

Maggie giggled and passed the lit stick to Biddy.

"Did you know that Queen Victoria of England smoked the weed?" Biddy rasped out from her filled lungs.

Maggie shook her head.

"Oh, yes," Biddy said. "For her menstruals. Relieved the cramps."

"Why, the old bitch!" Maggie exclaimed.

Biddy laughed and lost the smoke.

And that was the other reason Maggie liked the old woman. She was so damned interesting with her encyclopedic knowledge and facts.

"How's that imaginative little daughter of yours?" Biddy asked.

The first rush of the marijuana washed over Maggie. She sat back with a smile. "You won't believe what Andi's come up with now."

"Tigers in the closet?" Biddy asked.

"Oh, no. Nothing so humdrum for my little girl. She's got a little man, a dwarf she calls the finder-keeper, living in caves just beyond the basement wall. And with interconnecting holes to every house in the neighborhood."

"Fascinating!" Biddy said, feeling the effects of the drug and sitting back herself. "What does this finder-keeper do?"

"As soon as someone loses something or misplaces it, the finder-keeper takes it and stashes it in his cavernous horde."

"My stars, and all these years I've been coming up with the most very wrong theories for my husband's socks."

Maggie giggled.

"But what a fun thing to think about," Biddy said. "I was just remembering all the watches and earrings and rings—not to mention all the small change—I've lost over the years. Now multiply that by a few thousand households."

"Quite a treasure trove for Mr. Finder-Keeper," Maggie said.

"You know, I recall reading some of the old Indian legends. Something about the Monadnock tribe in New Hampshire trading with dwarves for objects stolen from their neighbors. Called the dwarves Wapi, if I'm not mistaken."

"What else?" Maggie encouraged.

"Let me see. There was something, too, about the Massachusetts tribes. One group in the Boston area that believed in a creature that was half insect and half man. This sprite used to steal objects and leave something in return."

"Anything about treasure troves?"

"Not that I can recall," said Biddy. "Though there was another tribe here in Massachusetts that believed in a little man who'd steal away a young wife or two."

"Where's a good dwarf when you need one?" Maggie said.

"Afraid this little gentleman's tastes ran into pedophilia," Biddy said. "He liked to steal away little girls as well."

That night Maggie and Brad had a fight. It was about the electric bill.

"You're the one home alone all day," Brad said. "You're the one running all the electricity."

"It's the washer and dryer and iron going all the time," Maggie said.

"It's also because you never turn a light out when you leave a room."

Maggie was just high enough from the afternoon to let it go, to let it wash over her and not fight back. Yet, when they got into bed and Brad dropped exhaustedly to sleep, she turned to him and whispered: "Where'd it go, Brad? The fun times? Damned money is tearing us apart."

Saturday, Brad left early in the morning on a business trip over the long July 4th weekend. He'd be back late Monday night, which left Maggie alone to finish the painting in the living room.

Maggie had breakfast with Andi, then Maggie shooed her off to play on her own. An hour later, Maggie was in the living room mixing up the paint. She had just finished applying the first brushful when Andi came running down from her room in near hysterics. Andi paused at the entrance between the living room and the kitchen.

"What is it, Andi?" Maggie said. The paint dripped down the brush handle and onto her hand. She grabbed a rag.

"He can't have her," Andi wailed. "He can't."

"Who can't have what?"

"Bundy. He's taken Bundy."

Bundy was her favorite doll.

"Who's taken her?" Maggie said. "Who?"

"The finder-keeper," Andi said. And she ran into the kitchen and threw open the cellar door.

By the time Maggie got to the door, Andi was halfway down the steps.

"For god's sakes be careful," Maggie said and descended with caution. "Andi, where are you going?"

The little girl mumbled something and Maggie saw her crawl on all fours into the pile of junk.

"Andi!" Maggie ran to the dryer, grabbed the big red flashlight and ran to the junk pile. She flashed the light and caught a glimpse of Andi's leg before it disappeared.

Maggie squeezed into the tunnel through the chairs, rugs, lamps and old clothes. She came to the stone wall, and in the stone wall was a crack just large enough for her to enter.

Maggie paused, heard her daughter, and squeezed through.

Maggie walked down the long tunnel that twisted and turned and was lined with a lichen that gave off an eery, green light. Off the tunnel were chambers and carved hollows. Each opening was piled with articles of clothing or small wooden objects or objects made of glass.

Maggie poked her head into each, flashed her light and whispered: "Andi?" Finally Maggie found her standing in a large chamber near a pile of junk.

"Andi," Maggie said. "What is this place?"

"I told you, mommy," Andi said. "It's where the finder-keeper keeps his things."

"Come on, sweetheart. Let's get out of here."

"Wait," Andi said. "There. I see Bundy there."

Maggie shone the light to where Andi pointed. Amidst the mountain of potholders, ties, towels and socks was the doll. Andi grabbed it and hugged it.

"Come on," Maggie said. "You got what you want. Let's go." She grabbed Andi's hand.

"No!" Andi insisted. She pulled another doll—her Raggedy Ann —from her blouse. "You've got to trade even with the finder-keeper or he gets mad."

"How's he going to know?" Maggie whispered. Then she heard a chittering noise behind her, like a cicada going off in a tree.

Maggie grabbed Andi, retreated several steps and aimed the flashlight. She caught whatever it was in the light for just an instant before it ran behind a boulder. Maggie had the impression of a small, manlike creature with huge and multifaceted eyes—like a spider's.

"Oh, god," Maggie said.

"Don't worry, mommy," Andi said. "He won't hurt. But he is kind of angry."

"How do you know?"

"That sound he makes. When it's real loud like that it's because he thinks you're going to steal one of his things." Andi put down the Raggedy Ann. "For this," she said, brandishing her Bundy doll in the direction of the creature behind the stone.

The cicada sound softened.

"See," said Andi. "It's okay."

Maggie grabbed her daughter's hand and backed toward the

chamber opening. Maggie flashed the light behind the boulder as they passed. She had another quick impression of the thing. A beard, thick and stretching to the ground. And a covering that could have been clothing—or hair. Then the creature disappeared.

Maggie moved cautiously along, her daughter in tow. As they were passing a gallery on the left, the cicada sound burst through the opening. Maggie stabbed the light inside. But instead of the creature her light flashed on something sparkling. Maggie paused and played the light around.

The room was filled with money—small change and bills—and diamond rings and watches and golden chains. The mound of articles and money was more than three feet high and twice as wide. Maggie crept inside the room. She knelt and picked up handfuls of the stuff.

The room filled with the angry cicada sound.

"He doesn't like you touching his things," Andi said.

Maggie threw the trinkets down. "Keep your filthy stuff."

Then a sharp, sweet odor filled the cave. The smell stung Maggie's nose. She felt a little high like she did when she smoked, but she led her daughter out into the tunnel and the long, winding way back to the wall.

Andi knelt in the center of the living room and hugged her doll. Maggie sat, her back against the wall. She still felt high.

"We should leave," she said.

"Why, mommy?" Andi asked.

"That thing in the cellar," Maggie said. She shook her head to clear it.

"He showed me where he lives," Andi said. "He showed me his stuff. He's real shy, mommy. And he's more afraid of people than we are of him."

"We should tell someone," Maggie whispered. "I wish your father was home."

Sunday morning, 3 A.M., Andi slept. Maggie could not sleep. She sat naked and cross-legged on the bed. If anything, the high had increased along with the ache in her sinuses and head. She no longer thought of the finder-keeper, but of his cache. The jewels. The rings. The money.

She thought of the financial struggle, the disintegration of her relationship with Brad.

Maggie rose from the bed, put on a jogging suit and went to check on Andi. The girl slept soundly, Bundy hugged in her arms. Maggie went out to the garage and got a pail. Then she went upstairs and got Brad's pistol from under the mattress. She had hated the gun in the house—but Brad had refused to get rid of it.

She went into the kitchen and grabbed the red flashlight where she had left it on the counter. She gathered up objects—statues, paperweights, books—and filled up the pail. Then she went to the cellar stairs and paused.

A part of Maggie screamed that she was crazy. The other, stronger part remembered the cache. Maggie descended.

She moved cautiously through the tunnels, the pail in her left hand, the flashlight in her right, and the gun at her hip behind the cinch of her jogging pants.

Maggie came to the high vaulted room and knelt at the mound. She examined a few coins—Indian-head pennies, sixty years old. She found some gold coins, tarnished but with dates from a hundred and twenty years ago.

She emptied her pail and started picking carefully through the pile of treasure. She took the most valuable coins and bills and jewelry, discarding the costume trinkets.

When her pail was half full, the cicada sound rattled behind her. Maggie grabbed the flashlight and swung the beam around—straight into the eyes of the finder-keeper, who scurried behind the boulder.

"Look," Maggie said. She held up the objects she had brought. "We'll trade. Even-steven."

But as Maggie held up each thing, the staccato noise increased.

"To hell with you," Maggie said. She scattered her objects and filled the pail.

Maggie rose with her heavy burden and moved toward the cave opening. The finder-keeper scurried from behind the rock and blocked her way.

"What do you want?" Maggie stabbed the flashlight beam into the finder-keeper's face. Its twisted, inhuman features were disgusting. She played the light down its gnarled body. It had three fingers on its left hand, seven on its right . . .

She pulled the gun and aimed it. And the creature stretched into something as thin as a worm and disappeared into one of hundreds of dime-sized holes in the ceiling.

The sun was up by the time Maggie left the caves and got to her room. She sat in the center of the bed and tipped the pail. She counted up the bills and arranged them in a neat pile. Then she sorted through the jewelry and gold coins and put those in separate piles.

There was enough to pay off the house—easily. With a down payment for a new car.

Maggie put the piles into three pillowcases and stored them in a bureau drawer. She went downstairs where Andi was waiting.

"You gonna paint, mommy?" Andi asked her.

"Yes, of course," Maggie said. Mechanically, she went through the motions of laying down the drop cloths, mixing the cans, dipping the brushes. Andi watched for a while, then she went to play upstairs.

Maggie had barely begun painting when she developed a headache that pounded and sent red flashes across her eyes. She went upstairs to lie down.

When Maggie got up at 3 P.M., Andi was gone. And in the center of Andi's bed was a brooch, tarnished and old.

Maggie crept through the tunnel of junk, the flashlight in her left hand, the pistol in her right. She entered the cave cautiously and spied her daughter on the floor of the first chamber.

Maggie knelt by Andi. The little girl appeared to be asleep but was otherwise all right. Maggie tried to awaken her, but to no avail. She reached her arms under the girl's body, but before she could lift her, the cicada sound vibrated menacingly throughout the room.

Maggie swung around, gun in hand. She got three shots off. The finder-keeper flinched backward with each shot. Then the creature elongated and disappeared into a tiny hole in the wall.

Maggie returned to her daughter. She lifted Andi from the floor and shuffled toward the opening.

An acrid scent filled the cave. Maggie sneezed. Her legs felt weak and collapsed under her. She dropped her daughter, who rolled on her side.

Then a blackness enveloped Maggie and she slept.

Maggie awoke. She couldn't move except for the fingers of her right hand and her head. She still held the flashlight.

By the light of the green lichen she could see the finder-keeper stooping over her daughter. What the creature did she couldn't tell. Maggie switched the light on the finder-keeper and tried to scare it. But the thing barely turned, and the acrid scent filled the cave.

Maggie slept.

Maggie awoke.

From her position, she could see past the chamber opening to the wall of the house. The finder-keeper was there, rolling stones, sealing them.

Maggie looked up. Dangling from the ceiling was a long, ropy tube —a stretched-out intestine. Attached at the bottom was a kidney-shaped organ. Blood dripped from the organ and onto Maggie's naked belly.

Maggie looked to where her daughter had lain. Andi was gone. Then several small, round objects dropped from the organ and stuck to Maggie's stomach.

She slept.

Maggie awoke. Her body was numb. Yet she felt elated.

It was quiet in the cave, except for an odd, chewing sound. She switched the flashlight on and aimed it around. She found the finder-keeper nearby. Or rather its remains. It was just a puddle of flesh with two red, ruby eyes rising from the center like islands.

The chewing distracted Maggie, and she lifted her head and aimed the light at her legs. A white caterpillar with a beard and bright red, faceted eyes stared back at her. Then it put its head down and resumed feeding on her flesh.

Maggie counted thirteen caterpillars.

She slept.

Maggie awoke.

And heard the chewing.

Dully, she remembered a conversation with Biddy Jameson. A discussion about insects. Biddy told her about a species of wasp that filled its prey with just enough poison to keep it paralyzed and alive. Then the wasp laid its eggs on the prey, and the larvae ate the prey.

But the larvae did it in such an insidious way—avoiding all critical organs, secreting a substance in its saliva to stop bleeding.

Then Maggie's thoughts turned to rescue. It must be Monday by now. Brad must've come home and discovered Maggie and Andi missing. He'd phone the police first. And maybe, just maybe, Biddy Jameson.

Biddy would come over. Reassure him. They'd have coffee. Maybe answer some police questions. Stay up together with their personal concern and fear.

And Biddy would remember. The story of the finder-keeper. She'd feel a little foolish bringing it up. Yet maybe Maggie did go down there with Andi, and that pile of junk so precariously piled may have fallen . . .

Then, miraculously, Maggie heard the sound of furniture being moved and a masculine voice—Brad's? And a feminine—Biddy's?

But the wall. The wall the finder-keeper put up. No. She heard the sound of picks. The mortar was too fresh, had fooled no one.

The sound of chewing distracted Maggie. It was much closer than it had been the last time. Much closer.

She closed her eyes and steeled herself. She switched the light on, opened her eyes and aimed the light where her calves should have been. Slowly, she played the beam up past her missing thighs, her hips. And finally to where her chest should have been.

The sounds of digging came closer and Maggie wanted to shout to them not to hurry, not to bother. For there wasn't much left to rescue, not very much at all . . .

On that previously mentioned trip to Okalahoma, I was struck by the high level of professionalism of all who attended the meetings and speeches. Many were already full-time writers in a number of different fields, and those who weren't were fiercely determined to become so. Cheryl Nelson is one of the latter, and once again I'm pleased to bring a delightfully, quietly, nasty first story from a state that I once thought had more quarter horses than people.

JUST A LITTLE SOUVENIR
by Cheryl Fuller Nelson

Rita Parker sat cross-legged on the braided oval rug. Beneath her, the hardwood floor creaked with her slightest movement. The aging house with its high ceilings and oak beams welcomed her, she felt secure in its protection.

Autumn sunlight filtered through the windows and illuminated gold in the thick mass of her auburn hair. Her hazel eyes were wide with anticipation. She looked up at Blanche Weatherby and waited for the old woman's words. "Please, continue the story. I don't remember ever hearing this one."

"Well, I was just a child at the time." Blanche paused, smoothing the folds of her girlish summer smock with liver-spotted hands.

"But it's something I'll never forget as long as I live." Her voice softened; she was lost again in the memory. "Poor LuElla. She loved Harlan from the moment she saw him, but she was too good for that man. Everybody tried to tell her. She married him anyway of course."

Across the room, Millicent Weatherby maintained the rhythmic motion of her rocking chair. She nodded in agreement with her sister. "Married him anyway," she repeated, never looking up from her needlepoint.

Rita nudged Bobby Freeman, whose lanky frame stretched full length beside her on the floor of the Weatherby sisters' living room. With one sharp glance, she halted the smirking grin spreading across his tanned face.

Rita had known the Weatherby sisters as far back as she could remember. They were her friends, despite the vast age difference, and she would not allow Bobby to laugh at them. She had been unable to keep him from intruding on her visit, but she would not permit any hurt feelings because of his rudeness.

"That marriage was doomed from the sorrowful day it began," Blanche continued. "He beat her. He never seemed to want LuElla after he got her. She must have really cared for him to put up with him for so long. Harlan Stone was as close to the devil as any mortal man can get. Why, I can remember Mama and the neighbors exchanging stories of the awful things he did. Don't think anyone was sad when LuElla finally left him and started making a life for herself. She got a job down at the Purity Drug."

"They served the best french fries we ever had," Millicent interrupted, once again capturing the attention of the teenage visitors.

"Yes, Milly," Blanche acknowledged her older sister. With an accomodating smile, she settled back into the soft pillows of her overstuffed chair. "Anyway, the poor thing only got a small taste of freedom. It wasn't long until Harlan wanted her back. He wouldn't take no for an answer. He followed her wherever she went right up to that tragic evening back in 1922."

"It was 1923." Millicent smiled sweetly.

"Milly, do you want to tell this story?" Blanche's polite tone was strained.

"Well, I could. I did know LuElla better. She was my age, you know. I even let her borrow my hat, a new one with lavender ribbon ties and silk violets. She was wearing it the day she died."

Millicent leaned forward, bringing the rocker to an abrupt stop. One strand of white-gray hair freed itself from a tightly drawn bun. She peered at Rita and Bobby through thick lenses, her blue eyes magnified, filling the wire frames of her glasses. "There were brains in that hat when they found it. And it holds the bloodstains to this very day!"

"You still have the hat?" Bobby's interest peaked.

Millicent nodded smugly. "Just a little souvenir. Shall I get it?"

"Yes!" A maniacal gleam made Bobby's green eyes sparkle.

"No." Rita disagreed too late; Millicent was already leaving the room at a slow, steady pace.

Blanche took advantage of her sister's absence. She spoke quickly, trying to finish before the inevitable interruption. "LuElla always walked home from the drugstore. She used to walk down our road out there. She lived on past the Maple Grove School, right on the edge of the woods. Well, one night, just as she came upon the school-yard, Harlan called to her. He was waiting there and somehow he persuaded her to stop and talk. They sat facing each other on two concrete benches at the school entrance." Blanche paused for a deep breath.

In the stillness of the room, Rita felt a sudden chill and pulled her sweater tighter. She had passed the deserted ruins of the old Maple Grove School so many times without even considering the events of its past.

"None of us were there to hear LuElla's last words, but the whole town heard the gunshots. There were two of them. One right after the other." Blanche's voice broke with remorse. "He shot her in the head and then took his own life. Harlan Stone went to hell straight from the schoolyard and sweet LuElla laid there with angels hovering over her."

"Dead and bleeding into my new hat." Millicent announced her return and offered the evidence to Bobby. "Isn't it lovely?"

Bobby took the hat and examined it with fascination. "Tell me more about LuElla," he urged, encouraging Millicent to begin her own version of the story.

Rita tuned out the conversation around her and sat quietly enjoying the ambience of the room. She was always enthralled when she visited the Weatherbys. She imagined that very little had changed here over the years.

Yellowed lace curtains moved gently with the cool breeze and fell silently back against the half-open window. Crocheted doilies covered a cedar chest where at least thirty pictures were displayed, reminders of just as many stories. Rita smiled with the thought, actually there would be twice as many stories, the Weatherby sisters never fully agreed on anything.

She walked across the room for a closer look at one of the older photographs. Three faces smiled, the image of youthful exuberance shone through the faded tint.

Rita could smell the sweet floral scent of Blanche's perfume before she heard the quiet voice drift over her shoulder. "I remember that day."

Blanche reached out to touch the picture. Rita felt the coldness of her hand. "That's Milly and I, of course, and that's LuElla with us.

See how her eyes were shining? She was so full of love and excitement. That was taken just before her marriage."

Rita was overcome with sadness for the girl smiling up at her. LuElla did not look deserving of her destiny.

Although she spoke quietly, Millicent was still holding Bobby's attention. "Some folks say, in the still of the night, you can hear him calling . . . 'LuEllaaa, LuEllaaa' . . . And then POW! POW!"

Rita jumped at Millicent's imitation of the gunshots.

"Millie, stop that," Blanche scolded. "You've frightened this poor girl half to death. Now that's enough ghost talk unless you are prepared to walk these kids home. They will be too scared to go alone."

Millicent's eyes widened. She glanced at the impending darkness beyond the living-room window and shook her head slowly.

Blanche took the picture from Rita's hands and returned it to the cedar chest. "Come with me for a moment, dear."

She led Rita out of the room and down a hallway to a linen closet. Stretching to reach behind the uneven stacks of quilts and blankets, Blanche found the small handgun and retrieved it. She placed the gun in the pocket of Rita's sweater and did not allow the girl to protest.

"Keep this with you," she ordered. "I love having you come to see us, but I worry about you walking all that way home. Don't let the ramblings of two old women make you frightened of ghosts, dear, but do remember there are real things out there that certainly deserve caution."

The expression on Blanche's wrinkled face changed; the smile was replaced with a worried frown. "Keep to the road on your way home now, don't go through the woods at Maple Grove." She patted Rita's hand. "A sweet child like you could wander into that darkness and never be seen again."

Bobby's voice filtered in from the living room. Rita could not hear the words but he sounded excited.

Blanche did not completely disguise the tone of jealousy in her own voice. "God only knows what Milly's been up to in there. She does love an audience. You better rescue your friend, though, there's not much daylight left and you two need to get going."

Outside, the cool air cleansed Rita, releasing the staleness she had carried from the old house. She wished she could so easily discard the tangible object she had been forced to take from the Weatherbys' collection of relics. She carried the hat awkwardly, careful that her fingers did not touch the bloodstains.

Bobby rested his arm on her shoulder as he walked her home. He tapped the straw hat. "Why don't you wear it?"

"Bobby, are you crazy? There's no way I could put this thing on my head. Someone died in this hat! I would never have accepted it if you hadn't insisted."

Bobby defended his actions. "The old woman wanted you to have it; she got a big thrill out of it. I didn't think you should hurt her feelings."

Rita did not answer him. He had no right to push her into taking the awful gift. She hated the way it felt in her hands. Tomorrow she would go back to the Weatherbys' house and return it.

"All right, don't wear the hat. It was just for fun anyway. But I don't want to hear one of your lectures tonight, not after wasting a date on an evening with those two. God, I thought they would never stop talking. We'd never be alone." He pulled her closer and tried to kiss her.

Rita gently pushed him away. "It wasn't a date, Bobby, we've been through this before. I want to be your friend, but I can't think of you in any other way." She chose her words carefully. Other conversations with Bobby had taught her that he could become enraged if she rejected him. On more than one occasion he had shouted at her; once she thought he might even hit her. Too often he had embarrassed her in front of her friends. She suddenly felt uneasy about being alone with him.

"I can walk the rest of the way home by myself, Bobby. There's no need for you to go so far out of your way."

As usual, he ignored the dismissal. "Let's cut through the woods. It's much quicker, and much more romantic for lovers."

She stopped to look directly into his eyes so he would not miss the intensity of her words. "Bobby, we aren't lovers. We're not going to be lovers. We're not even going to be friends if we have to keep playing this scene."

He seemed stunned. His eyes flashed with anger, but he withdrew from her and let her go on alone.

Rita walked slightly faster than before, following the dirt road home through the early evening shadows. After a while she no longer heard his footsteps behind her and she relaxed, slowing her pace. And then the dreadful thought jumped into her mind, shattering the calm. What if Bobby had taken the short cut through the woods? The route cut out more than a mile of the road she traveled, and then merged with it again. What if Bobby planned to wait for her? It wasn't at all like him to give up this easily.

She decided on a plan of action. She would simply take her time, even stop to rest for a while. Maybe she could avoid another confrontation.

If he was waiting for her somewhere up ahead, one thing was certain. He would not wait long. Soon it would be dark. Bobby was a city boy, still a newcomer to country life, not yet accustomed to night noises that whispered through the trees at Maple Grove. Tonight she had the advantage, having lived her whole life here. She would waste a little time and he would get bored or scared and go home.

Leaving the road, she made her way down a secluded path tangled with clusters of black-green underbrush. When the path spread to a clearing, she was able to see the remains of the school.

It crouched, abandoned, in the shadows of tall trees. Crumbling bricks, rotting wood, there was not even enough left to imagine the shape or design of the building that once had been. And there among the debris stood two concrete benches. Reminders of the story Rita had heard earlier, and the hat still in her hand.

She was cautious not to lose her footing through the rubble. Reaching the pair of benches, she dusted gravel from one and sat down. She placed the hat beside her, changed her mind, and picked it up once more. Her fingers traced the outline of the tiny flowers mounted on the rough straw texture.

The idea came from idle curiosity and grew quickly into an overpowering urgency. She placed the hat on her head and tied the ribbons beneath her chin. The night breeze caught long strands of her hair, entwining it with braided ribbons. A shiver started in the small of her back and worked its way up along her spine.

Slowly, she began to feel the familiarity, began to uncover sensations long forgotten. Sensations of sorrow, of torment. The dark mood folded around her and held her captive. In dazed semiconsciousness she summoned the memory from deep within.

The Weatherby sisters had both been wrong. It was 1921 when she last sat on this bench. 1921 when she consented to the pact that Harlan had proposed.

He had sounded so excited about the idea, had defended it with such passion. He had an answer for her every question. No, it wouldn't hurt. Yes, they would be together forever, their love undying through each lifetime. It would be simple, he had said, take the vow, repeat the words, deny the gods your soul.

How silly she had been, how willing to accept his scheme for his own immortality. She had agreed naively to it all, praising him for finding a way to continue their love forever. 1921. They had died here and begun an eternity together.

In her heart she felt the sadness of so many betrayals. She had no sweet memories of past lives, no love returned, no promise fulfilled. She untied the ribbons and let the hat fall to rest on her lap. Her tears fell on the silk violets and mixed there with the stains of LuElla's blood, her blood.

She heard the voice as he lied to her so long ago, saw the face of the man she had loved more than her own life. His green eyes pierced through her insecurities. And in that moment, she knew. She was not safe even now. The very purpose of the last eighteen years was about to be known. The ultimate and inevitable end to a short life as Rita Parker waited for her tonight, waited with a new name and a new face.

She left the school ground, carrying her hat in numb hands. Though often straying from the narrow path, she found her way to the road. She walked, spellbound, allowing her mind to drift. And, with all her soul, she felt him drawing her near.

"Rita?" His voice did not startle her.

"Rita." He called out to her again. "I've been waiting for you."

"Have you? And do you know where I've been, Bobby?" She did not wait for his answer. "I stopped at the old school. I stopped to sit on the bench there, stopped to remember." She moved toward him.

"Have you been to the Maple Grove schoolyard, Bobby? Why, of course you have. We've been there together, haven't we?" She smiled at the look on his face. He was obviously surprised, possibly a little frightened. She enjoyed this new feeling of control.

"Aren't you curious? Don't you even want to know how much I've remembered? I know who you are, Bobby."

He looked into her eyes. "Then call me by my name, Rita. Say my name and tell me our love is renewed." He reached out for her.

She moved away, unable to let him touch her. "No, the name means nothing to me now. And I haven't loved you in such a long time. I suspect you never loved me. But none of that matters."

Before she could resist, he grabbed the hat from her and held it close to his chest. "I remember how beautiful you looked in this hat. I just couldn't lose you. I wanted you forever."

His dramatic display brought wild spurts of laughter from her. "You wanted life forever. I was meant only to be a diversion, a game for your amusement. Something for you to track down. Something for you to kill."

She took the lightweight gun from her pocket. "Did I show you what Blanche gave me tonight, Bobby?" She paused to indulge in the power of making him wait, making him wonder. "It's even loaded."

She pointed the gun and took cruel pleasure at his reaction. Then she watched his transformation, saw the cunning shimmer return to his eyes.

"It could be as it was long ago. We could be everything to each other once more." His voice stirred some longing within her. "Come with me. It will be just like the first time. Give me the gun, LuElla."

"No." She was determined that his charm would not work this time. And yet some part of her wanted to hand him the gun.

"The transition will be glorious," he promised. "It won't hurt. It will all be over before you know it."

"It's over now." Her voice was a whisper. She did not give him time to move. She steadied her aim and fired.

The bullet entered his chest and for the first time she had found his heart. He slumped to the ground.

She bent over his body and removed the crumpled hat from his death grip. She carried it with her into the night shadows, careful not to touch the fresh bloodstains.

If you are ever in England, and you are lucky enough to meet Stephen Gallagher, get him to tell you about his garden and the cattle that fertilize it from the field next door. But until that time, read his stories —they appear quite regularly in American publications and are nothing like the not quite believable smile he has when he sits down to tell you a story. There's a dark about him that's difficult to explain, but that dark is readily apparent when he decides that face value isn't quite the way life works.

LIKE SHADOWS IN THE DARK
by Stephen Gallagher

Nikolai had done little more than to sit watching her for the first couple of hours, until he'd realised that he was making her nervous. That was when he'd moved from the fold-down seat to lie full length on the train compartment's upper berth, leaving Irina below to gaze out of the window at the passing landscape. This was continuous and unvarying, birch and pine forests standing dark in the moonlight; occasionally the trees thinned out for settlements of low wooden houses with small-paned windows and snow-laden roofs, but for the most part it was just a rolling backdrop for their dreams and fears.

He adored her. One dream, at least, seemed to be coming true for him.

He wondered if he ought to be more scared than he was; most of his feelings at this moment seemed to be of excitement. But then, he'd seen frontier checks before, and he knew how casual and routine they could be. More attention would be given to the body-sized hiding spaces in the carriage than to the two supposed foreign tourists whose bogus papers were all in order. From where he lay, he could see the seals that had been attached to the roof vent to keep anyone from crawling into the air duct above; even they were almost perfunctory, a piece of twisted wire with a lead crimp and a messy drop of wax on the head of a screw.

Easy, he thought to himself, and it was only when he heard Irina stiffen that he realised he'd said it aloud. "I'm sorry," he whispered, this time in English; it was their best shared language, and England their chosen destination. One overheard phrase of Russian now, with at least a dozen of the border police on the train, and their careful deception would suddenly cease to deceive.

Nikolai was twenty-two years old. He'd been a merchant seaman up until this night, when the old life was ending and a new one was getting ready to begin; he'd first met Irina only ten months before.

He adored her, even though he knew so little about her . . . but that would change, in the new life.

"Do you believe in ghosts, Nikolai?" she said, a question so unexpected that it startled him a little.

"No," he said, and he turned over on the bunk so that he could look down at her. "Why?"

She was still gazing out of the window. "We're passing through the land of the Winter War," she said. "Thousands died in the open. Wouldn't you think that would taint the ground forever?"

But a sharp rap on the wall by the door brought Nikolai slithering down from the berth. Irina was already standing as the guard came in, a boy soldier in an iron-grey uniform and with a deep cheek-scar that was like a cattle brand. He was carrying a short stepladder in one hand, their passports in the other; after setting the ladder down he read out the names on their papers, mispronouncing them, and then turned to the photographs. They were French passports, guaranteed stolen but not yet reported, and the flimsy visa forms inside were simple forgeries.

There wasn't much room. Irina was standing close beside Nikolai, her head only just level with his shoulder, and she was looking at the floor. Nikolai felt a small flame of apprehension coming to life inside him at this, and the flame became a steady heat as the guard—barely out of school but already as tough and as ugly as a board—looked up from her picture to find her avoiding his eyes.

It was then that Nikolai found his fear.

Through all their preparation, one prospect had never occurred to him; that when the pressure came on, Irina might fold under it. Even though he'd done all of the legwork and worked out most of the arrangements for the journey, it had been Irina's determination that had always sent him forward. It was for her that he'd raised money on the clothes and the records and the music centres that he'd brought home from foreign ports, and it was for her that he'd hung around outside the big tourist hotels in Leningrad looking for chances to buy the dollars and the Deutschmarks and the sterling that they were going to need. She was his source of power, the generator of his confidence.

He looked to her now, in this moment of balance.

Irina lifted her head, and returned the guard's level stare; and for Nikolai everything fell back into place, as neatly as jigsaw pieces.

He could feel himself unwinding, notch by notch, as the boy soldier handed back their passports and then stepped up onto his ladder to check the luggage rack and the vent seals. He then unhooked a flashlight from his belt and shone it into the space under the lower bunk; this short ritual completed, he went out into the corridor and closed the door on them.

Nikolai felt shaken, beaten, and ready to celebrate. But Irina's touch on his arm silenced him, and her warning look, even though it was tempered with a slight trace of a smile, told him that it wasn't yet over.

There was no baggage check. They'd anticipated one, putting foreign labels in all of their clothes and even including a few postcards and wrapped souvenirs to make the effect convincing, but after their customs forms had been collected their door stayed closed. There was a lot of movement up and down the carriage and occasional shouting along the corridor outside, but the two of them stayed where they were and waited for the tide of officialdom to wash on over. Theirs was a "soft-class" compartment, the best they'd been able to book, with teak-effect fittings and a lot of fresh linen, attendant service and even piped music if they wanted it; as a piece of bravado it had seemed like a good idea, but now it was serving to isolate them. Every time Nikolai heard a muffled shout, he thought that he could make out his name.

The train rolled on slowly. Irina lay back in the shadowed corner of the lower berth, and this time Nikolai sat beside her. The scene outside grew more and more empty, the forests cleared back from the trackside in a sure sign that the border was approaching. He saw the ruined remains of old concrete-block bunkers, many of them roofless and all of them half buried in the snow; they glided on in near silence past the tracks of earlier ski patrols and the occasional bulldozed vehicle road, the snow thrown up at its sides like dirty concrete.

Then there was daylight in the darkness as they came under the first of the searchlight gantries. These straddled the track every fifty metres or so, and the effect was of a slow pulsing as the thousand-watt arrays passed over. There were other lines here with other trains, all of them freightcars and none of them moving; it was like a forgotten railyard, the place where all the ghost-trains ended their runs, the only sign of life a small fire that had been lit under one of the diesel engines to free its iced-up brakes. The fire's attendant was a silhouette that stepped out to watch them go by, an eyeless, faceless shadow of a man.

Irina hitched herself up and moved closer to the window. The train was slowing in its river of light, fighting the sluggish waters that were taking it down to the sea of freedom. They were being watched from a two-man tower out across the tracks, a dark shape sketched in darkness that stood taller than the pines. Nikolai could feel Irina tense against his shoulder, and he looked at her; even in this harsh light she was a wide-eyed madonna, and it was as if he felt his heart turn over. His family, his friends, his job . . . they were nothing when he held them up against the promise of a life with Irina Iva-nova.

And he knew so little about her.

But that would surely change.

They'd stopped. Somewhere further down the train a heavy door was thrown back, and there were voices out at the trackside that were stifled almost to nothing by the double glass of the window. They were in a wooded clearing with just a single green-painted building that stood about a hundred metres back from the line, with the deep shadow of a snow-cut path narrowing away to it.

Away along the path, coming in at the extreme left of Nikolai's field of vision, trudged the frontier police and the border guards in single file, all in heavy overcoats now and with the first man carrying the black valise which would be holding all of the forms and the official stamps and the inked pads that went with them. His staff followed him in ranking order, with the two junior soldiers at the end of the line. The train was already moving again by the time that these came into view; the heavy door slammed, and nobody looked back.

Nikolai got off the bunk and moved to the door. He hadn't even wanted to try it before, in case he found it locked from the outside; but it unlatched easily, and he took a cautious look out into the corridor.

The American in the next compartment was still patiently quizzing his teenaged son on the statistics of the USSR: square mileage, the total length of all the rivers, the population of Moscow. Further down, he could see a tall blonde girl in a red coat and glasses, standing in the place where she'd been as they pulled out and from where she and her friend had waved to the boys who were seeing them off. One minute after departure the two of them had been in a consoling hug, the short, dark girl patting the blonde, who'd cried and cried and shown no signs of letting up as people going by stepped carefully around them. Now she was leaning on the chrome rail and looking out into the night.

He saw no uniforms, excepting a brief glimpse of the grey waistcoat of one of the carriage's two attendants as he carried a tray of tea-glasses around and into the washroom. Somebody had their compartment music turned up high and it was playing a bland, Westernised Muzak-version of "Kalinka."

Nikolai turned to Irina. She was watching him, waiting to see what he'd say. Keeping his voice low and sticking to the agreed English, he said, "Looks like that's all the checking they're going to do."

Even though he tried, he could barely keep his excitement down. Irina quickly got to her feet, stepped to the door, and closed it gently. Then she looked up at Nikolai, with understanding but also with a knowledge that went beyond his own.

"Better not to celebrate too soon," she told him.

"But we're as good as in Finland!"

"Others have been this far before, and the Finns handed them back."

And she was right, of course; Finland stood too much in the shadow of the Bear to be able to risk the delicate balance of its independence over a couple of nobodies on the run. They watched together as they passed the border marker, a simple blue-and-white pole showing above the snow at the trackside. Irina found his hand with her own and pressed it, briefly.

"We'll celebrate when we get to England," she said. "I promise."

But less than ten minutes later, the train was stopped again.

Nikolai lay tense, and began to worry. It didn't seem much like a signal-halt. When somebody passed below their window at track-

level, he swung himself down so that he'd be able to see better. Irina
was already sitting up, her face pressed almost to the glass. Now
someone else went by, blonde hair and a red coat; the passengers
were out on the tracks, wandering down towards the engine to see
what was wrong.

When he turned around, Irina was already up and buttoning herself into her mid-length overcoat. "We'd better take no chances," she
said, and so Nikolai reached for the boots that he'd kicked off and
placed in the corner behind the door. As he sat and pulled them on,
he saw that Irina had opened her case and was taking out the carrier
bag that they'd agreed would be their only luggage if the time came
to cut and run. It held their passports, all of their money, and one
item each that would give them some sense of continuity with the
lives that they'd left. Nikolai had chosen his grandmother's Bible—a
risky choice if there was a search, and so he'd wrapped and labelled
it like a gift. He didn't know what Irina had brought.

Seeing this, he said, "You don't think we're safe?"

"Of course we're not safe," Irina said, and then with the bag
folded up tight and tucked under her arm she opened the door and
led the way out into the corridor.

The pre-dawn chill began to seep into them from the moment that
they took the long step down from the carriage. Nikolai paused to
look around, his breath misting in the grey air as he tugged his gloves
on a little further and zippered his overjacket a little tighter. They
seemed to be at some anonymous spot in the middle of nowhere,
with the endless woodland crowding right up to the trackside and
cutting off any chance of seeing what lay beyond. There were faces at
most of the windows above him, and people hanging out of the open
doorways at the carriage-ends as they craned to see what was going
on; up ahead was a crowd of perhaps two dozen or more. Those
further along in the hard class seemed dazed, rumpled, slightly
shocked to find themselves still active and awake at such an hour.

Two trucks of the border patrol were blocking the track.

With a sudden movement, Irina hustled Nikolai towards the trees.
The trackside boundary fence had mostly collapsed, and it was easy
enough to step over the wire. The immediate cover was sparse, just
leafless silver birch that stood as straight and as narrow as threads;
even though they'd reached the first of them in three strides it would
be some distance before they could be certain that they were out of

sight. Nikolai was expecting a shout at any moment, and he was running hunched as if he anticipated it coming as an actual physical blow between the shoulders. Canelike undergrowth whipped at his legs, and he almost turned his ankle when he hit some stone or branch that had been buried under the snow. Irina moved ahead, light and fast, breaking the new trail and cutting across to where the forest grew denser and offered a better screen.

He caught up with her amongst the pine trees, where she slowed and stopped and turned her head to listen; they were both breathing hard, and she put a hand on the nearest trunk to steady herself. Nikolai felt the cold air in his lungs like broken glass, but he forced himself to keep it under control so that he could listen as well; after a few moments, there came a sound that could equally have been interpreted either as a danger or as a reassurance.

The train was leaving. Without them.

Irina didn't speak, but walked on. The only prospect for safety lay in the assumption that their empty compartment had been noted, and in the hope that only a limited search could be conducted here on the western side of the wire. Nikolai wanted to ask if Irina agreed with his thinking, but this would have to wait until some of the sickness of the fear and the hard running had left him. He shivered occasionally, and not only because of the cold.

After a couple of hundred metres, they met a well-tramped path that was too deep to have been cut by anything less than a snow-blower. This immediately punctured the impression of wilderness, and made their situation seem a little less bleak. The ground sloped up and away, part of a low ridge; the early morning air was still, the only sound the occasional rustling of tree branches shedding their snow. Nikolai wished that Irina would look to him for reassurance a little more, the way that he looked to her. But just wait, he told himself. His ship had been to England before, and he'd actually been to London a couple of times. Irina would realise how much she needed him there.

This was what he was thinking, as a distant whistle cut through the air.

They looked at each other. Nikolai wanted to say that it had perhaps been the cry of a bird, but he couldn't bring himself to believe it. Irina took the lead and said, "They're following our trail."

Another whistle answered, from further down the ridge. This one was more distant, and less expert. It was definitely no bird.

Nikolai couldn't see that they had any option other than to keep moving and to try to stay ahead, but Irina seemed to have another idea. "Listen," she said, not too loudly and glancing around, "we'll split up. I'll try to lead them away from you."

"I want to stay with you," he protested. But she gave him a hard shove, much harder than he would have expected from her, sending him on his way and nearly pushing him off his balance on the slippery path.

By the time that he'd recovered enough to protest again, she'd gone.

The darkness was giving way to that strange northern twilight that took a little of the colour out of everything but which sharpened up edges and outlines and presented them in a range of greys that shone like opal. It wasn't daylight—it wasn't even full dawn—but daylight couldn't be so far away.

After a few minutes, Nikolai came to the end of the snow-cut path and found himself facing a clapboard house with a cyclone-fenced yard stacked with bags of peat. Peat, in a forest? But he didn't have time to wonder; he gave the house a quick once-over and saw that it was well-shuttered and the lean-to shed at its side protected by a heavy padlock, and then he went out and around by the fence to get to the back of the house.

As soon as he was sure that his new tracks wouldn't be seen from the path, he struck out into the woodland again. There was a trail of sorts leading out from the house, but it didn't look too heavily used. The trees here were bigger, more mature, and their height cut down on the effect of the lightening sky and sent him forward into shadow.

He was thinking about what she'd done, launching him away like that, and he was wondering how she planned for them to get together again. After all, she still had the passports and the money, and he had nothing. Unable to help himself, he found that he was thinking about all the times that he'd asked her about their future together; about all the times that she'd turned his questions aside and promised him explanations later.

For the first time, he began to wonder. He began to wonder about being used.

He was walking upslope, still trying on the idea for size, when his shin cracked against something hard enough to make him stumble. He held his leg and waited for the pain to subside, and when it did it left him staring at the uncovered shoulder of stone from which he'd kicked the snow.

He reached out and brushed away some more, uncovering a name: *Jenny Matilda* something, the rest of the gilt carving filled in by snow which had set hard. When he stood up and looked around he saw more of them, different sizes of stones and cast-iron crosses half buried in white on the slopes in amongst the trees. Some were straight, others leaned at odd angles.

This, at least, explained the bags of peat; the house had been the grave-keeper's house. Leaving Jenny Matilda's marker behind, Nikolai pressed on upslope towards the crest of the ridge where the sky showed through the trees.

Generations lay around him, silent under the forest. Some lay under flowers, preserved but as brittle as thin glass in the sub-zero, whilst others lay forgotten under plain wooden crosses. The highest part of the ridge seemed to be the oldest part of the burial ground; his best hope, he thought, would be to get through and beyond this, to get over the horizon and out of sight.

He glanced back, ploughed on. His tracks were easy to see but there were others, days old, that helped to confuse the picture. Up ahead, on the skyline, were leaning arrows that pointed to heaven; these were the oldest markers of all, crosses roofed with shingle that stood almost seven feet tall, dark and weathered relics of the old country.

The whistle came again, a distant note from over beyond the grave-keeper's house.

It was answered from somewhere close to the right.

Nikolai started to run, but the depth of snow slowed him down. He had one immediate aim in mind, to reach the edge of the world and to leap over into safety, leaving the sick thrill of the chase behind him. This was all a mistake. He was a seaman, not a criminal, an ordinary boy of modest ambitions whose only flaw lay in the fact that he'd do anything that was asked of him by the girl that he'd met in the line for the Sadko restaurant. He wondered if they'd understand, when they gathered him in and took him home. He wondered if they'd look at her, and forgive.

Only one thing was certain. He'd lose her for sure, if they caught him. He scrambled through the stand of tall crosses, and looked down over the edge of the world.

The boundary of the burial ground was just a few metres away on the now falling slope, no more than a couple of strands of barbed wire showing along with an exposed corner of a low stone wall. Away and beyond, about a kilometre distant and a long haul down the hill, was the near edge of the frozen lake inlet which stretched ahead almost as far as he could see.

It took his breath away, suddenly to be presented with so much cold blue air and open space. Looking out, the ice seemed to get darker and darker in lines and layers until it suddenly became a covered snowfield; this carried on flat and white and featureless until the trees of the far shore abruptly rose out of it like a piece of the earth newly burst through. The horizon was a long, sinuous pine-clad ridge, a broken edge against the sky.

He ought to start down. But why? There was no cover ahead. The few features that he could see were simple and stark, the only hopeful sign a footbridge linking to an inshore island with some low, deserted-looking wooden buildings on it. But as a prospect it was too far, and seen too late.

Nikolai turned to go back.

The border guard was waiting for him by the tallest of the old crosses. He looked no different to the rest of them, a junior rank with cropped hair and a flat, glinty-eyed expression that said nothing at all. Nikolai saw the rifle that he was carrying, and he felt his heart stop and his bowels go weak as he wondered frantically if there was any way that he could turn the clock back twelve hours or so and get himself out of this.

All of his senses told him to stop and raise his hands. The guard was covering him with the rifle and would barely have to aim, the distance between them was so small. But Nikolai realised with horror that he was turning and floundering, kicking up loose snow as he went, his body responding with disobedient flight because it didn't have his mind's understanding of its own mortality; the guard was shouting something after him, but Nikolai couldn't make it out.

Perhaps he could lead them on a chase for a while, at least draw them out and give Irina a chance to get away. He was considering this possibility when he heard a sound of some kind, and then he got a hard punch in the back that sent him sprawling forward into the snow. He'd managed about three paces.

He wasn't badly hurt, but he wished that he had his grandmother's Bible to hold on to. He wondered if they'd let Irina bring it to him.

He wondered for a while longer, and then he stopped.

Irina knew that it was all over as soon as she heard the shot. It had come as she was stepping through the undergrowth to get to the lake shore; in spite of it being little more than a flat whipcrack from the upper slope of the ridge, its exact nature in the still morning air was unmistakable. The second party caught up with her only minutes later, before she'd even reached the bridge, but in her mind she'd already conceded defeat. With her hands raised and her head bowed, she let them march her towards the shore road where one of the trucks was waiting.

They didn't bring Nikolai aboard as she'd expected, so she was left to wonder whether he'd been captured, or hit, or was even dead; instead she was seated between a couple of the guards with nothing to hang on to as the truck was driven hard over the ridge road and into the forest. They stopped only once, to pick up another patrol at a point where a roll of barbed wire stood ready to be dragged across the track. Irina's guess was that they were entering some kind of military no-man's-land, and that as far as she was concerned she could consider herself to be home already. The guards stared at the floor of the cab, like meat machines that ran on only a spark of power in the absence of orders to set them going. None of them even looked up as the truck made a turn into a clearing amongst the trees, but as it stopped they clambered to their feet and Irina was prodded roughly by the butt of one of their guns.

What she saw as she climbed down was that they'd arrived at some kind of encampment, a group of perhaps half a dozen one-storey huts that looked for all the world like snowed-in summer lodges. Overhead floodlights fixed to the taller of the pines washed the snow yellow in the morning twilight, giving the camp a look of a warm oasis in a cold blue world. But Irina wasn't fooled, and knew that no welcome or forgiveness waited for her.

The room where they put her smelled stale and damp, and was warmed in only one corner by an old cast-iron stove. She stood by this and shivered, and wondered miserably what was ahead. One of the boy soldiers—it might have been the one from the train, save for the absence of the scar—sat between her and the door on a hard chair whose paint had been almost completely chipped and worn away. The room contained one other chair and a table, on which stood the small emergency bag that she'd been carrying.

A senior man came in a few minutes later. He must have been close to sixty, he limped, and when he looked at her his eyes glittered like sawn metal and seemed to contain about as much warmth. She had to stand and watch as he emptied out the bag, grunted as he thumbed through their stolen passports, and then tore the gift-wrapping from Nikolai's package and examined the Bible that he found inside. He didn't seem able to take it at face value as a book, but riffled through the pages looking for hidden documents before taking a clasp knife from his pocket and slitting the spine along its length. Her own souvenir, a crude little jewellery box that her father had made for her mother when they were both sixteen years old, was prised open and had its red lining pulled out in a similar search.

"You were lovers?" he said, those eyes looking at her again. They had about as much humanity in them as two small, wet river stones. Irina didn't miss the implication of his use of the past tense; and that, of course, was the only reason why he'd said anything at all.

"No," she said. *I'm sorry, Nikolai,* she thought, *but it's true.* "I hardly knew him at all."

He ignored her from then onwards, sending the boy soldier out to arrange an escort detail and then, with Irina as his only witness, helping himself to over half of their currency. The bag's contents were now a vandalised mess, scattered across the surface of the guard-room table.

When the three-man detail arrived and stood to attention, the senior man gave them their orders without even looking directly at any of them. Irina was to be handcuffed and taken to the military post at Luzhaika, where she'd be held until collected by the state security services. She wasn't to be allowed to speak to anyone, or to use a telephone, or to send any messages; nor were the guard detail to enter into any conversation with her. On leaving Luzhaika they were to . . .

He stopped, and a puzzled expression came onto his face. Irina had been able to hear a distant whistle coming from somewhere outside the hut for two or three seconds by now, but she didn't know what might be causing it; now she saw his puzzlement draining out to be replaced by dismay as the whistle grew into an incoming screech that was arching up overhead. The senior man started to shout, grabbing the nearest of the young guards and pushing him towards the door, but his words were lost in the noise of a shockingly loud blast that lit up the windows and rattled the sides of the hut and caused Irina to clap her hands over her ears in fear and hurt.

The soldiers all piled out, the young ones as stunned as she but with the senior man pushing at them and shouting as they fumbled with their weapons and fell out into the snow. Irina was left alone, not knowing what the danger might be and with no idea of what to do for her own safety. Two more explosions came then, both of them closer and louder than the first, and she clearly heard a spray of dirt and stones come showering down over the roof above. Running to the open doorway, she looked out.

Border guards were scrambling past, their long coats flapping as they tried to follow their drill in the face of what was obviously a completely unexpected attack. It was clear to Irina that the camp wasn't fortified and that the notion of an assault of this kind was something new and shocking to all but the oldest of them. She saw the senior man who'd left her only moments before, still limping, still shouting, still largely unheard. The forest all around the camp was backlit as if by hidden fires and flares, and new explosions continued to rocket in and shake the snow from eaves and branches. Smoke was boiling upward into the morning sky from somewhere less than a hundred metres away, and the sounds of approaching machine-gun fire punctuated the blasts of what she imagined had to be incoming mortar shells. Of the actual enemy, there was as yet no sign.

Time for her to move.

With that first, physical wave of shock over, Irina ran to the table and grabbed her passport and what was left of the money. Gravel spattered against the window like a sudden storm of hail, but she barely flinched. At the doorway she paused, fearing a shot if she might be seen trying to leave . . . but nobody was looking her way, their attention was all directed outward as they finally got organised and began to return fire. She slipped out and around the corner, and no call to halt came as she ran along the back of the hut and into the woodland. It was heavy going because there was no beaten path to follow, and she knew that she'd be leaving a clear trail; but she also knew that anybody who might be inclined to follow her would have other things on his mind right now. She couldn't imagine what the attack meant, or who was behind it, and could hardly have cared less. All that she could see was the second chance that it had given her—a bet that she had to take, for the simple reason that she had nothing to lose.

She still had a vague idea of the direction of the Finnish territories, and she struck out towards them before she'd gone far enough to lose her sense of place. She'd have to pass close to the fighting, but it seemed to her that its focus was now over to the right somewhere. Along with the gunfire she could now hear the growling and churning sounds of what she assumed to be tanks, along with the occasional crash of falling timber. What she heard was in total contrast to what she saw, which was the undisturbed stand of birch and fir through which she moved.

Irina had only one purpose in mind, and that was to get clear of the borderlands. She'd do it on foot, if that was the only way. And then if she could find a car and a ride, she could be in Helsinki within a few hours and she could go to one of the embassies there. Let the Finns try handing her back *then*.

A few minutes later, she came out of the woods and down to a cleared and gritted road. She couldn't cross it, because its opposite bank was closed off by crossed stakes and barbed wire. It was obviously a military access road, perhaps even the one that they'd brought her in along, and it told her that she'd probably been heading in the right direction. But which way now? The wrong choice would take her back towards the camp, into the thick of the fighting, and quite possibly back into the hands of her captors. From the way it ran, there was no way of telling . . . and the longer she spent following it, the greater the risk of being overtaken and recaptured.

She made a choice and started to follow, her ragged breath feathering in the air. The woodland had been cleared back on either side of the road, so no overhanging trees offered any way across the wire. The sounds of the battle seemed to be spreading now, its area widening; she heard a ripping hiss as something passed high overhead, although she saw nothing, and moments later there was a blast some distance back in the forest along the way that she'd come.

Her choice was wrong.

She realised it when, after several minutes of walking, the road began to curve and to take her back. The battle sounds were no longer a guide, having spread to surround her on both sides now, but the direction of the light and her own inner certainty were enough to tell her that she was in error. A bank of white smoke was drifting across the road and filtering away through the trees, and in this she saw the pale spots of a pair of headlights forming as a vehicle of some kind came out towards her.

Irina turned to run, intending to throw herself down in the snow and hide until it had gone by, but the ice-packed surface of the road wouldn't lend itself to anything more than a plodding gait, and she fell heavily. She heard the vehicle braking to a halt only a few metres behind her, and saw the disturbed smoke cloud roll over her like a mist. She waited for a call, or a shot, or anything, but nothing came; all that she could hear was the idling of the vehicle's engine, a rough and unhealthy clattering like a roomful of children playing with hammers.

It was an ambulance, she saw when she turned to look, one of those big ageless military vehicles with the Red Cross symbol on its side almost obscured by a daubing of mud; her uncle had told her how they used to do that kind of thing in the old days to reduce visibility during their night runs. No-one had jumped out and the ambulance was simply standing there with the mist curling around it, the machine-heart of its engine beating steadily now. There was too much dirt spattered across the windows of the cab for her to be able to make out the driver, but she did see his raised hand through the swept-clean arc made by the single wiper. He beckoned to her, once, and then pointed towards the back of the vehicle.

Irina lay on the snow, gripped with cold and apprehension and unable to move. She didn't know whether she was facing a friend or an enemy, and she felt intimidated by the vehicle's presence as if it were some dimly intelligent and unpredictable beast. She looked to the cab again, hoping for some further sign that might give her reassurance, but she saw nothing.

A triple explosion sounded from somewhere further down the track, a certain sign that the battle was getting closer. As the echoes died, Irina could make out the definite sound of human screams.

The ambulance revved, its gears crashing noisily.

Irina scrambled to her feet and ran, shuffled and slithered across the road. The rear doors on the ambulance weren't secured, which saved her a couple of seconds as she threw one of them open and clambered inside; but even as her walking-boots left the ice the ambulance was moving, and it was only by grabbing some part of the bolted-in stretcher framework that she was able to prevent herself from being thrown out again. A moment later the doors bounced on their hinges and then came slamming back, sealing her into a darkness that was much deeper than the dawn outside.

It was all that she could do to hang on through the noisy, bucketing ride that followed. As her eyes adjusted she was able to see by a feeble light that came from a barred window looking through into the driver's cab; the window was tiny, and its illumination barely enough to sketch in the interior of the wagon's rear compartment. There were cots on either side of her stacked two deep, and on each cot was a blanket-covered form so close that she could have reached out and touched any one of them. There were no oxygen cylinders, no first-aid lockers, in fact no signs of any medical equipment at all; it was like being in a Lysol-scented tin box that had been fitted as spartanly as possible so that it could be easily hosed out after every use.

What she had taken to be an ambulance was, she suddenly realised, a mortuary wagon.

One of the corpses grunted as they hit a hard bump in the road, but there was nothing in the sound to suggest consciousness or even life. Irina was now hanging on so hard that her hands were beginning to hurt, so terrified was she of being thrown to one side or the other. There was no way that she could look that she couldn't see at least one of the sheeted dead; and as they slowed for a bend and the wagon began to lean on its springs, she saw one of the stiff blankets move. It was sliding, almost as if being withdrawn by a curious but hesitant child. She looked forward to the cab, but could see only the back of the driver's head and shoulders and knew that a shouted appeal wouldn't be heard; the noise-level was too high, and there was glass between them, and the driver was intent at the wheel. She saw him begin a turn to the left, and through the windshield beyond him she saw trees and undergrowth rising to meet them and realised that he was taking the wagon away from the road. A moment later the worst of the jarring began, and the inching blanket smoothly dropped away to unveil the contents of the stretcher beneath. Irina quickly screwed her eyes shut, but not quickly enough. An image stayed with her as if it had been burned-in behind her eyelids, of a face with its jawbone completely blown away to show a ragged hole from the upper teeth to the throat, the whites of its eyes still wet and turned towards her.

The wagon braked and stopped abruptly. Irina lunged for the doors and felt around for a handle. She wouldn't have believed that her panic could worsen, but it did when she realised that there *was* no handle on the inside, probably because there was normally no need for one; but then she put her shoulder to the doors with all the slight force of her weight behind it, and the doors gave way and flew open and Irina fell out headlong into the snow.

She was on her feet again within moments, and starting to move. She'd retained enough presence of mind not to head back the way they'd come, but instead she ran forward past the wagon and in the direction of the safer territory. The battle sounds were faint now, only the shrieking of the mortars reaching her with any distinctness. Only when she was several long strides away did she pause and look back.

The mortuary wagon stood in deep snow, its high axles raising it clear. The wiper made a single arc across the windscreen and back, and through the cleared glass Irina saw and recognised the face of the driver.

He sat with his hands resting on the wheel. His eyes as he watched her betrayed a feeling that she'd seen there before, but now it was tempered with a certain reproach for the love that she'd been unable to return. She started to take a step back towards him; but he raised a hand and made a single, brief gesture for her to go onward.

And as she began to comply, a single mortar whistle seemed to detach itself from the steadily warring background. Before she'd taken three strides it had grown almost deafeningly loud, and at the fourth it ended in an immense shock wave that rocked her in her tracks and caused her to hunch over simply in order to remain standing. Her ears hurt so badly that she thought they'd probably bleed.

And when sound crept in again, all that came with it was the dampened silence of the forest.

Irina turned to see what had happened to the wagon, expecting at least the burning remains of a direct hit. But where it had stood was simply a mound in the snow—no damage, no signs of a blast, not

even any tracks other than her own. She followed them back to the
mound.

Seen from close by, it was just about possible to make it out: the
general lines of the bodywork, the shape of the cab, where the glass
had been before an intense fire had melted it away. Where paint
remained, it had been blackened; and as for the rest of the metal,
only a filigree latticework of rust held the lines of the panels. Three
good-sized firs had grown through different parts of the wreck, pushing it even further out of shape.

Irina placed a hand on the cold shell of what had once been a
headlamp. The wreck must have been standing for more than forty
years.

"So, Nikolai," she said softly, her ears still ringing a little in the
woodland's healing stillness. "So, now you believe."

And then, with a final glance back in the direction of the border,
Irina Ivanova set out towards the west.

It isn't easy being a writer when you have a full-time job in the outside world, especially when that job takes you all over the country for days at a time. Yet Douglas Winter has managed not only to establish himself as a nonfiction writer of no small repute, he has also launched a career in fiction and, now, one as an editor. It isn't easy. But the time he takes with a story makes his infrequent appearances all the more worthwhile. This story is about law; it doesn't have to be, for those of us who remember what it was like to work for someone else.

OFFICE HOURS
by Douglas E. Winter

That night, the heavy cloud cover had broken, spilling waves of snow over the capital. By midnight, the purged sky shone in its clarity above the whitened city. From his eleventh-floor office on Pennsylvania Avenue, David Frankel could see, for the first time in days, the lights of the Lee Mansion beaconing across the Potomac from the lonely heights of Arlington Cemetery. Their pale glow warmed him; he felt that he, too, was being watched from distant heights. Tonight, this night after many nights, he was inevitable.

On the street below, a nameless vagabond huddled in search of warmth along the grillwork of a heating duct. Passing cars, spearhead of the coming rush hour, cut grey ribbons in the drifting snow. Four blocks distant, the President slept—and, perhaps, dreamed. But in the last hour before dawn, David Frankel had no time for dreams; there was a deadline to meet.

Settling in behind his desk, he gulped a cup of coffee before beginning his final markup of the brief. Typographical errors fell bleeding at the cut of his flickering red pen. He flagged suspect citations, mended split infinitives, massaged the full worth from each sentence. An early-overtime secretary would arrive at seven o'clock; she would run the sixty pages through a word processor, Frankel proofreading over her shoulder, and old man Weston would have a clean copy by nine on the button—office hours.

At eight-thirty, the offices of Kramer, Kohl & Davies began to shed the blanket of night. Two aproned food service employees made their rounds, priming the coffee machines and placing new flower arrangements on each of the six floors occupied by the law firm. Photocopy units wheezed to life; computer terminals offered blank green stares; messengers rolled mail-laden carts down mazelike corridors. In the eleventh-floor lobby, a receptionist squeezed a telephone headset over her carefully styled hair, then took her place behind the angled mahogany desk, ready to smile a welcome to each and every one of the lawyers, paralegals, and secretaries as they arrived. At nine-thrity, she would begin to place calls to the offices of those she had not seen, confirming absences for her morning report to administration.

As on most mornings, when she opened her log, she saw that neatly printed initials filled the IN column next to David Frankel's name.

The snowfall, first of the winter, had paralyzed Washington's morning traffic. Mary Helen McDonald left home forty-five minutes earlier than usual, but she found herself waving hello to the receptionist at nearly nine-fifteen. When she stamped into Frankel's office, complaining of skittish drivers and certain frostbite, she found him slumped over his desk, fast asleep. Glasses askew, he looked like a napping schoolboy, and she rubbed her hands to warm them before gently touching the back of his neck. His head rose with a groan. Dark half-moons weighted his eyes.

"Hi, Mom." His voice, slurred with sleep, burdened the long-shared joke. At forty-seven, Mary Helen McDonald could just possibly have been David Frankel's mother; her plump, jovial features and fierce loyalty emboldened the image.

She set a black coffee and doughnut on the desk before him.

"Bad night."

He rubbed at his wounded eyes and tried to grin. "No shit, Sherlock."

She only stared at him.

"Well, what are you waiting for?"

She passed over the mail and a printout of the day's schedule.

"Three calls came in this morning. Reception took them while you were in dreamland."

He read each yellow slip before consigning them to the corner of his desk.

"Mr. Weston, Tina, Mr. Weston again."

When he looked up, she was still staring at him.

"Do us all a favor, would you, Davey? Get this fucking brief done and go home."

Frankel was amused by his secretary's concern; he wouldn't tell her—no, not yet—that this had been the final night. As Mary Helen took her station at the desk outside his door, he carefully stacked the pages of the brief. Each sheet of paper was crisp, pristine in its whiteness, the edges razor-sharp; the sixty pages of heavy bond stood nearly half an inch in height, a monument to more than three weeks of labor.

He had started the brief on a Friday evening, flush with the chance to secure a partnership by singlehandedly demolishing the appeal in the most important hazardous waste litigation in years. The assignment had come from one of the firm's legends, Freddie Weston—former U. S. Attorney for the District of Columbia, onetime member of the Council of Economic Advisers, Undersecretary of Treasury during five years of the Eisenhower administration, and, for the past twenty years, one of the most visible and respected partners of Kramer, Kohl & Davies. Weston's blessing of his efforts would virtually assure Frankel his place in the firm.

With the brief firmly in hand, Frankel took the private elevator to the thirteenth-floor penthouse. Weston's office occupied a corner suite; its windows opened onto a view, over the rooftop garden, of the clock face of the Old Post Office across the street. From the outer entrance to the suite, Frankel could see that the huge hands of the clock signaled nearly ten. But Weston's office was dark; even the secretary's station was deserted. The ghost of a half-smoked cigarette ascended from a crystal ashtray at the center of her desk.

He thought for a moment of leaving the brief on Weston's leather chair, but it didn't seem right. He wanted to hand the brief to Weston, to watch his admiring eyes, his grateful acknowledgment of a job well done. He would go back to his office and wait for the old asshole, who couldn't even get to work on time, to arrive.

Frankel riffled through his in-box, tossing the tear sheets of recent court opinions, unread, into the out-box. He wasted fifteen minutes reviewing a draft set of interrogatories, then called Weston's line. There was no answer; with the sixth ring, a weary-voiced switchboard operator requested a message. He hung up without uttering a word.

He weighed the brief in his left hand; sixty pages at roughly four hours a page. He opened it at random, then restrained himself; there was no reason to read it again until he had talked with Weston. He exchanged it for the time sheets on his credenza.

Each Monday, he was required to submit the time sheets—mauve computer-coded forms—to the firm's accounting department, recording the precise amount of time, to the tenth of an hour, that he had worked on each client matter in the preceding week. Time was, after all, the lawyer's true commodity. His hours were billed to clients at the rate of a hundred and fifty dollars each, and the number had come to have a certain magic for him. Five dollars for every two minutes, he would think as he picked up the telephone, answering a client's call. Twenty-five dollars for the ten-minute minimum of dictating a one-paragraph letter. At that rate, he could bring in twelve hundred dollars a day, twenty-five thousand a month, three-hundred-fucking-thousand dollars a year.

And that was based upon eight-hour days and five-day weeks, not on lawyers' hours.

Frankel picked up his diary and pocket calculator. His diary was filled with notes on his time, but looking back on Monday last, the hours seemed to blur. He had worked morning and night on the brief, but the afternoon was eaten by some sort of meeting. Legislative affairs? The faces danced at the corner of his eyes—smiling paper shufflers from a trade association, nervously lost among the tailored three-piece suits of Big Law. It was something about tax reform, some subsidy program that fell annually into peril. When he punched at the calculator, the numbers ran to nineteen and three quarters hours.

He began his double check, recalling that Joseph Hollander and Richard Waite had also attended the meeting; the client could only have been Clausen Pacific. He entered the appropriate billing number on the form. This time, the calculator showed twenty-one billable hours for Monday. He shook his head, then abandoned the time sheets, with his diary, to the out-box. Mary Helen could muddle through the confusion.

He didn't have time for such games.

When the telephone rang, Frankel hooked the receiver nervously before his secretary could answer.

"Mr. Weston?"

"David?"

He breathed a sigh, settling back in his chair. How could he have forgotten to call his wife?

The month before David married Tina Beck, they had flown to London, nesting in a bed-and-breakfast in Bloomsbury and emerging from bouts of lovemaking only for the necessities: Le Carré paperbacks, the mummy room at the British Museum, dinner after dinner washed down with Peroni at the Pizza Express. It was the beginning of a year of bright omens: a smiling Democrat had stumbled into the White House, and change was in the wind. A sudden dip in the mortgage rate and a hefty bonus for associates at Kramer, Kohl & Davies brought the newlyweds a townhouse on a cobbled street in Old Town Alexandria.

It was also a time when David could believe in omens. Two years out of law school, he had joined the post-Aquarian forces of young urban professionals in the melodrama of inanimate objects. The townhouse was only a beginning. A Volvo soon replaced his rusted Firebird; suits by Halston, Dior loafers, rep ties filled his closet. And it was work, he realized, not some vague providence, that had brought him these symbols of contented success.

At first, Tina had not understood the long hours demanded by his practice; only the distractions of ever growing prosperity and children—one soon after their marriage, now a second on its way—had tempered her need for what she called a "normal" life. But normality, he assured her, was in the eye of the beholder. "Take a drive down to K Mart," he said. "Then tell me about the virtues of a normal life."

He loved his wife; he knew that as certainly as he also knew that he was alive, productive, in control, only while in his office, safe from the seductive promise of a happy family gathered at home for the mesmerizing glare of television. When they married, partnership in the firm had been six years distant, a rainbow dream of wealth, status, power. Now, nearly five years later, he could never be accused of standing in its way.

The voice at the other end said: "When are you coming home?"

"Tina?" She seemed suddenly distant. "Just a minute." A yellow

light flared on his telephone console; a call was being held on the
second line. He fingered the intercom key—where was Mary Helen?

"Honey," he said. "Let me put you on hold. Be right back."

Wishing for luck—and the voice of Freddie Weston—he punched
into his second line.

"Dave?" The hoarse drawl, whiskey-thick New Orleans, brought
on images of three weeks of trial in Pittsburgh, a head-hammering
million-dollar breach-of-contract action that saw the jury split the
baby, returning with a $450,000 verdict for his client, Civic Steel,
after less than an hour of deliberation.

"What can I do for you, Gage?"

Gage Chasen, the general counsel of Civic Steel, believed that life,
like Gaul, was divided into three parts: football, Kentucky bourbon,
and women. When such mundane matters as equal employment opportunity crossed his desk, they, being beyond his avowed expertise,
were referred promptly to Frankel. Today, he needed a draft of a
specialized sales contract—by the close of business. Frankel promised a telex by the end of the week, and conversation promptly
veered to the dubious likelihood of the New Orleans Saints snaring a
wild-card slot in the NFL playoffs.

When Frankel hung up, he checked his watch, then opened his
diary and tolled one half hour's worth of time to Civic Steel's billing
number.

He returned to his other line.

"Tina?"

It was dead.

At eleven-thirty—he wrote the time on the yellow pad before him
with disgust—his umpteenth call conjured, after only two rings, the
polite, professional answer he had sought all morning:

"Mr. Weston's office."

The voice seemed familiar. What secretary was working for the
old man these days? Blond hair, glasses, frumpy dresses. It was coming . . .

"Gloria?"

"Excuse me?"

"This is David Frankel for Mr. Weston."

"I'm sorry," she said. "Who did you say was calling?"

"David Frankel. Is he in?"

"He's on his other line," she said.

"He stepped out for a minute," she said.

"He's in conference," she said.

"I'll see that he gets your message," she said.

By one o'clock, he had given up. The telephone offered him a silent smirk. He dialed his home number, but hung up before it rang. Then he scrawled Tina's name on the list marked URGENT that topped the growing mound of yellow slips at the corner of his desk. More than twenty other names preceded hers.

He felt guilty. Frankel despised guilt; it was a middle-class emotion, the *angst* of suburban mall shoppers, living out their nine-to-five worlds.

He lifted the brief from his credenza, centering it on the desk before him. His fingers stroked the cover page, tracing his name along the thirty-weight cotton fiber paper.

He turned the page and began to read.

There was no guilt here; he had stated the facts with fairness and precision, then set forth the cool, dispassionate logic of the law. It felt so right, this child of his sleepless nights. He held the brief to his chest and dreamed.

The door to C. Frederick Weston's office stood silent despite his repeated knocking.

His hand fisted for another assault. Over his shoulder, a woman's voice came. It was nearly a whisper:

"Are you looking for Mr. Weston?"

Frankel turned, swallowing a sarcastic rejoinder in favor of hurt surprise.

"It is imperative that I see Mr. Weston . . . " But his words were lost. The woman at the secretary's station was beautiful; her black hair, sleek and straight, angled across her face, and he knew the urge to brush it away.

"Mr. Weston's out of the office." She spoke in a flat monotone, looking away from him. A half-burned cigarette dangled from her right hand.

"What do you mean, Mr. Weston's out of the office?"

"Well," she said, glancing up. Her hair fell back, and her lips parted with a glossy taunt. "I mean that Mr. Weston's out of the office." She paused, opening a notebook slowly and reading from the blue-inked spaghetti of her stenography. "Board of directors meeting for Lamark Industries."

He returned to Weston's door and twisted it open. He saw only darkness, presided over by the massive clock face beyond. It was two forty-five.

He spent the next hour pacing his office.

For a time, Mary Helen sat complacently as he tried to dictate. He waved her away after repeatedly losing his train of thought. He had caught himself estimating the square footage of the room, comparing its diminutive size to the expansive floor space of Weston's office.

Each time that he turned to face the window, his eyes fell upon the brief, waiting on the credenza. The top pages, he realized with a frown, showed the signs of his reading. But there was something else, something he had not realized until now, something that stung him more deeply than Weston's intransigence.

He did not need Weston, not at all. The cards had been on the table since October, at his annual partnership evaluation.

Frankel despised the dog-and-pony-show mentality of the evaluations: the thin manila files of partners' assessments, announced in paraphrase by Harry Kohl with comfortably guarded optimism, words of encouragement framed as uncertain truths. For the listener, it was a private form of penance, the act of kissing the papal ring, each associate reminded of his or her servitude to a smiling-faced autocracy that hired twenty-five law school graduates each year with an eye toward making three of them partners after eight long years. Frankel could not help but embrace each tentative insinuation of hope for his partnership in the firm, yet the message was clear: the opportunity was theirs to give and theirs to take away.

He understood then, as he had understood from the day he joined Kramer, Kohl & Davies: hard work would be rewarded. It had been rewarded from the time of his first paying job, sweeping the floors of his father's shop in suburban St. Paul, to the dean's list at the University of Minnesota and the 770 LSAT scores that had, in turn, carried him to Harvard Law School. Work was a matter of using time; and time was money, time was the bottom line—time was the measure of life, and of lawyers.

As Harry Kohl closed the last folder with its words of diligence and best efforts and jobs well done, he eased back in his chair, his voice softening with a sudden semblance of emotion. "We," he said, drawing himself up as if swollen with the corporate whole, "we feel that you should give some thought to the hours you've been putting in here at the office."

Kohl forced a cough. "Of course, you are the best judge of things." His eyebrows arched in a laughable mockery of concern. "But our experience is that the kind of pace you've set for yourself . . ."

Frankel nodded, and began to smile—not outwardly, but inside, where Kohl couldn't get at it. He knew now that he had won; the white flag was being raised against his lengthy siege, and the gates had opened. The final gauntlet was about to be run. One year remained; nearly nine thousand hours.

He did not need Freddie Weston, but he wanted his blessing. Then there would be no doubt that he had spent his time well.

The call from Victor Briggs came at five-fifteen. Frankel set the brief aside, marking page forty-two with a paper clip. He buzzed Mary Helen, asking her to pull the pleadings files on the Whitcomb-Lean litigation.

"There's just one problem with practicing law," he said to her as she entered. "Every once in a while, you have to deal with other lawyers."

Minutes earlier, a motion to compel had arrived on Briggs' desk, claiming that documents Frankel had produced to opposing counsel from the files of Lean Newspapers were insufficient to fulfill certain discovery requests. Briggs, the partner in charge, had panicked; his vacation started the following week.

Frankel took the files from Mary Helen, found the reference he needed, and stalked from his office.

He was stunned to find, as he crossed the elegant eleventh-floor lobby, that C. Frederick Weston sat at one of the couches, smoking peevishly and wrestling a *Wall Street Journal*.

Frankel slowed his pace across the embassy-sized Persian carpet, glancing at the receptionist; she was lost in a Sidney Sheldon novel.

"Afternoon, sir."

Weston flushed with the interruption. There was nothing in his appearance—tailored navy suit and crimson cravat notwithstanding —to suggest his significance. Indeed, Frankel felt almost a sense of pity as he viewed the finely etched skin, the subtle shaking of his hands. Weston was well into his seventies, his blunt nose reddened with a cold, his white, feathery hair brushed in polite embrace of a growing bald spot. Only his eyes cautioned Frankel; such unforgiving eyes.

"Well. Good afternoon to you, son." Weston folded the *Journal* carefully in his lap. "French, isn't it?"

"Excuse me?"

"Daniel French?"

Frankel glanced again to the receptionist.

"Frankel, sir. David Frankel."

Weston chuckled apologetically. "Of course it is. Of course, Mr. Frankel. It's just that . . ." He gestured vaguely; Frankel watched as Weston's eyes roamed the lobby. Together they took in the eclectic blend of abstract modern art, antique furniture, oriental rugs. "It's just that, well, things *have* changed since the days on Lafayette Square, haven't they? Sixty lawyers then, young man, and we thought that *that* was large . . ."

"Sir?"

"We thought that *that* was large, son, and now . . . we're what? Two hundred plus, Sam Summers tells me. Option on the seventh floor. Saw the plans. Can you imagine . . ."

"Excuse me, sir," Frankel interrupted. Weston drew back from his revery.

Frankel cleared his throat and stepped closer.

"Did you want to speak with me?" he asked.

"Hmm." Weston scratched at his upper lip with the stem of his pipe. His eyes glimmered with frank appraisal.

"Hmm," he repeated. "Not at all."

Frankel tripped over his own feet, staggering from the lobby back into the corridor to his office. He felt the eyes of the receptionist questioning him as he passed.

He remembered the brief, waiting on his credenza, sixty pages and two hundred and forty hours, more than thirty-five thousand dollars' worth of work. He remembered the nights, alone in the library, stale coffee thick on his tongue, working the brief toward perfection.

For what?

He knew. He knew now.

Ahead, the shadows at his office doorway seemed to merge. A woman stood there. Her black hair, sleek and straight, angled across her face.

Frankel lurched forward. The hand grasped him high on the shoulder.

"Whoa there." Victor Briggs patted his back and chuckled. "Walk, don't run, hoss."

Frankel looked to him. Further down the hallway, the woman turned toward him with a smile. Beyond her, a grandfather clock, a fragile antique dislocated in the stark pastel corridor, mutely signaled the hour of six. Her hair fell back, and her lips parted with a glossy taunt. She entered his office.

"About that motion to compel . . ." Briggs massaged his chin with mock thoughtfulness.

Frankel shook off Briggs' hand; he tried to think of her face. Had he ever seen her face?

"Route me the papers," he barked. "What've we got? Ten days? Served by hand?"

Briggs nodded numbly, stepping back with surprise.

"I'll give you a draft by Friday." Frankel followed the woman into the shadows, calling over his shoulder:

"I've got all the time in the world."

He eased the door to his office shut behind himself, patiently making his way forward.

The woman stood behind his desk. Her eyes were downcast. She held the brief in her hands, raising it as a shield as he advanced.

"Why . . ." He brushed the papers aside. They floated toward the desk top, spilling like waves of snow. His hand was chilled with the pain of their touch. As he reached forward again, her voice spoke from the deepening shadows.

You

His hand slipped inside her dress, caressing her bare left breast, then descending to the taut flatness of her stomach. Their lips grazed, and her tongue flickered wetly, pulling his mouth full upon hers. His hand pushed deeper, sinking into the warmth between her legs . . .

cut

The knife slipped inside her dress, descending to the expanded

roundness of her pregnancy. His mouth closed upon hers, hungrily
smothering her scream as his hand pushed the knife deeper. He felt
the flow of warmth across his hand . . .

your

His hand slipped inside the pages, caressing the blank white surfaces, then tearing the sheets, crushing them into balls. His mouth
bent in laughter, and he felt the flow of warm tears . . .

finger

The pen slipped across the paper . . .

"You cut your finger."

He nodded dully, engrossed in the task before him.

"I'll need an overtime secretary," he said.

"Not tonight, Davey." Mary Helen had tucked her hair up beneath a wool stocking cap. She handed a stack of freshly typed time
sheets across the desk. "It's already past nine."

His face dimmed as he looked uncertainly at his watch. "Oh, yeah.
Well, tell you what. Can you run this tape for me before you go? It's
just a couple of memos . . ."

She shook her head. "Davey, I've really got to go. It'll wait till
morning. Believe me. It'll wait."

She frowned at the stain that covered his right hand.

"You cut your finger," she repeated.

He only smiled. She saw then that the surface of his desk was
covered with blank sheets of typing paper. Some were crumpled;
others were torn into jigsaw pieces. All were covered with an unread-
able scrawl. The red ink had pooled into a dark blot beneath his
hand.

"I've decided to revise the brief," he said.

It was difficult for him to wake up.

The office was dark, but here, curled in the embrace of the leather
chair, he could see the clock tower of the Old Post Office; it was just
after two.

The night was still young.

The desk before him was clear. There were no memo pads, no
yellow slips complaining of unreturned telephone calls.

There were no time sheets.

There were no briefs.

This is how it should be, he realized.

This is how it will be. In time. All in good time.

He left Weston's office, heading for the bathroom. There, he scrubbed the oily sweat from his face and looked up into the bruised hollows of his eyes. The mirror rippled, shimmering a false fluorescent dawn.

He smiled. The mirror man frowned and walked away.

"Listen," he said, but there was no one left to hear. He palmed the washroom door open, returning to the hallway. To his left, the elevator shafts gossiped with the wind, then hushed as he approached. In the lobby, he opened the receptionist's log and neatly printed his initials next to his name in the IN column. Then he left a yellow message slip, noting that Mr. Weston had called for Mr. Frankel.

The library bridged the tenth and eleventh floors. In its midst, the law waited in neatly ordered rows, its letters and numbers forming the cipher that he, for his entire adult life, had sought to crack.

And he would, in time. All in good time.

He selected a book at random, a worn volume of Wigmore on Evidence, and began to read. After a while, he worried a yellow pad with notes. There were so many things he had not considered, so many things to learn; it was little wonder that he was not yet worthy of Weston's recognition.

The brief, he was certain, would change all of that.

But it had not been ready. He knew that now.

So he had decided to start again.

And this time, he would get it right.

I first met Nancy Holder at, of all things, a romance writers' convention in New York City. Both of us were working in the field at the time (she much more successfully than I, I ought to add), and we were working like mad to get out and into something we could not only use to pay the bills, but, in many ways more importantly, something we enjoyed, something that wasn't, or at least didn't feel like, work. I made it first, though it wasn't a race; now it's Nancy's turn, and from the praise her stories have received, there's no doubt in my mind that she'll soon be at the top.

WE HAVE ALWAYS LIVED IN THE FOREST
by *Nancy Holder*

Brittle bones, aching joints. I hate growing old. And these children of mine make life less than simple, though that is why we have always lived in the forest.

But you know the young: they never listen to you; at least, mine never do. They struggle and thrash and escape at the first opportunity, thinking they can outrun me—pity's sake, I'm not *that* old!

But not to fear, I always catch them and bring them back. I'm a good mother.

But they try me, they do. Just yesterday, one of my older ones, Victoria, made the break while I was dressing her for dinner. (Such a lovely creature, all in white lace like a bride, a velvet ribbon at her throat.) Just as I was stitching up the back of her gown, she whirled around, shoved me to the floor, and took off shrieking.

The young. So restless and foolish. At least, mine are.

After I regained my balance I watched her for a moment, lace flying as she stumbled and panted, calling to her brothers and sisters to follow—but they stayed where they were, my good darlings. (Besides, I build my fences high.) A few began to cry, others to shout encouragement—*that* will have to be dealt with, no egging on the deserters—but no one joined her.

I thought, Let her go. Let her see what lies beyond the forest. If she won't listen to my warnings, she deserves what she gets.

But I couldn't bear the thought of stumbling on her one day, after they finished with her—the agony would far outweigh the satisfaction.

We have always lived in the forest to enjoy the simple life. And to hide from the town, of course.

After a stern warning to the others, I ran after Victoria; and for a while I thought she was going to make it. I had bruised my hip on the hard dirt floor and my pain slowed my progress. My girl fairly flew among the trees—I couldn't help the pride that surged through me at the sight of her, so beautiful and lithe, ducking heavy oak branches and bearded webs of Spanish moss. She led me a merry dance, though I called to her that she was going too far, getting too deep; the town waited with its maw wide open, slathering its lips to devour her. I believe tears came to my eyes—I care for all my children, though I have so many—and I reached out for her, clutching my sore hip, not at all angry with her for pushing me. For I understand the young, you see. A good mother always understands.

We raced into the bowels of the forest; despite my concern for Victoria, I shuddered and considered turning back. It was too dank and shadowy, too like my image of the town. But I pressed on into the bracken, so dense and thick my perspiration iced my skin.

I tired; I'm growing old, you see, and they take bigger chances than before; and all seemed lost. My, how she flew, my little gazelle! What a girl she was!

We raced on. The ground grew damp and my feet sank into it, but it caught Victoria, too, and I knew I still had a chance.

She stumbled over a large exposed root and pitched forward into the mud. Even then, she was not daunted—she crawled on her hands and knees, screaming for help. I wanted to ask her who she thought would come. There was no one but us and the town, and she surely didn't want Them to hear her.

But that was my Victoria: looking before she leapt—literally! I almost laughed aloud as I realized the aptness of the phrase, but poor Victoria still pitched forward, positively hysterical. She was almost naked; her dress had caught on the thorns and brambles and ripped in long pieces like bandages, and blood-soaked they were, too, with streaks from her scratches. Her thighs looked like ribbon candy.

"Oh, Vicky," I said sadly, and then I caught her. I embraced her like a huge mother bear, my breast heaving upon hers, and I scooped her up in my arms as if she were an infant.

She was beyond struggling; she hung limply in my arms, begging, "No, Mother, no. Please, not me."

"You've been very silly," I told her. "What did you expect to accomplish?"

"Oh, please, Mother," and suchlike. I have often told them not to whine. It is distasteful in a young person.

Halfway back, she rallied and tried to escape again, but I held her tightly (and gave her a tap on the chin, I must admit, though not too hard).

Now all the children were crying, a few on their knees, sobbing out my errant daughter's name. She held out a limp arm to them, staring over my shoulder as I carried her into the house.

I bathed my darling girl, in the big tin tub by the fireplace. She had exhausted herself, for which I was grateful—I was tired, too, and she might have been able to make it if she rallied herself one last time.

The others kept up their wailing, even after the sun set. I lit some candles and eased Victoria out of the tub, dried her, and patiently dressed her again, this time in scarlet to blend in with her wounds.

And then I ate her. She was as delicate and sweet as I had imagined, and I felt proud of her all over again.

In the forest we live a simple, self-sufficient life, and I protect my children from the horrors of the town. You would think they'd understand, and stop fighting me, but that's not the way of children, is it? Has it ever been? One can only sigh over their ignorance and do one's best.

In the forest, at least, it is easier. I can't bear to think what happens to those of the town.

As, still, I can scarcely bring myself to think about the poor thing who dragged herself here shortly after I devoured Victoria.

I sensed her presence before I saw her. I knew there was a stranger near, and though my hip ached and my meal made me sluggish, I roused myself from the warmth of the fire and staggered across the room.

I heard footsteps, and for one awful instant, I thought we were in terrible danger. I fumbled behind the door for my club and tiptoed out the back to the pens, warning my girls and boys to be quiet; which, in the contrary ways of children, made them shout the louder —oh, children! Sometimes I wish—but no, that's cruel. I wouldn't have life any other way.

I made my way back from the pen to the house and stood behind the locked front door, club at the ready. But what can you do against one of Them? They're practically invincible; I've never heard of a death among Them. Of course, we live far away and I know little of Their ways except Their savagery; perhaps one day my ignorance will prove my undoing, but in this case, I was fortunate.

After a murmured prayer I crept to the window and pulled back the curtain just a little, steeling myself for what must surely be the messengers of a grizzly, tortuous death.

To my delight, a small girl leaned against the door, head bowed, panting. (I couldn't hear her, of course, for the screaming of my own children; but I saw her red face and her bony shoulders convulsing.)

Now I'm sure you know that many would have sent her on her way; but as I stared at her my maternal instinct rose in my breast like a flame, and I knew I had to help. Without a second thought— for she could have been part of a trap—I opened the door.

She saw me and flung herself into my arms. "Oh, help us!" she cried, and collapsed.

Poor little waif, her feet were pulp. I lay her on my bed and bathed her; in her sleep, she flinched when I touched her. She was in worse shape than Victoria had been, and I knew without a doubt she had escaped from town.

It chilled me. This lovely child, at Their hands—

I was so upset I was sick. I lost my dinner in the same spot behind the house I go to periodically—that's another trial of growing old, that one has trouble digesting now and then—and when I came back, the dear creature was sitting up and clutching my quilt to her chest. Her eyes were huge and filled with tears.

"Where's my mother?" she asked when I came into the room.

I didn't know what to say, but I was saved from answering by a soft thumping on the door.

"Mama!" the child cried, though I shushed her, and "Angel!" a desperate voice carried through the heavy door.

When I opened it, a gaunt, pale woman fell at my feet.

"Take me, take me," she murmured. "Only spare the child."

Her words confused me, but I helped her onto the bed beside her little one and urged her to rest.

"You're safe here," I assured her, but she shook her head.

"Nowhere is safe."

"But you're in the forest."

"Nowhere is safe," she repeated, and fainted.

They slept for an entire day and night. Both had fevers and I placed cool cloths on their foreheads, but they appeared to grow worse.

I lit my big stove and made them some gruel from my newest, little Jamie. He was most compliant, though he cried at the end. Silly boy. I shall miss him.

I fed the gruel to the mother and child, but they spit it all back up. I gave them bread, and they managed to keep that down, and some water, which I have little of, and all that seemed to have some effect. So I tried the gruel again, with no luck. It seemed to make them sicker.

Then the mother awoke with a start; her feverish gaze searched the room until it fell on me, and I smiled, saying, "Don't you remember me?"

"The kind old lady." She sighed and put her hand to the forehead of her child. "She's burning up."

"I gave you some gruel, but it didn't seem to agree with you," I told her. "Maybe you should try again."

"You're most generous."

"Not at all."

She accepted a bowl from me and looked at me with big, brown eyes that melted my heart. In the forest, there are no visitors. I don't believe I had ever seen another grown person in my life. Of course, I'm getting old now, and they say one's memory begins to slip. Why, I couldn't even remember all the names of my children. But then, there have been so many.

She looked strange as she drank the gruel, but finished the bowl and handed it back to me.

"If you don't mind, may I have some for my daughter?"

"Of course."

I began to ladle some into the bowl, but the woman became violently ill, vomiting everything back up on my granny-stitch quilt.

"Oh, I'm sorry. I'm so sorry," she said, weeping. "What shall I do? I'm sure They're following us."

I finished wiping her off and sat beside her on the bed. "Just rest. It will be safe. It's safe in the forest."

But I wasn't at all sure of that. If she were right, and They were following her, They would punish me for harboring her. And my children, oh, Lord, what would They do to them? I couldn't eat all of them. Yet if I hid them, they would be sure to start their caterwauling, not understanding the situation at all—which I wouldn't expect them to, they're just children.

You can certainly understand my dilemma.

She slept fitfully after that, and I wished there were something I could do. I had a bowl of gruel—it was tasty, of course; Jamie was a good little boy—and sat by the window, looking for the first sign of Them.

I awakened in the morning. I had dozed in the chair all night. My bones were stiff and I knew that, if any of my children tried to escape that day, I would probably be unable to stop them, unless they were tiny infants.

The woman jerked awake and began dressing herself and whispering to her child.

"May we have some water, please?" she asked. "And then we'll be on our way."

I didn't begrudge her the cup, but it worried me—I use so much with my gruels and stews and such, and my supply was growing low —and then she asked me for a second, for the girl.

"Is she better today?" I asked.

The woman felt the brave little forehead. "I think so. She seems cooler."

I touched her myself. "The fever's completely gone," I told her, surprised she couldn't discern it. Then I felt her own skin. It was as hot as the inside of my oven.

"I'm sick, aren't I?" the woman wailed. "Oh, poor Angel, what shall we do?"

I have never been one to offer advice unless it's asked for, but this poor lady was dreadfully in need of some clear thinking.

I took both her hands in mine and said, "My dear, it's obvious that the child is well enough. Mine apparently aren't agreeing with you."

She looked puzzled.

"It's time to eat her."

You would have thought I'd told her to set the house on fire.

She backed away from me on the bed, nearly trampling the child, who cried out, and scrabbled into the corner.

"Do *what?*" she cried. "What?"

"You must have nourishment if you're to survive," I said, quite reasonably. "My children are making you sick."

She stared at me for a long time, her eyes so big I was afraid they might fall out. Then she stared down at her stomach and let out the most bloodcurdling scream. My children must have heard it, for they answered in kind, ringing my eardrums. (I have since made myself a charming set of earmuffs, which I wear when they are in their moods.)

"I've been eating your . . . ?" She didn't say any more, only fell to crying and screaming and thrashing around. I was afraid she had gone mad from her high temperature.

And then she spied her little one, who had awakened (naturally; not even the dead could have slept through her hysteria), and she clasped the girl to her breast. The child struggled, then grew still, and I thought for a moment the woman had taken my advice and smothered her.

But she crawled off the bed, her child clinging to her like a baby monkey, and fell to the floor. She pitched herself forward to the door, and I was so reminded of Victoria that I smiled across the room at her shredded white dress, which I planned to wash and repair so my other girls could wear it.

"Oh, my god, my god," she muttered, over and over, flailing at the doorknob. "My god, she's crazy."

"If you want to leave, you have but to ask," I said. Naturally, I was confused, and a little affronted as well. I had offered this stranger the comfort and sanctuary of my home, and in return she insulted me. I was of a mind to point out that *she* was the one going off her head, not I; and so just who was the madwoman around here?

But I have been well brought up, and I reminded myself that she was quite ill; so I turned the knob and opened the door.

She slithered out on her knees, dropping and gathering up her child, throwing her head back and yowling.

My children, as you can imagine, were in such a state I knew there would never be any peace again.

The woman staggered to her feet and quit my door, then looked at the tall wooden boards of the pen.

"And is that where you keep them?" she screamed. "Your children? You herd them like animals?"

"Mercy, no, they're children," I said carefully, for I knew now that she had indeed gone insane. It was as if she didn't hear my wee ones, though their pleas were deafening. I had to bellow like an ox to make her hear me.

"God, god," she moaned, and lifted the latch.

It was as if that motion waved black fortune into the forest.

For on the horizon, I saw the devil carriages of the town; and I knew inside They would ride, in Their black cloaks and hoods, with Their knives and hooks and syringes. With a wail of despair, I knew all my care was for nothing. My darlings were in mortal peril.

"We must all run," I cried, "but first help me eat the little ones, oh, do; it will go cruelest for them."

She burst into tears. I think she meant to hide herself and her daughter in the pen, for she threw open the gate and jumped inside; and then, though the death coaches were lunging ever closer, she shrieked with horror and gestured to my babes.

Her entire body shook. Her child tugged at her skirts, crying, "Mama! Let's go! Please!" but the woman only trembled.

Then she began to laugh. It was frenzied, awful laughter, and she pointed at me and said, "Your children are made of mud! You've made little statues to amuse yourself!"

She was clearly beyond reason, but I simply could not abandon her.

"Quickly, before They come, eat her. You know it is your duty."

She couldn't stop laughing. "Is that what you did?" she asked me, and her voice was high-pitched like a maniac's.

"We must go," I warned her.

But it was too late. The devil carriages swooped down on us and They clambered out, full of fury and evil, and the woman collected herself just as They stormed the pen.

"What have I done?" she cried. "I have failed my Angel!" She fell on her knees before Them, arms outstretched.

"Take me," she whispered, but the tallest of Them replied, "You know it is not you we want."

Their knives flashed. Their teeth sparkled behind Their masks. I saw the hooks of Their hands and the heavy boots, made for grinding little bones.

They seemed to pay no attention to me, almost to pretend I wasn't there. I darted around the leader and whispered to the woman:

"My oven is lit. Better to toss the girl in than—"

But the leader heard me. He took a menacing step toward the woman and said, "You know it is too late. We will not be cheated."

I turned to my children. "It is your turn to do a good deed! Eat her!"

But they cowered and ran the other way. Who can blame them? They are only children.

Eventually, of course, They tore the girl away from the mother, though she held on as if her own life depended on it. In fact, They hacked her out of her arms, carving great, gaping chunks of flesh from her bones and breaking her fingers. Had I not looked after her, she would have died. But she mended, though she lost use of most of her fingers.

And one night, while I was asleep, she left. A note beside my cooking pot read, "Gone to Town. I am too lonely here. I miss . . . almost everything."

I was most distraught, for I had grown to care for the dear mad thing, but perhaps she would be happier there.

As for me, I prefer my own company, and that of my children. Which is why we have always lived in the forest.

Mona Clee is another Texan, recently escaped to the Bay Area in California. She has, however, that Texas touch with a shadow, a way of looking at the world that is both disturbing and chilling. All you need to do is take something that is sometimes a joke, sometimes a cliché, and give that quarter turn to bring a new, dark face around for a look. Sunday supplements sooner or later show photographs of people who resemble their pets. "Just Like Their Masters" tells you something those newspapers don't.

JUST LIKE THEIR MASTERS
by Mona A. Clee

I

"Dogs sure do take after the folks that own 'em," Dub McCalley said. I looked up and saw Heywood coming toward us, followed by his little black dog.

I'd never thought about it before, but Dub, the grocer, had a point: like Heywood, the dog was too skinny, and had big dark eyes that were afraid of you. It slunk; it walked along in Heywood's footsteps like it expected you to chunk a rock at it, though you always got the feeling it hoped you might stop and pet it instead.

Funny—Heywood was that way, now that I thought about it. He'd duck his head when he saw you coming and make sure to avoid your eyes, but even so, you always sensed he was lonely and wistful inside.

"You know, you're right," I said. "I wonder how they get that way?"

Dub stretched out in the heat of the stove. "Beats me," he said in a low voice, and then, "Hello, Heywood."

Heywood shut the door behind him and nodded, jerkily.

"What can we do for you?"

Heywood shook his head and pointed through the side door to the post office.

"No groceries today, huh?" Dub smiled at him, a big, beaming smile, but Heywood darted through the door and disappeared.

"Poor thing," said Dub.

"I'd better be going." I got to my feet. So did Dub. He stretched again, and gave a big sigh.

"You off to see Cecily?"

"Yeah. Thought I'd come in here and get warm first. It's the half-way point."

Dub laughed. "Why do you walk all the time, boy? You've got a good car."

"I just like it. It feels good—and I see a lot of things." I opened the door and went down the concrete steps, Dub following me.

He looked up at the sky. "You'd better hurry. Looks like there's rain coming."

Behind us the door slammed. Heywood came down the steps carrying an armful of packages and a big manila envelope.

"You take care, hear?" Dub called to him.

Heywood's eyes darted toward us; he opened his mouth and almost said something. But then he scurried off down the main road toward home, the black dog at his heels.

"Now I wonder what's in all those packages," said Dub.

"You and everybody else in town."

Dub squinted, and looked down the road in the other direction. I looked too. Pretty soon I heard the sound of a pickup truck.

"Oh, hell," Dub sighed. "There's Earl, comin' back from Nacogdoches."

At once I turned my head to see how close Heywood was to home. He was still short a good quarter mile. "Oh, no," I said.

Earl passed us and waved. I knew the exact moment he caught sight of Heywood—just opposite the Burrows house, he threw the truck into neutral and let it coast.

Heywood had opened the manila envelope and was reading while he walked. He always did that. I guess it gave him a good excuse not to meet people's eyes when he passed them. At any rate, he didn't seem to hear the pickup coming, which was just what Earl wanted.

When the truck was right at Heywood's back, Earl leaned on the horn. I saw Heywood jump, and all his packages fell to the ground. Earl waved at him and gunned the truck on down the road; I was sure he was laughing.

"Someday Heywood's going to turn on Earl," I said. "I can't wait to see it."

Dub considered. "Earl's sure got it coming."

Heywood crouched in the road, picking up his packages from the red dust, while his dog waited beside him. I thought I saw it raise its head once to stare, stiff-legged, at the disappearing truck.

"Well," Dub said, clapping me on the shoulder, "you say hi to that little girl for me."

I turned and headed down the road toward Cecily's. The wind picked up, and I heard it rustling in the pine needles, so I quickened my step. Overhead, a bank of low clouds was pushing in from the northwest, which meant we'd have rain. My feet went crunch, crunch in the piles of sweet gum and poplar leaves by the side of the road; the sound made me wish I'd covered the next two miles and was already at Cecily's house, sitting in front of her big stone fireplace.

An extra strong blast of wind hit me, and I shivered. On the right as I passed was the Burrows house. It was an effort not to turn and look at it, for I knew Miss Berneice was sitting in the parlor with the curtains drawn, just as she always did, peeking out through the dusty Venetian blinds.

In towns like Y'barbo, it's hard not to know too much about your neighbors. You have to work at it; you have to shut your eyes on purpose just to keep from hearing things. I know that's true. Otherwise, tell me how the whole town knows that Miss Berneice never goes to a doctor or a dentist—that when her teeth go bad, she pries them out with a big silver serving fork?

I pushed myself to hurry. I passed the Harmon house, with Earl's oddly menacing pickup parked crooked on the lawn. I wondered why his old mother didn't make him stop, because it played hell with the grass. But some folks said not even she could tell him what to do.

Except for his Doberman sitting on the front porch, there was no sign of Earl. I felt relieved. At least there would be no bellowed hello on this trip, no slap on the back that knocked the breath out of me. And most of all, no prying questions about Cecily—no needling reminders that he had gone with her first, back when we were all in school together down the road in San Augustine.

When I drew level with Heywood's house, though, I knew I could look at it. Somehow you didn't picture Heywood peering out the windows like Miss Berneice. But it wasn't pleasant to look at the old place; you looked at it the way you'd look at something going wrong, when you knew it was none of your business to point it out.

Nothing had been done to the house since Heywood's parents passed on, nothing at all. The paint peeled. The curtains, glimpsed through the dirty windows at the front, dropped. Even the front walk buckled, bent, and fell prey to the encroaching weeds. Heywood never cared for the house. He never even went outside, except to visit Dub McCalley's store or the post office. Even his dog stayed inside with him, as if it belonged to a little old lady and not a man who, calendar-wise, was still in his twenties.

Again I shivered, and picked up the pace of my walk. I'd imagined Heywood sitting all alone in that house, hidden in a big chair as far from the outside world as he could get, reading whatever was in that envelope—reading, with all the hatred he must feel toward Earl and the rest of the town bottled up inside him. Simmering, threatening to explode one day.

The picture bothered me so much that when I finally got to Cecily's I told her about it. I told her how Heywood had come into the post office, and about Earl sneaking up behind him and startling him.

Cecily listened, holding her little cockapoo dog in her lap and stroking it.

"Earl won't ever change," she said when I was through. "He's tormented Heywood since we were children. He enjoys it, and no one will stop him."

"Maybe Heywood could stand up to him sometime."

Cecily fixed me with a look, and shook her head. "Not now. It's too late."

"Cecily—" I began, and stopped. I had wanted to ask her something for a long, long time.

"What?" She shifted the cockapoo in her lap.

"Why'd you break up with Earl?"

She looked down at her pet and smiled. "Because of his cruel streak."

"How so? He wasn't mean to you, was he?"

"He was mean to Heywood, and Heywood was my friend."

I was stunned. "Heywood?"

"Well, he was quiet and kind. And he never hurt anyone!" I could tell Cecily was ruffled. "He was different when his folks were still alive. He used to sit and talk with me sometimes, not about school or the football team or why I wasn't going away to college, but about things that really mattered to me. He brought me poems he'd copied out of books, and after I read them, I always felt like they said things I was struggling to say. He understood me."

I could feel myself redden. "I never knew he liked you."

Cecily looked at me reprovingly. "I said, Heywood was my friend. That's all. You know, sometimes I think about walking up to that old house and knocking on the door. Now that his parents are gone, he's shut himself away from everybody. The only thing he's got left in the world is that dog."

I nodded, but didn't hear what she said after that. I was suddenly staring at the little cockapoo. I'd never realized it before, but the cockapoo was somehow very much like Cecily.

Where my girl was small and dainty and very, very pretty, so was the cockapoo. Cecily had curly blonde hair, and damned if the dog's fur wasn't just the same color, and curly to boot. Its disposition was even like hers, and that was the strangest thing of all—both of them were gentle little things, but I'd never try to lean on Cecily when she had her mind made up, or try to take a bone away from that dog.

"Hey," I said, "do you and that dog get your hair done at the same beauty parlor?"

Cecily's eyes widened, and she just looked at me.

"I'm only kidding," I said at length. "It just looks like you both get your hair done the same way."

She pursed her lips and for a minute I thought she was going to be mad at me. But then she lifted up the cockapoo and looked at it intently.

"I guess we do sort of resemble each other."

II

The next week it got cold, vengefully cold. I remember having the impression that we were supposed to learn a lesson from it—something about buying heavier clothing and refusing to take quite so much for granted in our lives. People huddled around their space heaters or around wood-burning stoves, like at Dub McCalley's, with no heart for friendly visiting. Coming upon folks, I would feel their stares rise up to me with cold questions I couldn't answer.

I even abandoned walking at grocery-shopping time; that day I took the car into town. Everything was still—the leaves in the trees, the animals, the people—but not in a peaceful way. It was like winter was holding its breath, telling no one what surprises it was planning.

When I got to the store, I saw Dub and Earl and Joe Posey from Martinsville, drinking hot coffee that would have scalded them a week before. I had some warning that Earl was there, because his pickup was parked crooked in front of the building, taking up two full spaces.

He'd put his Doberman in the back of the truck. It was shivering but trying to look mean all the same.

"What've you got your dog out there for, Earl?" I asked when I got inside. I've always liked animals, and the pooch had looked miserably cold.

"I'm tryin' to toughen him up," said Earl. "He's a real woman."

Dub and Joe Posey laughed, but I could see they didn't think much of it. I got my groceries, paid Dub, and poured myself a cup of coffee to drink before I headed back.

I had just sat down and wrapped my hands around the Styrofoam cup, when there came a whining and a yelping from the truck outside.

"He sees somethin'," Earl said.

The door opened, and Heywood and his dog stood there. He took one look at the four of us huddled around the stove, and I could tell he wished he hadn't come in. He looked as if he wanted to run, but he had come too far—it was too late.

"Close that door, boy!" Dub said. Heywood hesitated, and as he did so, a dark form appeared behind him. Earl's Doberman stuck its head through the door, caught sight of its master, and pushed past Heywood toward the stove.

Heywood hurried through the side door into the post office, and before long, as always, he reappeared with a stack of mail. This time he carried a single big package as well.

By that time the Doberman had warmed up. When it caught sight of Heywood and his dog, it rose to its feet and padded toward them. Heywood froze; I think we all held our breath as it started pushing its nose into the little creature's rump, smelling it and bullying it across the floor.

Then the little dog tried to get away. All at once there was a growling, one of those scuffles people can't make hide nor hair of, and Heywood's dog started screaming. It was a terrible sound, like a woman in pain. Earl's Doberman had its right front leg in its powerful jaws, and the sound of bone cracking made me sick to my stomach.

Heywood screamed too. He dropped his packages and flew at the Doberman like he was going to kill it. He managed a heavy blow to the head with his doubled fist, then snatched up his own pet and cradled it to his chest.

Both of them trembled. Both looked at Earl.

Except for the faintest shrug, Earl ignored him. But the rest of us kept staring at Earl too, so at length he got up, removed his belt, and sauntered over toward the Doberman. He hit it a few times on the face and, when it turned to run, the rear; then he tugged the door open and kicked the animal in the direction of the truck. Still ignoring Heywood, he dropped back into his seat near the fire.

None of us said anything for a moment. From the corner of my eye I could see Heywood's pet was badly hurt, the leg dangling uselessly. I wasn't surprised when Heywood stumbled outside, the dog in his arms, but I was glad. Relieved.

"Earl, dammit, your dog's not coming in here again," said Dub.

Earl looked up at him, but Dub meant what he said. It wasn't often people stood up to Earl, and he flushed. He looked away, sullenly, and didn't reply.

Pretty soon the quiet started getting to Earl. He got to his feet and stared out the window. Then he poked at the stove. I thought he was getting ready to go when he spied Heywood's package, lying on the floor where it had fallen.

He picked it up and shook it. "Wonder what's in here?"

"You better put that down," said Dub.

This time Earl ignored him. I suppose he was beginning to feel his reputation was on the line—if that's what he called it.

"Aw, he's just fooling around." Joe Posey sat back with a grin and watched him shake it again. "I wonder myself what's in it."

Dub sighed. "Probably books."

Earl looked up. "Books? You can get plenty of books in Nacogdoches. What kind of books d'you have to get through the mail?"

Joe giggled, and Earl's eyes lit up. "No, no," Dub said, "I just know Heywood's folks used to read a lot. I was inside the house once before they died, and it was full of books."

"What were you doing there, Dub?" Earl snickered.

"Delivering groceries. They were sick."

Joe got to his feet, walked over next to Earl, and looked at the package. "Well, the postmark says New York."

"New York!" Earl snorted. "Gimme your pocket knife." Joe tossed it to him, and he started to slit the package open.

"You stop that!" Dub said. "That's not right!"

"Aw, come on, he's just havin' fun," Joe said, overriding him. By then Earl had the package open and was pulling away layers of tissue paper.

The first thing he held up was a plastic-covered packet full of little cloth squares; the one on top had a flower design stamped on it. Earl stood back and held it up to the light. "Needlepoint from the Metropolitan," he read out loud. "Jesus! Heywood's embroidering!"

Joe hooted softly. Earl dug into the package again, and brought up several little skeins of brightly colored yarn, a tiny box of watercolors, a thin old book of poetry by someone named Brownlow or Browning, and an object wrapped in still more tissue paper.

He fumbled at it. He almost had it unwrapped when Dub drew in his breath sharply; we turned, and there was Heywood again, standing in the doorway with the cold wind at his back.

There was a moment of silence while we waited to see what he would do. There was an even briefer moment when Heywood could have shamed Earl, and taken back his belongings without any fuss. But Joe Posey snickered again, and that moment passed.

"Hi there, Heywood, look what we got for you!" Earl waved the box at him.

"Give it here."

"Oh, no!" Earl danced back. "I'm not through lookin' at it yet!"

Heywood looked at the rest of us. Then he lunged at Earl.

"Whoop!" Earl backed away from him, the box held high over Heywood's head. He worried at the wrapping paper that covered the last little object; then it fell away, and he was holding a little statue, no bigger than your hand, of a lady in Grecian-looking clothes with a spear and an owl perched on her shoulder.

"What the hell kind of sissy junk is this, Heywood?"

Heywood darted toward him, but Joe's foot jumped out and Heywood went sprawling across the floor.

"Give it back to him." Dub was very quiet, but made no effective move to help Heywood.

"In a minute," said Earl, engrossed in the statue. I moved closer to him and looked at it too. It was pretty; I thought it might be a copy of the kind of things they have in museums, like the one I visited in Houston when I was a kid, and I couldn't help thinking how much Cecily would have loved it.

Heywood got to his feet. He made a final lunge at Earl and grabbed him round the waist. Earl let out a cry of surprise and tried to push him away; and he dropped the little statue, which struck the concrete floor and broke.

Heywood let out a wail. He got down on his hands and knees and scraped the pieces into a pile. Dub pushed Earl aside, knelt down, and gave Heywood the box it had come in.

"I think maybe you can glue it back," Dub whispered.

No one noticed the little owl but me. It had skidded across the floor and lodged behind one of the stools at Dub's long Formica lunch counter.

Heywood swept the broken pieces and the tin of watercolors and the needlepoint and the ancient book into the box. Then he ducked his head and ran out the door.

Earl settled onto a stool, just above the owl, actually, and looked at the rest of us. He seemed uncomfortable. "I didn't mean no harm," he said resentfully. No one believed him, of course. Only Joe smiled.

"Go on, get out of here!" Dub's voice was harsh. "You, a grown man!"

Earl slid off the stool and stuck his hands in his pockets. "You talk to me about grown men? I'm not the one sendin' off to New York City for fancy work—"

"Just go on." Dub turned away from him. "I've got to clean up in here."

The others filed out and I followed, but not before I bent down, on impulse, and picked up the owl.

Outside, Earl was getting into his truck. His Doberman was already in the back, watching the rest of us with its mouth hanging open. It seemed to be grinning. I stood where I was and looked at it; I could swear it knew what had just happened inside, and was getting a kick out of it. The dog was smiling in the same sly-eyed way I'd seen Earl smile a thousand times.

"What are you starin' at?"

That was Earl, from the cab of the truck.

"Your dog," I said. "He's a mean one."

"Aw, Heywood's mutt probably nipped him. He's a good dog." Earl turned the key in the ignition and gunned the motor, eyeing me. "Say—I don't appreciate all of you taking up for that fairy."

With a lurch, he backed the truck away from McCalley's store and pointed it down the road toward the highway.

III

Several days went by before Earl came home again. I thought maybe he'd gone into Nacogdoches for a little night life, but when two days had passed, and then three, the boys at McCalley's decided he'd gone as far as Shreveport or Houston.

By the fourth day the weather was still cold, but I had been cooped up long enough, so I took to walking again. A man can get to where he'll adjust to most anything. I went to Cecily's for supper, and when it got dark I started home, though it had gotten so cold by then I thought I'd freeze to death before I reached the house. I hurried down the road, half walking, half running, and kept an eye out for somebody to hitch a ride with. But the road was deserted, and when I got to the middle of town there wasn't a soul on the street. I wished I'd taken my car, and not only because I was cold.

When I neared Heywood's house I looked for a light, but saw none. Nobody had seen Heywood since that day at McCalley's, either. I wondered if he and his dog were all right.

As I drew level with the house, I heard the rumble of an engine far away, down at the other end of town. It had to be Earl; sure enough, the pickup swung into view, speeding hellbent down the middle of the road toward me. His lights weren't on, and that had to mean trouble. I got up on the curb.

He didn't stop at his own house. He whipped past, threw on his brakes in front of Heywood's place, and stopped just short of the sagging fence that bounded Heywood's property. Earl staggered out, scarcely glancing at his Doberman; it sat, glowering like something wild, from a nest of empty beer cans.

"What the hell are you doing here?" Earl demanded when he saw me.

"I should be asking you that," I said softly.

He pointed at Heywood's house. "I'm gonna have a talk with that little bastard. Gonna set him straight once and for all. As for you, boy—you stay out of the way." He set off down the front walk, his gait unsteady.

"Earl—" I said, but he paid no attention. From the back of the pickup I heard a growl, and the Doberman looked right at me and showed its fangs. It dared me to try to stop him.

Earl pounded on the door, howling for Heywood to come outside. Down the street a light came on in Berneice Burrows' house; I saw the curtains stir and part.

For a long time there was no answer. Earl beat on the door, bellowing for Heywood to face him. He called Heywood every taunting name he could think of, and then, at last, there came a noise from the interior of the house.

I felt the back of my neck prickle. I imagined I heard the heavy breathing of a great beast in the night—but not, I sensed, Earl's dog, for it still sat motionless in the truck, watching its master.

In spite of my thick woolen gloves, my hands felt suddenly cold. I shoved them deep into my coat pockets, and my right hand touched something unfamiliar—the forgotten little owl. I clutched it tightly, as if it were a charm that would protect me.

Up on the porch, the heavy front door swung back. But I saw nothing opening it, nothing there at all—for a moment. The interior of the house remained pitch-black.

But behind me, the Doberman began to whimper, and I became certain that something stood in the open doorway. Toenails clicked on wood, the porch sighed with sudden and unaccustomed weight, and a black mass formed at the top of the stairs. It was a great dog, I realized, bigger than any mastiff I'd seen in pictures or with my own eyes. Its sleek coat gleamed brightly, so it seemed to give off a blue aura that shimmered around its massive shape. Perhaps the dimness played tricks on my eyes, but I thought the dog's outlines shifted and wavered as it started to descend the steps. I fancied I could even see through the beast in spots, make out the texture of the wooden steps straight through its shadowy black form.

Except—I caught my breath. Except that a small, opaque, faintly wriggling figure seemed to be suspended in the center of the apparition. It was, or I believed insanely that it was, Heywood's dog, encased somehow in that terrible Presence, its tiny right foreleg bandaged with white strips of cloth.

The dog advanced down the front walk, stiff-legged and silent, past a stupefied, gawking Earl. As it passed me, I saw its eyes gleam. It turned a knowing stare upon Earl's Doberman, which by now had cowered in the farthest corner of the truck, whining and scrabbling as if trying to get away. Then the thing sprang, bowling over the Doberman effortlessly. In seconds, it had closed its jaws around the other dog's neck.

Earl, forcing himself to move, blocked my view of what happened next. "Son of a bitch," he muttered, but stopped short when he heard a noise. I heard it too. It could have been soft laughter. Earl whirled, and as he moved we both saw Heywood framed in the doorway, his face paler than ever, but with his eyes dry and smoldering.

"Yes, get him too," Heywood whispered. "Get *him.*" The black creature in the truck opened its jaws and I heard a thumping sound. Then it was over the side, dropping to the ground.

Advancing, silently, on Earl. By the time Earl realized the danger he was in, it was much too late. Another whisper from Heywood, and the monster leaped for Earl's throat. It knocked him down as easily as it had felled the Doberman. I caught a glimpse of the awful, muscled neck as it slashed, and Earl's single, bewildered scream was cut short.

Down the street, lights came on over Dub's store. From far off I heard a telephone ring. I stared at Heywood, and stared at the creature. I stared most of all at the bandaged foreleg of the little dog at its heart.

Only when it raised its head again and moved toward me did I realize my own danger. Why had I assumed it would pass *me* by?

"Call it off," I got out, but the dog came even nearer, its eyes glowing. Heywood stood on the porch, expressionless, and said nothing.

"Heywood," I cried, "I've never tried to hurt you!"

Up in the dark, up there on the porch, I could hear his breath come and go quickly. "You never tried to help me, either."

Now the creature was close enough to spring. I remembered the owl then; my fingers tightened around it again, and I held it up for both of them to see.

"Look! I picked this up! I saved it for you!"

Heywood started. His face suddenly crumpled, just as it had when Earl dropped the statue. But his eyes seemed mad. "Where did you find it?"

"On the floor, underneath the lunch counter."

Heywood came to the edge of the steps, and I thought I saw tears on his thin face. A little of the crazy look left his eyes, and at that, the yellow fire in the dog's eyes died too.

"Here," I said. I stepped forward as carefully as I could, putting the owl into his reaching palm.

Heywood clutched at it. He held it up, looked at it keenly in the faint light. Then he came out of his trance, or whatever it was, and looked about—first at me, then at the still form that had been Earl's Doberman, and then at Earl himself. His eyes widened. He gave a mournful, wailing cry that jarred on my ears and turned me cold as ice. The black creature in front of me turned, fled noiselessly up the steps, and disappeared into the depths of the dark house.

Heywood took one last look at me and slammed the big door shut behind him. From inside, I thought I heard another cry.

I waited there for Dub or the sheriff to arrive, trying not to look at the place the creature had been, then trying to figure it out. But then a gunshot sounded behind the closed door of the old house and, only a moment after that, a second shot. It was silent then, so quiet I thought my heart might stop beating.

When Dub and the sheriff finally came, we beat on the door until our knuckles were raw. At last we got a pine log and broke the door down that way. Dub turned his flashlight on the front parlor, and we had to look no further. Heywood lay there, shot through the head, and beside him was the body of his little dog, its right foreleg bandaged and its brains scattered across the hardwood floor.

Nobody else had seen the monster, and so I made myself stop wondering about it and driving myself crazy with questions.

We buried him, and I never saw the creature again. I asked Cecily to marry me when Easter came, and she said yes. I was relieved, because that meant I didn't have to walk past Heywood's house on the way home anymore.

I tried to forget about it. I made myself stop wondering about the dog. I stopped making up stories to explain it away, for deep down, I knew what had really happened.

Eventually, I thought it was all over. Some folks from Nacogdoches bought the house, renovated it, and planted flowers all over the yard. They never had any trouble that I heard of.

But now I'm not so sure. Tonight I took a different route home from buying groceries at Dub's. I walked down one of the dirt roads just west of town, past a cluster of what used to be sharecropper cabins, where a lot of poor whites now live.

As I walked, I suddenly became aware of the cold and the growing dark around me—of the pine trees pressing round, shutting out the light. I turned to cut through the forest to my own house, when I caught sight of a woman watching me. She stood on the porch of one of those old cabins, her hands on her hips—a frowzy, beaten-looking woman, the sort who has been poor and ground into the dirt all her life, with no help from the other side of town.

I saw the banked resentment in her eyes—the hatred, even—as I passed. And suddenly I was reminded of other eyes, in an earlier time. Of course I tried to tell myself I was imagining it, and that I had nothing to fear. I blinked and forced myself to look past the woman, to turn my thoughts toward home. But there, beside her on the rotting porch, sat a great golden cat, with glittering teeth and ivory talons. It watched me with merciless, gleaming eyes; they followed me as I turned and ran toward home.

For quite some time, Al Sarrantonio has been making his mark in the field as a writer of short stories. As his talent has settled and grown, so has his reach, and now, though his stories are not as numerous as they once were, his work can be readily appreciated, not to mention envied, in novel form, especially in his latest, The Boy with the Penny Eyes.

PIGS
by Al Sarrantonio

The day they took Jan was like any other day. The sky over the Vistula was fat with billowy gray clouds, "thick puffs from God's pipe," as Tadeusz had once said of such smoky formations. He stood on the bank of the river with Jan and with Karol, leaning on the thin rope bridge, the three of them sharing one cigarette as they waited for their solemn friend Jozef, who did not smoke, and did not approve of it. It was November, but felt like late September, cool but muggy. Karol dropped pebbles into the river below, his flat, open face spreading into a grin as his "depth charges" disappeared into the water. "Just like that American Clark Gable, in *Run Silent, Run Deep,*" he laughed. "Captain, we've been hit!" Tadeusz had his cap pushed back on his head, which always forecast the weather because Tadeusz would pull it down tight over his ears in cold or wet times. He did not like the cold and complained bitterly when it rained, calling it a punishment from God for some great sinner in the city. "In Warsaw," he once told Jan, as they sat hunched over the smallest table by the smallest window in their tavern, so close together their pints of beer were pressed into their coats. The noise in the cafe was nearly unbearable. They looked out at the rain pelting the tiny window, at the thick wash it sent across the four panes intermittently, because it was either look at that or into each other's close faces, or into the coats of the standing patrons surrounding them—damp wool that would suffocate their conversation. "In Warsaw, when a great man, some member of the Party, commits a great sin, there is rejoicing in heaven. They laugh loud and long, because another Communist has proved himself weak and human, not equal in purity and character with God himself. You know," Tadeusz continued, poking Jan's nose lightly with his thick finger, an annoying habit, "that this is the great fault of Communism. In seeking to abolish

God, it merely replaces him with Man. This is why it's doomed to failure. And God knows this. So, when a Party official commits a great sin, one of greed or lust, God and his angels laugh until they can no longer contain themselves, and God allows his angels to relieve themselves on the city of Warsaw. It is a just and mighty retribution—as well as a great relief for the angels. Unfortunately," he said, shivering at the rain outside, "it's a pain in the ass for those of us who live in Warsaw."

"What about God?" Jan asked him, gently warding off Tadeusz's finger, heading toward his nose to make another point. "Doesn't God ever piss?"

"Of course he does," Tadeusz answered, offended. "But he is God, and his bladder is vast. It's as large as the Milky Way galaxy. And if you're going to ask me if he'll ever use it, the answer is yes. He's saving it, though, for a very special occasion." Tadeusz leaned close, pushing Jan's head around so that only his ear would hear his next words. Jan smelled the sourness of Tadeusz's breath, the odor of sausage and beer and stale tobacco, before he felt the rough stubble of Tadeusz's mustache at his ear. "God is waiting until that biggest man of all, the Big Man himself, the one in Moscow, commits the biggest of all sins." He turned Jan's face around, moving his own back. He smiled. "And then—BOOM! The big rain, right on you know where, and then you-know-where won't exist anymore."

"And then?" Jan asked, smiling in a friendly way.

Tadeusz held his hands out in his confined spot, palms upward, indicating what surrounded them. "And then this is ours again."

They looked out through the small window silently, before Tadeusz added, slyly, "There's only one catch. I have it on very good authority that you-know-who in Moscow has already fucked a chicken, and," he sighed, "nothing happened."

They turned to their own thoughts, watching the sliding wet sheets of rain on their tiny window, in their tiny space surrounded by heat and the smell of damp shorn sheep, until Tadeusz added, "And why do you ask about God, Jan? I thought you knew all about him. It's you who was going to be a priest."

At the bridge, leaning lightly on the rope railing, smoking and waiting for Jozef, who now approached them sullenly, the words of his disapproval of their smoking probably already forming on his never smiling mouth, Jan thought of the priesthood and wanted to laugh.

"And what do you find so funny?" Karol said. "Are you thinking of pigs?" Seeing Jan shudder, he quickly changed the subject, nudging him to look at Jozef. "Now *there's* something worthy of laughter. Our friend Jozef was born with a frown on his face." Karol, who almost never frowned, laughed heartily.

"He doesn't even smile when he gets off a good fart," Tadeusz said, throwing the remains of the cigarette which had been passed to him into the river and turning to meet Jozef, who had now reached them.

"Save your breath," Tadeusz said, slapping Jozef on the shoulder. "We've heard all your lectures on smoking. And we're late for work as it is."

The look on Jozef's face made him stop his joking.

"What's wrong?" Karol asked, as a cloud of seriousness descended.

"They're looking for Jan," Jozef said.

"What do you mean?" Tadeusz nearly shouted, and then he barked a laugh. He laid the back of his hand on Jozef's brow. "Are you ill? Have you been drinking? Who is looking for Jan?"

"The police."

"A mistake," Karol spat.

"No," Jozef replied. His dour face was pinched tight. He turned to Jan. "I saw them come out of your mother's house as I passed. They must have just missed you. I waited until they were gone, and then I went in. Your mother was at the kitchen table, weeping. I asked her if they had hurt her. She said no—but there was a pot of oatmeal broken on the floor, by the stove."

"Bastards," Jan said, angry.

"She might have dropped it herself, when they came in," Jozef continued. "She was very upset, Jan. She said they wanted to speak with you, but she could tell by the way they came in, knocking once and then nearly throwing open the door, that they were there not to talk but to take you away."

"*Why?*" Karol shouted, indignantly. "What could they possibly want Jan for?"

Jozef shrugged. They saw now how frightened he was, his big-knuckled hands working one over the other, his thick coat pulled tight around him, the collar up as if protecting him from a chill wind.

Jan said quietly, as much to himself as to the others, who now faced him as if waiting for an explanation, "I've done nothing."

"Of course you've done nothing," Tadeusz said, scratching the black stubble on his chin. "But we have to hide you. We can't let them take you. When the storm passes over, it will be like nothing ever happened."

"There is no place to hide," Jozef said, his eyes on the ground.

Karol, in anger, grabbed Jozef by the front of his lapels. "Of course there is."

"I've done nothing," Jan repeated, as if in shock.

Tadeusz said, "We must get him to my house, off the street, then move him to a place that can't be connected to him." He took Jan by the arm. "Quickly."

Jan looked at him. Comprehension of what was happening to him on this fine day, with its cool, late summer breeze and fine gray clouds—on this day when he had smoked a cigarette with his best friends, and leaned on a rope railing overlooking the roiling water of the Vistula—dawned on him. Something out of his control was closing in on him, a machine in the form of a hunting hound had been set in motion, with his name imprinted on it, and unwavering instructions to bring him to a tree. The police would not go away. They had been told to take him, and they would.

"I'll give myself up to them," Jan said.

Karol's face came before his own, flushed and angry. "Come with us," he said. *"They're not going to take you."*

Tadeusz's grip on Jan's arm tightened. Karol took his other arm. For a brief moment he felt as though he was going to faint. But then the world, the gray sky, the billowing gray clouds, the smell of the moving river, came back to him.

They moved briskly away from the bridge, Jozef darting glances behind them, and ascended stone steps to the street above. "Walk casually," Tadeusz ordered. They began to converse, trying to keep the tension out of their voices.

The street was filled with late factory workers hurrying to their jobs. Some wore winter coats, since the last few days had been colder than today, but they were opened at the collar, enjoying the last hint of warmth before the damp winter settled in. Most carried black lunchboxes.

They walked along with the workers. The pace quickened as the clock in the church steeple near the end of the street began to toll the hour, promising reprimands for those not at work by the time it had ceased. Jan and his friends hurried along until Tadeusz said, "This way is quicker," and brought them through a narrow alleyway, lined with discarded boxes, to the next street. "Stay back," he ordered when they reached the end. He went ahead, slipping out onto the street before motioning for them to follow. They crossed the road and mounted a flight of wooden steps to the second floor.

Tadeusz fumbled a huge iron key out of his pocket and turned it in the lock. Below them, on the street, someone rounded a corner, a man in a trench coat and brown hat. "Shit, he's right out of the movies," Karol said as they pushed Jan into the flat. The man in the trench coat was followed by two uniformed policemen, who kept a discreet distance.

They watched through the window as the man in the trench coat stopped and waited for the two uniformed men to catch up with him; there followed a discussion over a piece of paper which the man in the trench coat produced. The discussion escalated in volume, with the uniformed cops arguing and the man in the trench coat waiting for them to stop.

"Are they the ones you saw come out of Jan's house?" Tadeusz asked Jozef.

"I think so." He squinted hard through the window, then pulled his head back. "Yes."

"Jesus," Tadeusz said, "they must have gone right to the factory and found we weren't there. They're looking for this place."

The man in the trench coat suddenly threw his hand up and his companions ceased arguing immediately; the three of them then proceeded down the street away from them.

"They'll be wanting a telephone, and then they'll find the correct address," Tadeusz said. "We can't wait here. There's no time to waste." He reached into his pocket, pulling out a clip of bills, and handed it to Jan. The others did likewise, Karol cursing when he could produce nothing more than one small bill and a handful of coins.

"You must get to a bus," Tadeusz said to Jan. He held him by the shoulders, looking hard into his eyes to make sure that Jan understood what he said. "You must get out of the city. Do you know of a place away from here?"

Jan shook himself from his torpor. "There's a town called Kolno. It's about a hundred kilometers northeast of here. My grandfather had a farm there, once. I remember . . ." A sharp memory flashed across his mind, was gone. "There was a hotel outside the village, I think. I can't remember the name. It had a pot of flowers by the sign out front."

"Good," Tadeusz said. "On Sunday, two days from now, I'll meet you there. We'll get money together. I'll go to the priest and he'll help. They all will." He squeezed Jan's shoulders tight, bringing him close. Then the three of them, Jozef muttering goodbye, Karol punching Jan on his arm with his fist, looking angry and impotent, were gone, leaving Jan alone in the room.

"They'll all help," Tadeusz had said to him. But even as his friend was saying it, even as their eyes met while he was uttering the words, they both knew that, in the end, the police would find and take him.

Jan stood in the middle of the empty, cold, dark flat. He looked down at the money in his hand. Suddenly, for no real reason except that he refused to give up, a sort of life came into him. *Maybe they won't take me.* Maybe there was escape. Even if there wasn't, he would not let his friends down by not trying. He owed them something. He thought of his mother, in her tiny kitchen, cleaning the remains of his breakfast which he had cavalierly refused because he was anxious to get out of the little stuffy house, to smoke cigarettes with his friends ("No, Mother, I can't eat it, I'm not hungry"), the almost arrogant way he had refused her cooking. He thought of all the little things she did for him, her mending of his boots, the way she had replaced the lining of his coat after he had had it ripped during that brawl in the pub the previous September. She hadn't even scolded him about his fighting—though, later, he had seen her in her bedroom, the faded, colored quilt tucked still under her pillow, the mattress of the bed high and uneven from the old filling it possessed, kneeling with her elbows on the quilt, hands clasped around her rosary, head bowed. When he went to his own room he would find a holy picture tucked under his pillow, just as he had every night since he was a boy, since his father was killed during a worker's strike. Jan thought of his mother, and his eyes filled with tears. She would never see him again. She had been in her kitchen, probably scraping the remains of his uneaten breakfast back into the pot, to save for later, perhaps to serve with the potatoes with dinner, and the policemen had come into her house, and had asked her rough questions, and then had left her, not laying a hand on her perhaps, but, just as well, striking into her body, into her heart. He cried not because he would never see her again, but because she would never see him. He was the one thing in her life she truly cared for—Jan, her only son, the image of her husband, the boy who would, perhaps, be a priest. He had told her that once, when he was young, with his tongue connected to a boy's confused heart, mostly because she had wanted to hear it so badly. Yes, he had said, he would become a priest. Later, when he had realized that he was now a man and not a boy, he had almost stopped speaking to her because he realized that he could never be what she wanted of him. He resented her for wanting him to be something he could not be. She had never said anything to him about it, had never mentioned the priesthood again, but still, every night, under his pillow the holy pictures, the image of Christ, the Sacred Heart burning in his open breast . . .

I'm sorry I couldn't fullfill your dreams, Mother, he thought. *I'm sorry I didn't tell you mine.*

More than anything, he must get away for his mother. If she knew he was safe, she would be all right.

Jan's eyes were dry by the time he opened the door. The street below was empty. But it would not stay so. At any moment the man in the trench coat and his two thugs might reappear, heading with certainty toward the very spot where he stood. That would be the end of it. He would have betrayed his mother. He would have betrayed his friends—and their money, which they had thrust into his hands and which the police would quickly confiscate, would be gone.

He turned his collar up and descended the stairs. As calmly as possible, he crossed the street, heading for the alleyway Tadeusz had taken them through. From the next street he could reach the bus depot by mingling with the shoppers in the marketplace.

"You there, just a minute."

He was turning into the alley when someone called to him. He thought of turning with his fists out. He could use the boxing move Karol had taught him, which they had used to such good purpose during the bar brawl this autumn. But there were three of them. There was no way he could overpower them. The one in the trench coat would be a few steps behind him, his two companions to either side, guns drawn, already aiming at a point between his shoulder blades. There was nothing the cops loved better than a prisoner resisting arrest. It was sometimes a quick road to promotion to add to one's record the shooting of a wanted man attempting to escape.

"I—" he began, turning around. Confusion was replaced by elation. It was one of Tadeusz's friends, a man named Jerzy who had sometimes observed their chess matches. He was a pensioner who lived alone, and, though he never spoke while he watched, Tadeusz claimed that he recorded every move in his head, learning the game voraciously. "One day," Tadeusz said after one of their matches, when the old man had limped down the stairs to his own apartment, giving Tadeusz the chance to bring out his good tea, which he hoarded, "he will beat us all. His eyes are a hawk's eyes."

"I say, Jan," the old pensioner said. The glow of concentrated purpose that Tadeusz had spoken of was in the man's eyes. "Do you think I might have a game of chess with you sometime soon?" He trembled; he must have practiced the speech before approaching Jan. His great shyness, and the great need bursting now from within him, made Jan reach out and put his hand on the man's arm.

"I—"

Behind the old man, Jan saw the man in the trench coat with his two henchmen approaching Tadeusz's flat.

He gripped the old man's arm tenderly.

"I'm sorry, Jerzy, not any time soon."

He turned away, nearly as much in avoidance of the disappointment on the old man's face as in haste.

As he had hoped, the marketplace stalls were busy. He was able to blend with the crowd of haggling women, schoolboys playing hooky and the young marrieds out together to buy vegetables and, perhaps, a little meat for dinner. He mixed with the hagglers, arguing himself over the price of a bag of chestnuts, which he leisurely ate as he strolled.

When he reached the last stall, Jan thought it must be at least noon. But, to his great surprise, the clock over the bus depot showed it to be only twenty minutes past nine. His initial feeling that the bus station would surely be watched by the police was replaced by a conviction that it was not. They had only been looking for him for a little more than an hour. At this point, there would only be the three men he had seen after him. When he was not located, there might be more, and a general alert would be posted, but now it was three against one.

His theory was proven correct when a covert inspection of the station revealed no sign of police activity. Jan's spirits were further lifted when he discovered that a bus heading out of the city in the direction he wanted was preparing to leave. He had no difficulty hiding his features from the ticket seller, who was more intent on his magazine than on studying the faces of bus passengers. He took the same precaution handing his ticket to the driver, using the opportunity to glance out over the driver's shoulder to see if his three pursuers might have shown up. They had not, and a few moments later, as Jan reached an empty seat halfway toward the back of the bus and away from the driver's direct gaze in the rear-view mirror, the bus lurched forward.

Twenty minutes later, they were out of the city and passing into the rural region north and east of Warsaw.

Though Jan never actually closed his eyes, a great feeling of lassitude overcame him. He felt as if he had been detached from himself, floating above the unfolding drama of his life, watching his own plight on a television screen. With some interest, he wondered what would happen next. In the drama, the man had eluded his pursuers, but now what would the script call for? In every television crime show he had ever seen it was easy to plot the destiny of the felon. If he was a good character, he would elude his hunters and ultimately triumph. If he was a villain, he would be caught and brought to justice. But what was Jan? Was he hero or villain? If the police wanted him, did that not make him an automatic villain? On the television productions, whenever the state wanted a man he was obviously a criminal, to be judged and sentenced. But what had been Jan's crime? Why did the state want him? It didn't matter.

About halfway to Kolno, the bus stopped to let passengers off. Jan waited for them to continue but instead the driver left the bus. Jan nervously waited for his return. After fifteen minutes he was sure that word had somehow spread and that policemen would appear momentarily and drag him from the bus. But as he was rising to leave, the bus driver suddenly reappeared, reclaiming his seat and pulling the door shut behind him.

Jan was filled with anxiety, undecided as to whether he should stay or rush to the front of the bus, throw the door open and flee, until he overheard one of the passengers in the seat in front of him laugh and say to her companion, nodding toward the driver, "There he is with his loose bowels again, it never fails." And the other one replied, knowingly, "Sausage for breakfast as a habit will do that. I tried to tell him that our last trip, but he wouldn't listen."

"Men never do," the other woman answered, and they both laughed and nodded their heads.

Jan settled back into his seat.

The trees thinned, showing dry farmland. Somewhere in the distance he thought he saw the remains of his grandfather's farm, the fire-blackened ruin of the house which had sent him and his mother to Warsaw, his grandfather's burning cries from the cellar mingling with squeals . . . But then trees reappeared. And then, suddenly, they had reached Kolno. The two women in front of Jan got out ahead of him, stopping a moment to scold the bus driver on his breakfast habits. The bus driver waved them on impatiently, and Jan hurried out behind them, keeping his face averted from the driver and from the two women, who were nosy enough to remember a face. The bus doors closed with an airy hiss and the bus groaned off. Jan noticed that it leaned slightly to one side in the back, another state vehicle in need of repair it wouldn't receive.

The bus had left him at the edge of the small town square. So as not to draw attention to himself he went to the base of the statue at the other end and sat down on one of two benches there. An old woman occupied the other bench. She was blind, one of her hands rubbing softly at the blue-veined wrist on her other arm. Her black cane rested against one hip. Her eyes calmly stared into blackness.

"Excuse me," Jan said.

"I'll tell you anything you want," the woman said, "if you buy a pear from me." She lifted the corner of her cloak, revealing a small wicker basket of pears nestled beside her. "It will cost you five hundred groszy."

"Certainly," Jan answered, drawing out one of the coins Karol had given him and pressing it into her hand. "Can you give me change for this?"

"I don't have change to give," she answered.

Jan was about to say that she could keep the whole coin, but realized her game. "I'm sorry," he said, reaching to remove the coin from her palm, "I can't buy your fruit, then."

"I'll give you change," she said, smiling mischievously. She pulled a purse from beneath her cloak. She drew out coins, shorting him one to see if he would notice. When he protested she handed him all she owed him.

"I'm looking for the hotel with a pot of flowers out front," he said to her.

"Oh, I can't help you," she said. Her mischievous smile returned.

"You promised to help me. I can tell you you won't get another groszy from me, old woman."

"I was playing with you," the old woman laughed. It was a hoarse, unpleasant sound. "It's just outside of town. There's a horse path behind us, and you take that for about a half kilo. It's on the left side. A man named Edward runs it." She laughed again. "A skinflint like me. Don't let him cheat you. There isn't a room in the place worth more than ten. The best rooms are in the rear, where there's plenty of sun in the morning."

Jan stood up. The woman's sightless eyes followed him. "Are you going to stay long? Perhaps there are other things I could tell you, people you should watch for."

"Thank you for your help," Jan said, not trying to hide the annoyance in his voice. He moved on.

It was a longer walk than the woman had said. After what must have been a kilometer the road narrowed, leaving space for barely a cart, certainly not two horses abreast. The day had grown almost oppressively hot, an anomaly for November. There were thick hedges beside the road, the branching trees getting their brown coats of turning leaves overhead. It was like walking through a close burrow. Jan began to feel claustrophobic. He carried his coat over his arm. He rolled his shirt sleeves up, and loosened his tie. It felt like August, the humidity in the air palpable. He wanted to sit and rest but the hedge was cut so close to the road, there was nowhere to do it. His entire former life seemed like a dream, something he had left behind only a few hours before but which was a lifetime away from him. He tried to conjure up his mother's face, or Tadeusz's, but could not precisely remember what they looked like. If someone had told him a day ago that in twenty-four hours he would be stumbling through a darkling, hot tunnel, hiding from the police, running from a crime that was unknown to him, he would have laughed or executed the fighting move with his fists that Karol had taught him—the quick one-two.

Or maybe he was dreaming. Perhaps he would awaken at any moment, pushed gently on the shoulder by his dear mother, and would look up into her face, and tell her that he had had a dream of guilt, that he loved her more than anything, that he was sorry he had not told her of his feelings for her in such a long time. He would tell her that he was sorry that he had grown arrogant and distant, perhaps embrace her. Hopefully, the breakfast he had left on the table this morning was yet to be faced, waiting for him out of this dreamland on the kitchen table at this moment; and his mother stood over him right now, ready to end this guilt dream, about to give him that gentle nudge, this mother who had awakened him so many times, gotten him off to school, changed the sheets on his beds, seeing the stains he had sometimes left there with his wet dreams—his mother who was closer to him than anyone . . .

Oh, mother—

He did not wake, because it was not a dream. But suddenly he came up short, nearly walking into a black wrought-iron post curving out above the road to hold a brass basket of white and red roses. Riveted to the pole was a tarnished sign that said, KOLNO INN.

Flanking the sign was a lane, and he turned into it.

The path was lined with rose bushes, trellised up to nearly Jan's height. He could see where some had been clipped for the basket out front, strong green stems covered with thick red thorns, which suddenly ended in sharp, slanting lines. But there were more than enough, in various states of bloom. The largest, in full flower, was wider than his closed fist. He vaguely recalled that roses normally bloomed in June. Wasn't it November? But these vague thoughts, which battled with all of the other fears and anxieties that had been in his mind since the morning, were pushed aside at the sight of the hotel.

It seemed to appear before him out of thin air. One step he was on the rose-enshrouded path and the next step he was in the courtyard. His first thoughts were of a peasant cottage on a monstrous scale. There were three stories. The front was flat, lines of ornamentally shuttered windows set on a dark, chocolate-brown facade of diagonally laid planks of wood. The roof was edged in scrollwork, and at the four corners there were turrets, each with a small, square window.

The front door of the inn was low and wide. Dark flat stones led up to it.

Fearing only what lay behind him more than what lay ahead, Jan walked to the door and used the heavy brass knocker.

The sound echoed once and then was swallowed from within. No one came to let him in. He pulled at the wrought-iron handle, curved against the door in the shape of a long, bristled boar-pig. His fingers drew back; a memory came whole into his mind, was instantly blurred. He remembered this door handle; the image of a pig, large blank swinish eyes staring into his own, his screams, his grandfather lifting him, pulling him away from that bristled face, those blank button eyes ("What, no sausages today, Jan?" Tadeusz always kidded him. "But you're Catholic—not Jewish!").

He put his trembling hand on the door and it opened, letting him in.

At the end of a short hallway, through an entranceway, was a small lobby. It looked as though it might once have been a taproom. The ceiling was oppressively low. The front desk might once have served as the bar. Above it, butting the ceiling, was a thick square beam which ran the length of the desk. On it were intricate carvings of animal grotesques. Jan shivered. There were bloated pigs with the faces of wild men, mouths grinning, sitting on their haunches, bellies sliced open to reveal hanging strings of sausages and bacon slabs immersed in twisting clouds of smoke. There were pigs with the heads of women, sprouting great tufts of hair, open mouths full of sharp teeth. Some were biting themselves; one had its head thrust into the gaping stomach of an adjacent sow. Above these fantastic animals, at the line of the ceiling, had been carved scenes of violent weather: fat thunderclouds with thick jets of rain pelting down, hailstones square as bales of hay, blizzards of snow stacked up in leaning drifts against the unheedful animals below. Jan studied the bizarre scenes, moving along the desk slowly from depiction to depiction. The thick black beam drew him, mesmerized. Again, he knew this place—

"What do you want?"

The rough sound of a human voice startled him. A short man was now facing him from behind the front desk. A door behind him, which had been closed, was now open wide. The man had a shock of white hair like those of the fantastic swine-women above him. But there was no hog body below his neck, only a hard torso sporting a green felt vest. In one sharp-fingered hand he held a piece of bread which had been torn from a loaf and a slice of sausage, which he now pressed together before bringing them to his mouth. Half of this meal disappeared into his mouth and he chewed, waiting for Jan to speak, regarding him with his unfriendly eyes.

"Are you Edward?"

The other continued to chew, his hand holding the remaining sausage and bread pressing them together. He started to bring his hand up to his mouth but stopped and said, "You have a reservation?"

"No. Your hotel was recommended to me by a friend."

"Recommended, eh?" For a moment the man's stare softened, but then he put the rest of his meal into his mouth and wiped his hands across the front of his vest. "It will cost you extra if you don't have a reservation."

"How much?"

"Twenty for the room. And ten more for not phoning ahead."

"That's too much," Jan bluffed, remembering the old blind woman's warning about the proprietor being a skinflint. "When my friend stayed he said it was ten for the room."

"Twenty." Edward shook his head. "Costs go up."

"I could stay at the other hotel."

"Go on, then," Edward said, but he added, "All right. Ten it is for the room. In advance. And ten more for not reserving."

Remembering the blind woman's other words, Jan said, "I want a room in the rear of the hotel."

"Fine," Edward said, impatiently. "Just pay in advance."

Jan paid him, and was taken to a small room in one of the back corners of the third floor. It was hot. It looked out onto an oppressively close stand of oak trees. What little light reached the room filtered through the sway of branches. Looking out through the small window, he saw that the entire back of the hotel was suffocated by encroaching trees. *Damn old woman.* So much for her advice about morning sun.

When Edward had left him Jan lay on the bed. He found it lumpy and tilted annoyingly to one side. It smelled of old feathers and mildew. He laced his hands behind his head, finding with his fingers a rip in the pillow. He stared at the ceiling, trying to think of nothing, to make this day, what had happened to his life, vanish. But it would not. He saw it all again, as if played on a television screen: the haunted look on Jozef's face as he approached them on the bridge with his news; the smug visage of the man in the trench coat, sure of his job and his prey; and his mother's face, looming over him, telling him to get up for work, then weeping alone in her room after the police had gone, her rosary clutched in her praying hands, kneeling over the quilt, crying and praying to God crucified over her bed on his crucifix—

He pushed himself up on his elbows at a sound of movement, and there at the end of his bed was a girl he had never seen before, holding her hand out to him. She was short, her pale face suffused with freckles, her hair straight and red. She did not look Polish. But when she spoke she spoke Polish to him.

"Don't worry, Jan."

He reached his hand out to her, and she took it in her own. Her touch was gentle but in the fingers he felt a fierce hardness. He sensed that, if she wanted, she could grip him so tight it would feel as though his hand was in a vise. And yet she held his hand now as gently as a lover.

"Come with me," she said, in her beautiful, soft, enigmatic voice, letting his hand go.

He rose from the bed. She walked into the far corner of the room. He thought she had disappeared. But then he saw that the shadows in the corner lengthened, and that the walls did not meet. There was a hallway there.

Jan entered the shadows, leaving all but faint tendrils of light behind. He felt the walls with his hands. Abruptly the hall ended, and there were stairs. He climbed. Above him the stairway ended, and he faintly saw the girl turn away from him. There was only a wall ahead. When he reached it he found himself in another hallway which turned to the left. The girl was ahead of him, opening a door.

"Come on, Jan," she called tenderly to him.

He reached the doorway. Inside was a huge attic. At first he did not see the girl, but then he located her at the far end of the room.

The girl was bending over something in the midst of a forest of stacked boxes.

He hurried to catch up to her. There was dust on the floor, as deep as fallen snow. He had to kick it aside to walk. He covered his mouth to prevent his lungs from being filled with it. He began to cough. He had kicked up so much dust that he could not see.

"Where are you!" he shouted to the girl, but there was no answer.

Suddenly the room was very dark. There was a noise off to his right. He turned toward it but found only darkness and settling dust.

Something ran by him, brushing his leg and kicking up more dust. "Help me!" he yelled in fright. He could not see through the dust and darkness. There was a cold grip on his ankle, and he cried out. The grip released and the thing was gone in a cloud of soot.

"Where are you?" he called to the red-haired girl. "Help me!"

The dust settled to the floor like a cloak. She was very close to him. "Don't worry," she said, soothingly. "Follow me, Jan."

He looked, and saw that there was a stairway at her feet.

He followed. They went down a steep flight of steps. It was like the one in his grandfather's house that led to the cellar. Another memory washed through him. He had gone down there to see something. He remembered squeals, the sweet red smell of blood, his grandfather's face turning up under the bright overhead bulb to look at him, his spectacles red-spattered, the drawn dripping blade held at the sweeping height of its arc, the limp pink thing held in his other hand making a weakening whooshing sound like air escaping from a gasbag, Jan's own cry mingling with the wheeze of the dying pig, rising past it to reprise its lost squeal, his feet slipping, falling—

Jan felt a movement of cold above him. A sudden, unshakable fear took hold of him. He stopped, head level with the floor of the attic. He saw the girl proceed ahead of him; a moment later she was gone. It became very dark again. He reached down, gingerly, and touched the step he was on; it felt exactly like the steps in his grandfather's cellar, dry wood cracked to splinters.

The air was cold all around the upper part of his body. He became filled with terror. When Jozef told them that the police wanted him he had felt fear, but it had not been like this. That was a formless thing; this was concentrated to a sharp, needlelike point that seared his middle, making him want to scream. He felt on the verge of becoming a mindless thing; he wanted to push the fright from his lungs with his shrieks and thrust it away from him.

In the darkness above him, there was the slightest of movements. He heard a tiny scratching sound, like a fingernail across slate. He thought he heard even breathing, above the sound of his own ragged breaths.

Something touched his head. It was a tap, as of a hard fingertip tapping a blackboard. The carvings in the beam over the bar in the lobby rose into his imagination. A shiver swept over him. He remembered the pigs with the faces of wild men, stomachs happily revealing processed innards. One of those creatures, he was sure, was crouched above him, leaning over the stairwell, a mere inches from his head.

The step he was on sagged. Something moved past him, down the stairway. There was a passing hot breath on his face. A grunt of laughter.

It ran back up the steps; something hard and bristly (a paw?) brushed his face.

He screamed.

The hardness of a nailed foot tapped his head.

Suddenly the coldness left the upper part of his body. The thing crouching above him scuttled into the darkness of the attic.

Below him, the stairway became visible again.

She was waiting for him.

"Don't worry." She smiled.

He descended after her. He found himself back in his small room. The girl stood by the bed, silently smiling at him. Wordlessly, not taking her eyes from him, she removed the shoulder straps of her gown. The gown fell to her feet, revealing her naked to him. She was a mixture of girl and woman. Her face, the perfect white lines of her body, were childlike, yet the rise of her breasts, the V of deep red hair below her belly, the loving smile and the magnetic sexuality of her look and stance aroused him deeply. She held her hand out. He went to her, and as he took her hand she lay back on the bed, pulling him down above her. She lay very still, looking into his eyes. Her hair was almost the color of cherries. She let his hand go so that he could touch her. He wanted to kiss her. She looked into his eyes. "Someday," she whispered, a moan.

And then her eyes became huge and blank, her skin bristled as she vanished beneath him.

Someone struck Jan roughly, on the back. He was pulled away from the bed and turned around, then pushed back, feeling the lumps of the old mattress under him.

The man who had pushed him now held him with his hand on Jan's chest and sat down next to him on the bed. It was the man in the trench coat. Behind him, to either side of the window, stood the two uniformed policemen. They looked tired; one of them yawned into his hand.

The man in the trench coat took his hand off Jan's chest and flipped open a small notebook.

"You are Jan Pasek?" he asked, matter-of-factly.

Jan said nothing.

The man in the trench coat looked down at him; when he spoke he sounded almost bored. "I can make one phone call from downstairs," he said quietly, "and it would be very hard for your mother indeed."

He looked at Jan dispassionately.

"I am Jan Pasek," Jan said.

The man in the trench coat wrote something in his notebook and then closed it, putting it into his pocket. He studied Jan's face for a moment. He, too, looked as though he wanted to yawn.

"You caused me great inconvenience," he said, and then he swung his fist in a high arc over the bed and hit Jan squarely on the nose.

Jan felt an explosion of pain followed by numbness. Another blow struck his face. Dully, he looked up to see that the two uniformed cops had moved to the bed. The man in the trench coat stepped back. The uniformed men began to beat him methodically, raining blows on his ribs and stomach. He tried to roll into a fetal position. They struck his head and legs. One of them pulled him to the floor between them, and they began to kick him.

Through a curtain of torment that was lowering him to unconciousness, Jan heard the man in the trench coat tell them to stop. He heard the word "dinner." Turning his head, he saw through one nearly closed eye the man in the trench coat leave with one of the uniformed men. The other sat on the bed, trying to light a cigarette with an uncooperative lighter.

Jan attempted to sit up. The uniformed cop put his lighter aside on the bed. "Feel like fighting?" he laughed, dipping his boot toe into a sore spot in Jan's side, rolling him over onto his back.

Jan felt another deep push of pain in his side and then blacked out.

When he awoke they were carrying him through the lobby of the hotel. Edward, the proprietor, had another sandwich of sausage and bread in his hand. He turned his face away from Jan as he was dragged through the front doorway, his shoes scraping over the flagstones outside. Jan caught a glimpse of the roses through nearly closed lids. He could smell the flowers; their sweetness was mingled with the odor of his own blood.

He was carried a long way. They dumped him once on the way to rest. Jan heard one of the cops grunting, the other making fun of him for being out of shape.

"You would be too if you relied on using your head instead of your fists," his partner replied. The other mocked him in return until the man in the trench coat told them to stop bickering.

They dragged him to the town square, near the statue, where a dark sedan was parked at an angle. The blind woman was still in her accustomed spot. She cocked her head up and smiled at Jan as he was taken past her.

"You found your way to the hotel?" she said, giggling throatily, but Jan didn't know whether she spoke to him or the policemen.

He was thrown into the back seat of the car. One of the uniformed cops got in heavily beside him. The other drove, the man in the trench coat beside him in the front seat.

The car wouldn't start. The driver cursed, the other uniformed man, next to Jan, mocking his friend's ability as a chauffeur. Sharply, the man in the trench coat told them to shut up. The engine turned over, the driver shouting in triumph as they pulled away.

Jan lay on the back seat, watching the slate gray of the sky go past through the rear window, mingled with denuded trees. The face of the uniformed cop hovered over him. "Enjoy it now," the cop smiled. He nodded at the sky with his head. "You won't be seeing that where you're going."

They turned the car from the square onto the tree-lined road. It was then that Jan remembered. The cop's face rose over him again, the pink, stiff bristles on his face spreading into a grin. He put his hard-nailed foot on Jan's chest to keep him from rising. Through the window Jan saw the flower pot outside the inn as the car turned into the lane. He smelled the flowers. Again he smelled the blood in his grandfather's cellar. He saw the knife in his grandfather's hand, felt his own four feet slip on the cellar steps, heard his mother's barren cry at the top of the steps, begging for a son her dead husband had never given her.

And, finally, as they led him from the car to the attic, he saw once more the look in his lover's blank huge eyes as he was lifted squealing away from her, the lover who now waited for him within, the look that promised, "Someday."

Charles L. Grant is one of the most respected writers and editors in the field of horror and fantasy. He is the winner of two Nebula Awards for science fiction writing, a World Fantasy Award as the editor of the original *Shadows* anthology, and winner of the World Fantasy Award in the categories of Best Novella and Best Collection (for *Nightmare Seasons,* a collection of his own horror fiction). His most recent novel is *The Pet.* In addition to the popular *Shadows* series, he is also the editor of the anthologies *Greystone Bay* and *After Midnight.* He lives in New Jersey.